# THE CIRCLE

# THE CIRCLE

*A Grand & Batchelor Victorian mystery*

# M J Trow

CRÈME de la CRIME

This first world edition published 2016
in Great Britain and the USA by
Crème de la Crime, an imprint of
SEVERN HOUSE PUBLISHERS LTD of
19 Cedar Road, Sutton, Surrey, England, SM2 5DA.
Trade paperback edition first published 2016
in Great Britain and the USA by
SEVERN HOUSE PUBLISHERS LTD.

British Library Cataloguing in Publication Data

Trow, M. J. author.
  The circle. – (A Grand & Batchelor Victorian mystery)
  1. Baker, La Fayette C. (La Fayette Curry), 1826-1868–
  Death and burial–Fiction. 2. Murder–Investigation–
  Washington (D.C.)–Fiction. 3. Private investigators–
  Fiction. 4. Detective and mystery stories.
  I. Title II. Series
  823.9'2-dc23

ISBN-13: 978-1-78029-083-6 (cased)
ISBN-13: 978-1-78029-567-1 (trade paper)
ISBN-13: 978-1-78010-755-4 (e-book)

*All Severn House titles are printed on acid-free paper.*

Severn House Publishers support the Forest Stewardship Council™ [FSC™],
the leading international forest certification organisation.
All our titles that are printed on FSC certified paper carry the FSC logo.

Typeset by Palimpsest Book Production Ltd.,
Falkirk, Stirlingshire, Scotland.
Printed and bound in Great Britain by
TJ International, Padstow, Cornwall.

To Cathy and Rick, of Knoxville, Tennessee -
all good plots start with meeting new friends!

# ONE

At first, he didn't want to go near the window. Then, he couldn't stay away. He waited in the shadows as the clouds of evening boiled up over the city and he didn't light the lamp. He had always gone armed, for as long as he could remember, but now his gun never left his side. There was a knife under his pillow too, and another one next to the door. No one was going to catch him napping, not that bastard from Steubenville, nor any of them. Allan Pinkerton claimed his boys never slept; well, neither did he.

There was a solitary cab parked across the street, the horse dozing in the traces, the driver muffled against the night airs. The street began to glow as the lamplighter came along, tapping his way along the sidewalk, bringing his eerie, green light to the city.

He saw the couple walking towards him, the girl leaning into the boy, laughing and joking. So young, so much to live for. He dodged back into the darkness of the room, his scalp crawling. Were they all they seemed; just a young couple in love out for the evening? Nothing was that simple, not any more.

His heart jumped at the sudden rap on the door. He didn't move, except to cock the pistol in his pocket. Another rap. And a third, in quick succession. That was the signal, the one he'd worked out with his people months before. Even so . . . He crossed the room, careful not to make a target of himself against the window and listened at the doorframe. He heard muttering outside. 'It's me, for Christ's sake. Let me in, will you?'

The gun was in his hand, his arm rigid, his finger on the hair trigger. With his left hand he turned the key and let the door swing inwards. His visitor froze, both hands in the air, a Navy Colt muzzle resting on his forehead, cold and deadly.

'You alone?'

'Of course I am.' The visitor let himself be hauled into the room and stood there. How long, he asked himself, could this nonsense go on? 'I brought your beer. Look.' He held up the flagon. 'Laff,' he said softly, looking at the man in the green light from the street, 'are you all right?'

'I will be,' Laff said, and eased the hammer forward, lowering the gun.

'Do you want a drink, Laff?' The visitor saw the glass on the cabinet and uncorked the flagon, pouring the amber liquid that frothed and bubbled. Laff closed the door and locked it. Then he reached for the glass and drank deeply, sighing as he drained it.

'You're a good man, Wally,' he said, wiping his mouth. It had been dry all day. Now everything tasted bitter, strange. Wally's eyes flickered to the door. He had done this once too often and after all this time he had nothing to say. Laff was afraid of his own shadow. The rest of his friends, if he had ever had any, had long gone.

'I should be going,' Wally said.

'Of course. Yes, of course.' He unlocked the door and stood behind it as Wally left, glad to be out of there, away from that peculiar smell. It was dark on the stairs now and he couldn't make out the figure waiting at the bottom. He could make out the bag, however, and he knew the sound of gold coin when he heard it.

'I can't do this any more,' he said to the man in the shadows.

'Don't worry,' came the answer. 'After tonight you won't need to. You're a good man, Wally.'

Wally grunted and gestured back up the stairs with his head. 'That's what *he* said.' He reached out and took the bag, feeling its weight before stashing it under his coat. 'My thirty pieces of silver,' he said solemnly.

'Now, don't go all Biblical on me, Wally, not now. We're doing this great country of ours a favour – you know that.'

Wally did. With every step he took as he crossed to his waiting cab, he kept telling himself he was doing everybody a favour.

*Offices of the Telegraph, Fleet Street, London*

It was the nose you saw first, bulbous and defiant above the walrus moustache. Then you saw the little eyes, mischievous and twinkling, darting here and there, never missing a thing. Only then did you notice the clothes, elegantly cut, expensively tailored in a Savile Row way. And the gardenia, clipped to the lapel just *so*.

With his trained journalist's eye, James Batchelor saw all that. But then, he had seen this man before, many times, and he had gone in awe of him on every single occasion. He was George Sala, doyen of the London reporters, friend of kings and frequenter of brothels. He knew everything about everybody. And what he did not know, he made up. The *Telegraph* didn't ask too many questions; *The Times* asked even less. Men in high places were afraid of George Sala. So, most of the time, and certainly this morning, was James Batchelor.

'Well, George?' The younger man could bear the silence no longer. The last thing he wanted was to hurry his old mentor, but he had sat in the great man's office now for the best part of half an hour, listening to Sala sucking his teeth, sighing, tapping his cigar stub on the ashtray. Batchelor would not have minded, but Sala had had his opus now for nearly six months. Perhaps he should have sent it to Mr Dickens after all.

Sala looked at him over his rimless pince-nez. 'Well, James,' he said.

'Is it . . . any good?' All James Batchelor's powers of language had deserted him this morning. This was no time for flowery prose; he had a living to earn.

'I don't think "good" is the word,' Sala said.

Batchelor looked at him. Was the great man being cryptic? Was he about to explode into a rapture of effusive praise? Offer to serialize Batchelor's first fumblings himself?

'I'll be blunt, James,' Sala said. 'It needs work.'

'Ah.'

'Why did you bring it to me?'

Batchelor spread his arms as though the question needed no answer. 'You used to write this stuff,' he said. 'Further . . .' Batchelor was choosing his words carefully. He knew that George Sala was the vainest man in London and perhaps, even now . . . 'You were *the* master of the art.'

'Penny bloods?' Sala sneered. 'Yes, I was rather good, wasn't I?' He smiled at the memories. 'Charles and I . . .' Suddenly, his face straightened. 'Then I became a serious journalist; put the bloods behind me.'

'They're called penny dreadfuls now,' Batchelor could at least prove that he moved with the times.

'Yes,' Sala sighed, reaching for his cigar again. 'And, in view of this,' he tapped Batchelor's sheaf of papers, 'that's rather unfortunately apt, isn't it?' He looked down at the title page in Batchelor's immaculate copperplate. '*Lady Costigan's Revenge*,' he read aloud.

'Too racy?' Batchelor was trying to read the great critic's mind. 'Too bland?'

'There's nothing wrong with the title, James,' Sala said. 'It's the rest of it that's woeful.'

Batchelor's heart sank. For a long, ghastly moment, he felt himself shrinking, sliding to the floor until he was a speck of dust on Sala's carpet.

'But I thought you were sleuthing these days,' the journalist said. 'You and that American fellow . . . what's his name? Grunt?'

'Grand.'

'Yes. Consulting detectives, aren't you?'

'We prefer "enquiry agents".'

'Of course you do. Not going well?'

Batchelor sighed. 'Divorce cases. Dog stealing. We did have a goat murder last month.'

'Riveting,' nodded Sala.

Had it not been for the tick of Sala's clock, the silence would have been deafening.

'Why don't you go to the hanging?'

'Hanging?' Batchelor repeated.

'Barrett, the Fenian. You know, the Clerkenwell outrage?'

'Of course.' Batchelor may not have been a journalist any more, but he could still read the papers. Irish prisoners had been set free from the Clerkenwell House of Detention last November. Their rescuers had overdone the dynamite and a wall had collapsed, killing innocent passers-by. Michael Barrett had claimed he was in Glasgow at the time; but then he would, wouldn't he?

'It'll give you a feel for the thing,' Sala went on, remembering his own experiences. 'I've been to more than a few. Dickens. Thackeray. All the greats. Believe me, there's nothing like a turning off to catch the horror of the crime. It'll help your writing.'

'If you say so.' Batchelor slid the manuscript towards him.

'Besides,' Sala leaned back, puffing his cheroot to give it new life, 'it's a chance to witness history. You know they're going to take hangings indoors from now on? Turn them into sneaky, hole-in-corner affairs.' The great journalist shook his head. 'It's a terrible indictment of our times, James. So,' he brightened, 'you will have one last chance to see that old idiot Calcraft at work, making yet another pig's ear of some poor bastard's last moments on earth.'

They had hanged men outside Newgate for decades. And, for most of that time, the job had been done by William Calcraft, a white-bearded old man who styled himself 'Executioner to Her Majesty' and bred rabbits. He was also an incompetent and many was the poor wretch who slowly strangled to death at the end of one of Calcraft's wrongly measured ropes. This was one reason he drew the crowds, so that they could roar their delight as the old rabbit-breeder jumped up to grab the twitching legs and haul the poor bastard down to snap his spine.

Increasingly, these days, William Calcraft travelled by night, clutching his leather bag with its ropes and pinions. He was at Newgate long before dawn, watching as the first of the crowds began to assemble. This would be an Irish hanging, and it was well known that the Irish looked after their own and always gave the hangman short shrift. Calcraft would have to watch his back, even if the drop went well.

'Good day for a hanging!' Somebody slapped James Batchelor on the back as the crowd carried them both forward. It was. The spring sun shone bright, flashing on the helmets of the Metropolitan Police that ringed the perimeter. The commissioner was taking no chances. Twice in the past two years, Sir Richard Mayne had offered his resignation. He had been commissioner longer than James Batchelor had been alive, and the years were beginning to take their toll. As white-haired and cranky as Calcraft, Richard Mayne was an exhausted and bitter man. But it was not his idea to have the cavalry on standby. That was the brainchild of Gathorne Hardy, the Home Secretary. And a move more calculated to enrage the Irish could not be imagined.

'What are they doing here?' Batchelor murmured, as he saw the sun glancing off the helmets of the Life Guards waiting patiently in Limeburner Lane.

'Waiting for a chance to blow our feckin' heads off,' an Irish voice grunted nearby. Batchelor looked around him. Along with the costers in their fustian jackets and caps were dotted dark-haired men with cold fire in their eyes. He noted that several of them held their arms close to their sides, as though they cradled something precious up their sleeves. There was a ripple of laughter and Batchelor saw a knot of ladies of the night, unusually up before noon, intent on making a holiday of the occasion. Toddlers were whimpering and grizzling, tired already after the long walk from their homes and frightened by the sheer numbers of the crowd.

The lemonade sellers were out early and the chestnut vendors and the toffee-apple men. Two sharply dressed bucks were accosting the arriving crowd, offering the last confession of Michael Barrett, neatly printed. Somebody else was calling his wares, giving the great British public a once-in-a-lifetime chance to own a brick of the very wall from Clerkenwell, blown down by the Fenian monster himself.

George Sala had been right. The ground outside Newgate was solid with people. Both sexes, all ages, all social classes. A Rechabite in silk sash and tall hat was trying to get a hymn going, but the Catholics had other ideas and made religious noises of their own. That was all right, Batchelor reasoned. Just so long as no Fenian airs struck up or things could get ugly. Such was the press of people that Batchelor could not reach his notebook to jot anything down; he would have to trust to memory. Anyway, his right hand was firmly on his wallet.

There was a sudden roar from the direction of the prison and the black flags lifted in a gust of wind. The white-robed chaplain was leading the way out of the dark doorway to the left, looking down, with a Bible in his hand. Behind him, the gaudier priest of Rome, who had spent the night with the condemned man, stared straight ahead at the sea of faces, his fingers twitching at his rosary, his lips moving in prayer.

In the crowds, the cheers of the Protestants were drowned out by the boos of the Catholics and vice versa until the noise around the rooftop platform was deafening. Michael Barrett himself was a small man, perhaps five foot three – although no doubt Calcraft would have argued with that – and he may have been in his mid-twenties. He was pale and sad-eyed, but he walked unaided, and there were those who swore he had a spring in his step. To each side of him, burly prison officers kept pace and, three abreast, they climbed the scaffold steps.

To Batchelor, the whole scene looked like a play; some weird open-air amusement for the children. Whatever anyone was saying on the platform, no sound carried to the crowd, which had a life and a roar of its own.

'God bless you, Mickeleen!' a woman shouted.

'Feck you, body snatcher!' a man bellowed at Calcraft.

'Calcraft! Calcraft!' The cry was taken up, swirling in its deadly, rhythmic cacophony, bouncing off the brickwork around the prison. The white-haired hangman took centre stage now in Batchelor's view of it, partly obscured by raised arms, flying hats and clenched fists. He stood behind Barrett, pinioning his wrists; then he bent and snapped the shackles around his ankles. The condemned man ignored him, looking steadily into the face of his priest, looking already for his God.

The police line of dark blue braced itself around Newgate's entrance. High on the rooftop, Calcraft and the others were safe from the mob – unless, that was, some Irish lunatic had a gun or a bomb. But the unarmed crowd would instinctively surge forward, especially if Calcraft was bungling his work. They would go for the blue line, for the men the older crowd still knew as Peel's Raw Lobsters, and they would take out their vengeance on them. By the time the cavalry arrived, God alone knew how many heads would be broken.

Batchelor felt his heart pounding, louder surely than the roar around him. He glanced to right and to left. Had no one else heard it? Had no one else heard the scream rising in his throat? Above him and far ahead, Her Majesty's Executioner slipped a white linen hood over Michael Barrett's head. He could just hear the Irishman still intoning the prayers with the priest, but they knew, all of them on that platform, that the choral speaking would soon stop and that one voice would carry on alone.

For years to come, James Batchelor swore he heard it – the

dry rattle as Calcraft slid the bolt, the thud as the trapdoor crashed back, the snap as Michael Barrett's spine broke at the third vertebra. He heard it because the crowd was suddenly, terribly silent. Anyone still wearing a hat tugged it off now and all eyes were on the rope, creaking taut on its housings. The body of Michael Barrett hung there, his head on one side, as though he were listening to some distant choir. His feet had not twitched once. Astonishingly, for this, his public swansong, William Calcraft had got it right.

Now they all heard the priest. 'And may the Lord have mercy on your soul.'

Like a riptide roaring along a shore, like the first kick and hiss of a paddle steamer, an eerie sound rose from the crowd, three thousand throats giving vent at once to the horror of the moment. Batchelor was too numb to take in the reactions of those around him. He only saw the prison governor shaking the hangman's hand and saw the old man toddle off to get his brandy and his blood money. The usual perks would come the rabbit-breeder's way. He would cut up Barrett's rope and sell it at ten bob per three-inch piece. The dead man's clothes weren't worth much, but Calcraft could probably get a bob or two at Spitalfields Market; he wasn't proud. It was a shame that Barrett wasn't a notorious killer – a poisoner, or something to catch the public's imagination. Madame Tussauds paid much better than the rag merchants for the clothes then, but beggars couldn't be choosers. And there was no blood either, that was a shame. A lot of the Irish would have paid good money to dabble their handkerchiefs and scarves in Michael Barrett's life essence, martyr to the cause as he was. Calcraft smiled to himself. Still and all, it had been a good day for a hanging.

For the life of him, James Batchelor could not see how he could work any of this into *Lady Costigan's Revenge*. Best to start again, perhaps, with a brand-new story. He was still working out a rough plot in his head when he realized he had taken a wrong turning. The crowds had thinned now, except those who had stayed to hurl abuse at Calcraft when he came back after an hour to cut Barrett down. The police were still in place, but mugs of hot tea were being passed along their line and around the corner;

the cavalry had dismounted to check their girths and stirrup leathers and ease their horses' backs.

Damn. Batchelor didn't know where he was. It was an alley, certainly, with tall buildings that blotted out the sun. Mangy cats prowled near him, skulking low down on their haunches, bellies close to the ground. He turned to go back the way he had come. Then he saw them. Four men. No, five. They were silhouettes at first, with rough caps at jaunty angles on their heads.

'That's him,' one of them said, his accent pure Leinster. 'He was in the crowd, chanting.'

'So he was,' another said, as bog-Irish as the first.

'Come to see our boy turned off, did you?' a third man asked.

'I came to see a hanging, yes,' Batchelor said. He weighed up his options. Any of the men facing him was bigger than he was and they outnumbered him five to one.

'You know what this is, Englishman?' The first thug raised a club, gnarled and knotted. 'It's a shillelagh. An Irishman's right arm.'

'You know what this is?' Another voice rang out from behind the men.

They turned as one. A tall man stood there, in a wideawake hat and duster coat, a pistol gleaming in his right hand. 'It's a .32 calibre Colt, known as a vest pocket. It carries six bullets. That means, for those of you with limited arithmetical skills, I can kill all five of you and still have a slug left over for if I miss. But – believe me – I don't miss.'

The Irishmen hesitated, caught between two fires. James Batchelor thrust a hand into his jacket pocket and pointed it forward. 'I'll concede,' he said, 'I'm not as good a shot as my friend here, and I've only got three bullets in my pistol. Even so, that's nine bullets to your none. Happy with the odds, sheep-shagger?'

The Irishmen still hesitated. Then they turned, dashing past Batchelor, who wisely stepped aside to let them pass.

'The thing about you, Matthew Grand,' he said, walking up to the bigger man, 'is that you keep turning up like a bad cent. No coincidence, I suppose?'

Grand shook his head. 'Going to a hanging is never a good idea,' he said. 'Oh, I'll grant you, it's a good ol' American pastime, but it's never a good idea.'

'I thought Inspector Tanner had told you to get rid of that.' Batchelor pointed to the gun that Grand twirled three times on his trigger finger and slid deftly into his shoulder-holster.

'Oh, ye of little gratitude.' Grand shook his head. 'I just saved your life, James Batchelor.'

Batchelor paused, looking the man in the face. 'Yes, Matthew,' he said, seriously, 'you did. And I *am* grateful, really.' He patted Grand's shoulder and walked on, back along the alley.

'Anyway,' Grand said, 'I *kind* of followed Tanner's instructions.' He patted his pocket. 'There are no bullets in this thing.'

# TWO

Alsatia was wide awake long before Matthew Grand peered over the coverlet. Below the offices of Grand and Batchelor, Enquiry Agents, the street hawkers were already pattering, crying their wares along the Strand, rolling their carts into position. The pigeons deposited their calling cards on the stone hat of Lord Nelson, perched as he was on his column, and they perched on him. Trafalgar Square was loud with the rattle of hansoms and landaus, barouches and gigs, as the huge civil service that ran an empire got themselves to work along Whitehall.

Grand sat up in bed. He could hear Mrs Manciple down below in the kitchen, rattling pans and talking to someone in a crooning, singsong tone. He and Batchelor had learned to deal with her frustrated maternal instinct and, indeed, often to take advantage of it. No boot could be too muddy, no hat nap too muddled for her to take it immediately to her ample bosom and buff it till you could eat your dinner off it. But that she was a little unusual could not be ignored. He listened more carefully to see if he could discern a pattern to her crooning. Sometimes she thought Batchelor was looking thin and decided to feed him up, usually with rather upsetting marrow sandwiches, but even she normally left those for later in the day. Grand shook his head and swung his feet round on to the floor. Time would tell whether she had gone that little touch madder, so they could incarcerate her somewhere, or whether today would just be another of those days. He hoped they could keep her a while longer. Although she talked to herself and wouldn't open the door on any account, she did cook like an angel, so leeway could be given. Wrapping himself in his dressing gown, he ventured out on to the landing. Batchelor poked his head out of his room.

'Matthew,' he said, surprised. 'What are you doing here? I assumed Mrs Manciple was talking to you.'

'Same here,' Grand said. He gestured to his dressing gown.

'I don't like to go down dressed like this if she has someone in the kitchen.' Somehow, they had never got used to eating anywhere but in the kitchen, and it was by far the best place to be when Mrs Manciple was doling out treats.

'It is our house,' Batchelor said, on his dignity, and then, without a pause, 'your house, after all.'

'True. Let's go down.'

And they marched down the stairs to beard – almost literally, poor woman – Mrs Manciple in her lair.

She looked up as they came in, but from a rather unfamiliar position; she was crouching in the corner of the room, in the warm spot by the range.

'Mr Grand!' she exclaimed. 'Mr Batchelor. Come and see.'

They approached with trepidation. Whatever it was, it was for the landlord to sort out. They peered over her shoulder and immediately recoiled. There was a mess of fur and blood and wriggling worm-like things. It was clearly Mrs Manciple's cat, but equally clearly she wasn't well.

'What in God's name has happened?' Batchelor said, pressing his hand to his mouth. 'It's horrible.'

Grand, who was not such an inveterate townie as Batchelor, thought he might have an inkling. 'Kittens?' he ventured.

'Yes!' Mrs Manciple clasped her hands under her chin and her eyes were bright. 'Five . . . oops, no, six, all healthy. Tabbies, gingers, all sorts. Who's a clever girl, then?'

'Umm . . . yes. Very clever.' Grand was a little lost for words. As a man of the world he knew that it wasn't as clever as all that. 'Is there to be any breakfast, Mrs Manciple?'

She looked at him aghast. 'But . . . what if there are more kittens? What if . . .?'

He took her gently by the arm and pulled her to her feet, no mean task. 'Mr Batchelor will watch over her, won't you James?'

Batchelor's face was still rather a strange shade of grey, but he nodded his head and stood as far as was possible from the mewling pile of new feline life. The mother cat seemed to be eating something; he didn't enquire too closely. His role of enquiry agent only went so far.

Mrs Manciple busied herself at the range. She turned a beaming face on Grand. 'Isn't it wonderful, Mr Grand?' she asked him, rhetorically. 'Six more little creatures around the house. Seven cats . . . that's probably good luck. It certainly is with magpies, that's for sure.'

Batchelor gave a groan and the cook and Grand glanced over to the corner.

'Oh, I tell a lie. Eight.' She chuckled as she spooned an egg into the boiling pan. 'Soon have enough, Mr Grand, do you think?'

Grand was a man who could usually come up with a suitable remark for every occasion. He had been brought up to genteel company and his small talk was the talk of Washington, back in the day. But he settled for a simple, 'Hmm.' The cook smiled at him happily and burst into song.

'Come, thou long expected Jesus,' she carolled, 'Born to set thy people freeeee . . .'

Batchelor looked round at Grand who was standing aghast. 'Don't worry, Matthew,' he said, raising his voice so he could be heard. 'She always sings this when she is boiling eggs. She says it is just the right length.'

And so it proved. As she came at last to the final line, letting out all the stops, so she scooped out the eggs with a flourish and set them on the table. 'Thank you for watching Calico, Mr Batchelor,' she said. 'I'll take over now.'

Batchelor nodded, confused for a moment. 'Calico? Oh, the cat. Absolutely delighted to do it, Mrs Manciple. She seems to have stopped . . . er . . . stopped, now. Eight. That seems a lot, somehow.'

'Oh, lawks, no,' the cook laughed. 'I've seen a dozen and more. We'll soon have enough, never you fear.'

Settling for a nervous laugh for a reply, Grand sat down and shook out his napkin with a flourish. It was so clean and stiff with starch it sounded like a thunderclap. Mrs Manciple was surely a wonderful laundress as well, but . . . perhaps he could ask James to have a word with her about the cats.

Batchelor pulled out his chair with a squeak which elicited a 'Shhh' from the cook, who was bent again over the cat and her babies. He picked up the coffee pot and poured as quietly as he possibly could and passed the cup to Grand.

'Thank you, James,' he said, looking across the table for the

sugar, which Batchelor pushed nearer. Grand glanced at Mrs
Manciple, but she wasn't looking, so he picked up a couple of
lumps with his fingers and dropped them in. She frowned on
fingers at the table – sugar nips were not there for nothing, in
her opinion. He picked up the post as he stirred and then stopped
abruptly, his spoon in mid-air. 'Well, well, well,' he said. 'A
letter, James.'

Batchelor could see that. 'Don't tell me,' he said, dipping his
toast into his egg. 'Tiddles has gone missing in Edmonton? No,
far too exciting. I know – "There's a man who lives across the
road and he keeps looking at me funny – with his glass eye."
My detective's nose tells me that one's from Dollis Hill.'

Grand shook his head, slitting the envelope with a deft stroke
of the paper knife. 'Uh-huh,' he said. 'It's postmarked D.C. The
city of Washington.'

'Oh.' Batchelor paused in mid-swig. A letter from America
always meant business.

'It's from Luther Baker.' Grand had turned to the end of the
letter. He leaned back in his chair as he read the rest. 'My God.
Cousin Laff is dead.'

'Cousin Laff,' Batchelor repeated. 'Lafayette Baker, Head of
the National Detective Police. You've spoken of him.'

'I have,' Grand nodded. 'And a bigger bastard never drew
breath.'

'Looks like his sins have found him out.' Batchelor returned
to his breakfast.

'In more ways than we know,' Grand said solemnly. 'Cousin
Luther thinks he was murdered.'

'"Well, well, well", indeed.' Batchelor didn't like the look in
Grand's eye. It smacked of the hunter.

'Know what this is, James, my boy?' Grand waved a piece of
paper under his colleague's nose.

Batchelor didn't.

'It's a Treasury Bond,' Grand told him. 'What you call a blank
cheque over here. We have a commission.'

'We?'

'All right,' Grand shrugged. 'Me. But you've often told me
how you'd like to see the good ol' U S of A.'

'The colonies?' Batchelor smiled. 'It might be entertaining.'

'Oh, it'll be more than that, I fancy,' Grand smiled. 'But first, I have to see a lady. Where the hell is St John's Wood?'

The house in St John's Wood was tall and imposing and Matthew Grand stood in front of it that Tuesday. Four storeys, an attic and a basement. Sash windows and a brass bell with the name 'HARDINGE' stamped into the metal. Grand rang it, listening to the echoes through the house. He had visited dozens of houses like this over the last two years, pandering to people who needed help but who had been turned down by the police, or to people too proud to call in the police in the first place. But something told him that this particular call would be different.

'Can I help you, sir?' A small black woman wearing an elegant day dress stood there.

'I'd like to see Miss Boyd,' Grand said. 'Miss Belle Boyd.'

The maid's eyes flickered for an instant. 'There's no one of that name, sir,' and she made to close the door, but Grand was faster. Few people opened their doors voluntarily to private enquiry agents and fewer still kept them open. His boot blocked the maid's attempt at exclusion.

'Who is it, Eliza?' a female voice called from the hall.

'Give your mistress this,' Grand said, and passed over his card. Eliza read it and scowled at the tall, handsome man who, with his voice alone, had brought her past to her, suddenly and without warning, this morning.

'It's a Yankee officer,' Eliza said, without taking her eyes off Grand.

A tall, dark-haired lady appeared at the maid's elbow. She was perhaps in her mid-twenties, her eyes as bright as her jewels, her dress a burning amber satin. She took the card.

'Captain Matthew Grand,' she read aloud. 'Third Cavalry, Army of the Potomac.' She looked up at him and smiled. 'You're not wearing your red cravat, Captain Grand,' she said.

'Forgive my little subterfuge, ma'am,' he said, tipping his wideawake. 'I no longer technically have the right to wear the red tie or even to call myself captain. I resigned my commission.'

'Yes,' she said, the smile still playing around her lips. 'We all have to resign ourselves to change, don't we? Won't you come in? Eliza, some tea, please.'

The maid was still scowling at Grand. 'If you say so, Missy,' she muttered.

The lady showed Grand into an opulent drawing room and they sat opposite each other in feather-bedded comfort in two matching armchairs.

'Eliza was a slave,' she said, 'and before you ask, I set her free long before Mr Lincoln did. She doesn't like soldiers.'

'Any more than you do, Miss Boyd,' Grand said. 'Er . . . you are Belle Boyd, the Cleopatra of Secession?'

She laughed. 'I am,' she said, 'but I prefer the Siren of the Shenandoah; so much more romantic, don't you think? I go by Isabella Hardinge these days.'

'Another alias?' Grand asked. From what Luther Baker had said in his letter, this was one belle of the South you didn't turn your back on.

'My real name,' she said, and reached across to a black-framed photograph on the piano. 'My late husband, Sam. He was an officer in the navy.'

Grand took the photograph. In it, a demure-looking Belle sat in a high-backed chair while a man in the uniform of the United States Navy stood beside her, his hand on her shoulder.

'A navy man,' Grand said, 'with sympathies for the South.'

Belle took the photograph back and smiled at the portrait. 'With sympathies for me,' she said. 'Sadly, dear Sam died.' She put the photograph back. 'You were lucky to catch me, Mr Grand. I sail for the States next month. I have enjoyed my time here, but without Sam . . .'

Her eyes cast downwards.

Grand nodded. 'London can be a lonely place,' he said.

'It can.' She looked up suddenly, smiling and clearing her mind of bitter memories. 'Now, how can I help you?'

'Lafayette Baker is dead.' Grand came straight to the point.

Her eyes widened. 'So, there is a God,' she said. 'Although I had never seriously doubted it.'

'He was murdered.'

This time her eyes narrowed and she drew herself up, ready to stand and call someone to throw him out. 'Did the government send you?' she asked.

'Indirectly,' Grand told her. 'I have received a commission from Luther Baker.'

Belle snorted. 'That reptile,' she said. 'If the Devil cast his net, Mr Grand, he'd have caught him too.'

'God or the Devil, Miss Boyd,' Grand said. 'You'll have to make your mind up.'

'Oh, I did, Mr Grand,' Belle smiled, 'a long time ago. Tell me, did you really have to bring your sidearm to talk to me?'

Grand's face flickered despite himself. His pistol was well hidden under his coat. Luther Baker seemed to have been wide of the mark in describing Belle Boyd's deadliness. 'Force of habit,' he shrugged.

'May I see it?'

For a moment, Grand hesitated. Then he slipped the Colt from the shoulder-holster and spun it in his hand so the walnut butt faced the woman. To his horror, she spun it too, cocked it, threw it from right hand to left and reversed it again, so that the butt faced Grand.

'Very nice,' she smiled, enjoying his discomfort. 'The first man I killed couldn't believe I could handle a gun either. Of course, it was a Dragoon model, a *little* heavy for a seventeen year old.'

'The first man?' Grand took the gun as quickly as he could and put it away.

'Oh, all right,' she trilled. 'The *only* man. I must say, Mr Grand, that most people I meet think one is enough. Or even, in nicer company, one too many.'

'Er . . . may I ask . . .?'

'He was a drunken Billy Yank, Mr Grand,' she said. 'He and a handful of brutes broke into our home at Front Royal. He first trampled on the flag of the Confederacy, then he insulted my mother.'

'So . . .?'

'So I shot the son of a bitch,' Belle said, matter-of-factly. 'The Boyds don't allow bad language in their house.'

Eliza returned at that moment with a tea tray. 'Thank you, Eliza,' Belle said. 'I'll be mother. You take little Grace for her constitutional now, d'y'hear?'

Eliza was still scowling at Grand.

'It's all right,' Belle told her. 'Captain Grand isn't a captain any more. He's just come to talk over old times.'

For a moment, Eliza hesitated. It was the old times she was afraid of. Then she snorted, turned her back on Grand and marched off towards the nursery.

'Miss Boyd.' Grand took the proffered tea as though in a daze. 'I don't understand . . .'

'How I escaped a hanging? Why, Mr Grand,' she put the teapot down and reached across, trailing her fingers over his hand. Was it his imagination or had Belle Boyd suddenly become deeper South than ever? Her words were pure honey, by way of Virginia. 'I was a seventeen year ol' maiden, whose honour had been sullied by an animal.' She dropped the deepest Virginian, 'or that's how the bastard's commanding officer saw it, anyhow. He was a sweetheart, that man. Had daughters about my age.'

Matthew Grand smiled. Then he laughed. 'I'm glad,' he said, 'that there's only one Belle Boyd. Otherwise the war might have had a different outcome.'

'You flatter me, sir,' she drawled. 'Now,' she sipped her tea and sat up straighter, back to business. 'Lafayette Baker's dead. Why should cousin Luther send you to me?'

'You knew the colonel?' Grand sipped his tea too.

'I did,' she nodded, remembering the hard eyes and heavy beard of the man she now knew to be dead. 'July Sixty-Two if memory serves. The Old Capitol Prison in Washington.' Her face hardened. 'Room Nineteen.'

'That was your cell?'

She smiled in spite of the memories that were already screaming inside her. 'Not exactly,' she said. 'Room Nineteen was Colonel Baker's private quarters. His torture chamber.'

Grand looked at her over the rim of his cup. He knew what the war had cost him, the loss of a love, a career, a home. And he had been on the winning side. 'He used torture on you?'

Belle Boyd left the side table and the chair and crossed to the window. Outside, the sedate suburb of St John's Wood shimmered in the summer sunshine, but all she could see was Washington in the late war, its streets clogged with marching men, supply wagons and mules. What greenery there had been had long been destroyed by cattle, milling around Swampoodle, searching for the grass that had gone. She saw the circles of white tents that stretched away from the river. She saw the Potomac sliding dark and deep and she fancied she saw the water run red.

She turned back, away from the memories, 'He was an artist, was Lafayette Baker.'

'An artist?'

'He knew exactly which wires to pull to make us dance to his tune. Like marionettes at the peep shows. He used iron on the men and his own fists. That was the thing about the Old Capitol; it had strange echoes. A whisper could carry for yards through the piping, around corners, down shafts. A scream could shatter your ears.'

She paused. Grand gave her time.

'And then, of course, the colonel liked to display his work. He would chain people, bloodied and broken, in the passageways and the halls. We walked past them every day on our way to eat or to the exercise yard. We saw what he was capable of and he made sure we saw it.'

Belle came back to her chair and sat down. 'No, with me – with any female prisoner – he played games strictly using his mind, and ours. Did I know that my father was dead? They had hanged him for passing secrets to the Rebs. Had I heard about my mother? She had been passed around the soldiers. He even knew the regiment. The Fifty-Fourth Massachusetts.'

'A black regiment,' Grand nodded.

'It was the constant drip, drip of hopelessness,' she said, 'making me believe that there was no cause left to fight for.'

'Was any of it true?'

'Not a word, as far as I know. My mother and father are alive and well and still at Front Royal. Oh, times are hard for them, of course . . . Baker kept me in prison for a month.'

'And you told him . . .?'

'Precisely nothing,' she said.

Grand had finished his tea and there was a clattering in the hallway. A young girl scuttled into the room wearing a little crinoline and poke bonnet, with Eliza not far behind.

'Darling,' Belle hugged the child to her and kissed her. 'This gentleman is Mr Grand. He has come all the way from

America to see us. Isn't that nice? Mr Grand, my daughter, Grace Hardinge.'

Grand stood up, 'Ma'am,' he half bowed.

Grace's attempt at a curtsey left a little to be desired, but she had given it her best shot. 'Pleased to meet you, sir,' she lisped.

Eliza shepherded the girl away. That was more than enough contact with soldiers for one so young. You couldn't be too careful.

'She's delightful.' Grand sat down again when the girl and her nanny had gone.

'She's a daughter of the Confederacy, Mr Grand. I wonder how she'll cope with it all when I take her home.' She looked at him. 'I still don't know what Luther Baker thought I could tell you, about cousin Laff, I mean.'

'Neither do I,' Grand sighed. He stood up again. 'You have been very kind, Mrs Hardinge,' he said, 'I'll see myself out.'

She stood up with him. 'There is someone else who may be of more help than I,' she said.

'Oh?'

'Judah Benjamin. You'll find him at Lincoln's Inn, inappropriately enough.'

'Judah Benjamin?' James Batchelor frowned, putting down his newspaper.

'Does the name mean anything to you?' Grand asked.

'Of course it does.' Batchelor climbed briefly on to his high horse. You could take the boy out of Fleet Street, but it was more difficult to take Fleet Street out of the boy. 'I know him to recognize him in the street – not to speak to, exactly. I used to see him when I worked at the *Telegraph* – he wrote the occasional article for them; might still do as far as I know.' Batchelor had shifted his allegiance and now read any other paper but the *Telegraph*, although he understood Mrs Manciple occasionally put it down when the cat wasn't well. 'Big, roly-poly chap, isn't he? There can't be two with that name, surely?'

'Belle Boyd had him down for Secretary of State in Jefferson Davis's Confederate cabinet,' Grand said. 'Do people like that write for the *Telegraph*?'

'Fortunes of war, I suppose,' Batchelor murmured.

'Well, if you know the man, James, I think you should be the one to go see him. Lincoln's Inn. Know where that is?'

Batchelor knew. He took a cab in the Strand, rattling northeast to Chancery Lane where the traffic was always murder. At the red-brick gateway a pompous flunkey in livery stopped him.

'I'd like to see Mr Benjamin, please,' Batchelor said.

'Is he expecting you, sir?' The flunkey spoke as though he had a permanent smell under his nose. To be fair to him, this near the river and with the prevailing wind, he often had.

'Not exactly. If you could tell him Belle Boyd would like a word.'

The flunkey looked Batchelor up and down. He seemed an ordinary enough young man, but you just couldn't tell these days. There were such stories, about St James's Park in particular . . .

'If you would be so good as to wait here, sir,' the flunkey said, and vanished up some stairs inside the gatehouse.

For a moment, Batchelor toyed with following him, but he hoped his announcement would provide incentive enough for an entrée to the great man. And so it proved.

Judah P. Benjamin, when he appeared in the wake of the returning flunkey, was every bit as roly-poly as Batchelor remembered him, though it was well over a year since he had seen him last. His frock coat stretched over his ample front and the beard curled luxuriantly over his several chins. But the eyes twinkled kindly and the smile was ever ready.

'Belle,' he said. 'The years have not been kind.'

Batchelor glanced at the flunkey, who looked so disapproving he thought he was going to faint. 'I'm sorry for the subterfuge, Mr Benjamin,' he said. The flunkey did not look any more reassured to hear that, so Benjamin took Batchelor by the arm.

'Let's stroll in the garden,' the lawyer said. 'One of the lungs of London,' and the flunkey was grateful to leave them to it.

'I know the face,' Benjamin said quietly, looking for his favourite bench in the shade of the rhododendrons, 'but the name . . .'

'Forgive me, sir.' Batchelor sat alongside his man. 'James Batchelor,' and he passed the man his card.

Benjamin's face fell. 'Enquiry agent,' he read aloud. 'If it's cases you're chasing, Mr Batchelor, I'm afraid I'm not your man.'

Batchelor had only heard Benjamin talking once before, in old Leigh Hunt's office at the *Telegraph*, and he continued to be fascinated by the accent – a mix of the West Indies, the Deep South and the clipped consonants of the Chosen People.

'It's about Colonel Lafayette Baker,' the detective said.

'Baker?' Benjamin raised an eyebrow. 'Don't tell me the old reprobate has sent you to arrest me.'

'Arrest you, sir?' Batchelor repeated. 'Why?'

'You used to write for the *Telegraph*, didn't you?' It was all coming back to Benjamin now.

'I did,' Batchelor smiled, oddly proud to be remembered by a man who had once virtually run the Confederate States of America.

'Then that explains your lack of knowledge of current affairs. Jeff Davis and I are traitors in the States, Mr Batchelor. We raised the flag of rebellion as far as the North is concerned. Laff Baker isn't the forgiving sort.'

'I thought Jefferson Davis was released without trial.' Batchelor was keen to prove that his knowledge of current affairs was not as woeful as all that.

'So he was, my boy.' Benjamin pulled a cheroot out of his cigar case but didn't offer one to Batchelor. 'But since when do the Lafayette Bakers of this world trouble themselves with little things like trials and due process? What does he want?'

'Nothing,' Batchelor told him. 'He's dead.'

'Well, well, well.' Benjamin blew delighted smoke rings to the dark-leafed canopy overhead. That seemed to be everybody's comment on the passing of Lafayette Baker. 'What's all this got to do with me? And, by the way, how is Belle Boyd involved?'

'She sent me to see you, sir,' Batchelor went on, leaving Grand out of the equation for simplicity's sake. 'You see, Colonel Baker was murdered.'

Benjamin whipped the cigar from his mouth. 'The Hell you say,' he drawled.

'Miss Boyd imagined you'd know something about that.'

The lawyer looked hard at the younger man then burst out laughing. 'Always had a sense of humour, did Belle,' he said. 'Tell me; did she say how I managed to kill the old bastard from three thousand miles away?'

Batchelor smiled. 'I don't think that Miss Boyd implicated you personally, sir,' he assured him.

'Well, now,' Benjamin beamed, 'that's hugely gratifying. Of course, there's nothing the Yankees would like better than all us Southern trash turning on each other, like rattlers in a pit.'

Looking at the well-fed lawyer in the civilized gardens of Lincoln's Inn, Batchelor found it difficult to balance the words 'trash' and 'rattlers' – especially since he wasn't totally certain what they were.

'I'll tell you this, Mr Enquiry Agent,' the big man smiled. 'For a while back there, in the war for the States, I guess you could say that Laff Baker and I were the two sides of the same coin. He ran the National Detective Police – which, by the way, is about as national as the City of London force over here. I ran the secret service for the Confederacy – that's how I met Belle. If I'd had my chance back then, I'd willingly have put a slug in Laff Baker's brain. But now . . . what would be the point?'

'Revenge, Mr Benjamin?' Batchelor suggested.

'Oh, yeah,' Benjamin's Louisiana came to the fore for a moment. 'A dish best served cold; yeah, I know. But sometimes,' he threw his cigar butt into the rhododendrons, 'it's a dish best not served at all. Tell me, Mr Batchelor, how are you involved? With Baker's death, I mean?'

'My colleague and I have received a commission to look into things.'

'I see.' Benjamin nodded. 'Are you going over there? To Washington? I don't see how you can solve a murder long distance.'

'We have booked a passage for next month,' Batchelor told him.

'Well, give my regards to the President,' Benjamin said, 'and to cousin Luther.'

'I will,' Batchelor said, and stood up. Judah P. Benjamin had walked the corridors of power in Richmond. He had thrown in his lot with the most desperate escapade of modern times and he had lost. But Judah P. Benjamin was a survivor. The Secretary of State of the Confederate States of America was now a lawyer enrolled at Lincoln's Inn, well known on the Northern Circuit and a man tipped for a QC. Could a man bounce back like this and *not* have anything to do with the murder of Lafayette Baker?

'And while you're over there,' the lawyer called as Batchelor took his leave, 'you might take yourself for a trip to the South. Specifically a little town called Knoxville in Tennessee. Ask for Mr Munson.'

# THREE

There was a strong wind from the southwest as the Guion Line's *Manhattan* braved the waters of the Atlantic. The black smoke belching from the funnels drifted almost flat to disappear into the rolling grey clouds. At least with the thud of the engines and the roar of the wind, Matthew Grand was glad he couldn't hear the fiddle and the bodhrán rising from the immigrants in steerage; the sons of Erin making for the land of the free but not willing to leave their music behind them.

'How long did Captain Price estimate?' he asked Batchelor as they huddled under the blankets on the deck. 'For the crossing, I mean.'

'Hmm?' Batchelor had his nose buried in a book and his mind was patently elsewhere.

'The crossing,' Grand repeated, 'to New York. How long did he say?'

'Hmm.' It was not a question this time, it was a statement.

Grand was patience itself. 'Still,' he said, 'I expect when we've rounded the Horn, all will become clear.'

'It certainly will,' Batchelor murmured. His eyes had not left the page.

'It's this new Suez Canal I'm looking forward to.' Grand's smile was frozen now and not just by the weather.

'Absolutely,' Batchelor nodded, turning pages furiously. 'It will make a huge difference, I have no doubt.'

'James!' The American had had enough and he shouted in his colleague's face.

'Sorry – what?' Batchelor looked up for the first time in over an hour.

'What *is* that?' Grand pointed to the book.

'Oh, it's riveting,' Batchelor assured him. '*Belle Boyd in Camp and Prison*. I can't put it down.'

'Clearly,' Grand muttered.

'It's fascinating. I wish *I'd* gone to see her now.'

'No, you don't, James,' Grand assured him. 'She'd have swallowed you whole.'

'For instance,' he turned back a few pages. 'Did you know she was Stonewall Jackson's ADC?'

'Uh-huh,' Grand nodded.

'She ran across a battlefield to warn him of an ambush.'

'Uh-huh.'

'Bullets were whizzing around her.'

'Yes, they would be.'

'Made holes in her dress.'

'They do that, bullets.'

'Anyway, the general was so impressed, he awarded her the Southern Cross of Honour.'

'Don't forget we spell it "Honor",' Grand corrected him. He could almost hear that redundant 'u' in Batchelor's voice.

'That's what I said. And she became his ADC.'

'James . . .'

'Hmm?' Batchelor was back in his book again.

'I wouldn't believe everything you read in there.'

'Oh, but . . .'

'You're a penny dreadful writer, for God's sake.'

'Well, I'd like to be,' Batchelor reminded him. 'Haven't got there yet.'

'My point,' Grand said, 'is that some literature should be taken with wagon-train-loads of salt.'

'Oh, really?' Batchelor was a little crestfallen. He had never met the mercurial Belle Boyd but, after the preface of the woman's book, he was with her, heart and soul.

'The South,' Grand said solemnly, 'isn't quite as romantic as Miss Boyd makes out.'

Batchelor closed the volume like a drowning man throwing away a lifebelt. He looked up at the ship's rail, dipping under then rising above the white caps as the *Manhattan* rolled her way west. 'Tell me, Matthew,' he said. 'It was July when we left Liverpool, wasn't it?'

Grand nodded.

'And it will still be July when we get to Washington?'

'Hopefully,' Grand said.

'So, it'll still be summer. You know, hot?'

'Oh, yes,' Grand smiled. 'I think I can promise you that the empire of King Mud will be hot as Hell.'

King Mud's mud had baked hard by the time Grand and Batchelor reached Washington. The train had taken them to the New Jersey Avenue Station, all snorting steam and bustle. Batchelor couldn't be sure, but the trains seemed to have American accents; even the dogs, weaving in amongst the travellers, didn't yap in quite the way London dogs did. From the station, a cab rattled through straight streets without number, following the orderly plan of all American cities, a logic of city planning that had never appealed across the Atlantic. After the Strand petered out, having run straight as a die for half a mile, all roads became the tangled rabbit warren of Alsatia, where a man, especially an American, needed a compass to navigate.

That was not a problem in Washington, District of Columbia. The city planners had hacked a city out of a wilderness, although – to James Batchelor's parvenu eyes – it still looked pretty much like a wilderness. He had to keep reminding himself that only three years ago, Washington was a city under siege, a battlefront full of the horrors of war. And just across the Potomac, at the end of Long Bridge, stood Virginia; already, inexplicably, the heart of the Confederacy.

Willard's Hotel, just off Pennsylvania Avenue, was comfortable enough; black flunkeys in bright livery carried luggage in all directions. Grand had booked a suite of rooms. He knew of old how crowded Washington always was, especially in the summer, although he had not seen it at peace for nearly eight years. And he also felt a little guilty; Luther Baker's Treasury Bond was open-ended, but even the United States government had its limits, and there would be other expenses down the line; *two* suites would be an indulgence too far.

'Why is it called Downtown, exactly?' Batchelor asked, finding hangers for his shirts. 'Is there an Uptown?'

Grand smiled. This foreigner had *so* much to learn. 'No,' he said, looking out at the trees on Pennsylvania Avenue, heavy with the leaves of summer. 'We've got Frogtown, Bloodfield, Swampoodle and the Mall. You'll soon feel at home, though.' He pointed east. 'English Hill is that way, not an American half-mile from Capitol

Hill – that's where most of the country's criminals live and work. And before you get hold of a map and start asking tricky questions – the Island is not an island. Hell's Bottom is north of here – and there's no Hell's Top.'

As Grand could have predicted, Batchelor looked confused.

'Cheer up, James,' he laughed. 'I'll show you the sights later. But tomorrow, we have to be in Murder Bay.'

Batchelor's eyes widened.

'It's not *quite* as bad as it sounds,' Grand told him, 'and it's where we'll find the man who's paying for this little sightseeing trip. You'll like Cousin Luther. But probably not much.'

James Batchelor had seen brothels before. Bawdy houses, bordellos, houses of ill-repute – call them what you will, every city had them. The Haymarket, Seven Dials, Whitechapel; those were the dens of vice in London. But Washington was different. The houses of Hooker's Division were opulent enough – you could find hundreds of them in the slightly less salubrious areas of Pimlico and off the Strand. But here, hard-eyed men lolled against railings, smoking pipes or cheroots and watching the passing trade.

'How can I help you gentlemen?' one of the pimps asked, tipping his hat in mock civility. 'We cater to all tastes. Black? White? Mulatto, maybe?'

'We'll settle for the Wolf's Den,' Grand said.

The pipe smoke blew out of the side of his mouth. 'Marble Alley?' he asked. 'Whaddya go there for? I got a fourteen year old fresh from the country.'

But Grand and Batchelor were already walking away.

'Somethin' younger, maybe?' The pimp had to try one last time, but turned away when he got no reaction, spitting copiously into the dried mud at his feet.

James Batchelor didn't like alleyways and the one they entered now was certainly not made of marble. It was narrow and dark and, unusually for a Washington street, kinked sharply halfway along. Was it Batchelor's imagination, or were the men sitting on the steps that led to the open doors getting larger? And uglier? Definitely uglier.

'Are you carrying your pea-shooter?' he felt constrained to ask Grand. The sticky summer sun had not penetrated Marble

Alley, not at this hour of the morning, and it looked as though it never would.

'Sure,' Grand nodded, counting the houses as they passed. 'And, despite Inspector Tanner, it's loaded. I won't reach for it now, but I've got a second in my stocking. It's only a two-shot Derringer but I suggest you borrow it.'

'I wouldn't know one end of it from the other,' Batchelor protested.

'Suit yourself,' Grand shrugged, 'but if things get ugly around here, don't rely on your fists. Use your boots, any furniture you can get hold of. And when a man goes down, make sure he stays down.'

'Sounds like one of Her Majesty's tea parties.' Batchelor's levity was not really working this morning. Not on him, at any rate.

Grand had stopped walking. He was looking up a flight of steps to where a huge black man stood lolling against the door-frame, arms folded. Batchelor watched as Grand pulled his hands from his pocket and spread his arms.

'Here I stand,' he called to the man. 'I can do no other.'

The man came down the steps. He was half a head taller than Grand and positively dwarfed Batchelor. 'You packin'?' he asked.

'Shoulder-holster,' Grand said. 'Left breast.'

The man reached under his coat and pulled the pistol free. 'You?' he grunted at Batchelor.

'He's from England,' Grand explained.

The huge doorkeeper scowled and nodded. Batchelor followed Grand up the steps and into the darkness.

A piano was playing somewhere; old, out of tune and, unless the pianist was a master of syncopation, there were rather a lot of notes missing as well. It was like no music James Batchelor had heard before, at any rate. The hallway was plain and drab with the dark stains of old mud along the carpet and up the stairs. The lampshades were fringed a deep crimson and the gas lights popped and flared. Grand knocked on a closed door to his right.

'Who's there?' a voice called.

'Childe Harold,' Grand said.

Batchelor looked at him. Had they both entered some sort of circle of Hell?

The door swung open and a waft of incense, sickly and

powerful, hit them like a wall. A single lamp burned on a circular table and someone sat behind it, playing solitaire. His hands were smooth and supple, snaking over the Devil's picture books with accustomed ease. His face was in darkness.

'Captain Grand,' the card player said. The hands paused. 'Who's this?'

'Introductions are due. James Batchelor, Enquiry Agent – say hello to Lieutenant Luther Baker, the gentleman who is kindly paying our hotel bill.'

'Lieutenant Baker,' Batchelor said, refusing to use the American pronunciation of the title.

'Just plain Mister these days,' Baker said. He tilted the lamp and for the first time Batchelor saw his face. Baker had a centre parting, the hair Macassared down. His beard was full and wild, deep black with streaks of grey. But his eyes were what held Batchelor's gaze. They were like coals in the pallor of his face. 'I seem to remember you hung up your saber too, Grand.'

'I did,' Grand nodded, sitting unbidden on a chair facing Baker. 'I guess Washington's still crawling with ex-soldiers.'

'It is,' Baker nodded. 'At least we're all handy for a reunion or two, huh?' What passed for a smile flickered over his face. He turned to Batchelor, who sat down next to Grand. 'So,' he said, 'you've doubled your fee at a single stroke, Grand.' He looked Batchelor up and down. 'And what makes you worth all that money, Mr Batchelor?'

'The codes threw me at first,' Batchelor said. '"Here I stand. I can do no other." That's Martin Luther, isn't it? The man who started the Reformation. That's what he said in court at Worms when the Catholic Church asked him what the Hell he thought he was doing. He's your namesake, Mr Baker. Then there's *Childe Harold*. That came to me as I walked into this room. It's one of Lord Byron's more noteworthy efforts at poetry – "Childe Roland to the dark tower came". And that's your second name, isn't it – Byron?'

Baker nodded. 'You coulda told him that,' he said to Grand.

'I could,' Grand agreed. 'But I didn't.'

There was a sudden rustle of silk and a sultry beauty swept into the room. Her skin was the colour of chocolate and diamonds sparkled from her ears and around her throat. Her scarlet dress was tight at the waist and her breasts threatened to escape from the top of it. 'Why, Luther, honey, I'm sorry. I didn't know you had guests.'

Batchelor was already on his feet.

'Don't get up, honey-child,' the girl drawled. She looked the Englishman up and down with rather more favour than Baker had. 'My, ain't you the cute one?'

'Gentlemen,' Baker said, slapping the girl's crinoline as she swept past him, 'this is Julep. She's the best thing – some might say the only thing of note – to come out of New Orleans.'

The girl laughed.

'Julep,' Batchelor said. 'That's an unusual name.'

She licked her lips and moved closer to him. 'It's 'cos I cost a mint, sugar,' she purred. 'Say,' and she was frowning now, 'that accent. Where you from, honey, New England?'

'Old England,' Batchelor told her. 'London.'

'London, England,' Julep repeated. 'Wow! Wanna try one of these?' She whipped a small packet out of her cleavage. Batchelor looked startled. 'Relax, honey,' she trilled. 'They're only Nonpareils.'

'Candy, Mr Batchelor,' Baker translated. 'It ain't going to kill you.'

Hesitantly, Batchelor helped himself.

'Get lost, now, Julep.' Baker slid the cards together and laid them face down. 'The grown-ups want to talk.'

The girl snatched her candy back. 'I'll be seeing *you* again,' she said, tapping Batchelor's nose with a jewelled finger, and she swept from the room.

When Batchelor had regained both his composure and his seat, and with Julep's perfume still swirling in the room, Baker looked at the enquiry agents. 'I'll come straight to the point, gentlemen,' he said. 'Stanton.'

# FOUR

'Edwin McMasters Stanton,' Batchelor was reading in the warm lamp glow of the Willard. 'Do you know him – personally, I mean?'

Matthew Grand was savouring his brandy. 'Our paths never crossed,' he said, 'but, after Lincoln was killed, he was a law unto himself. Ran the government. What have you got there?'

'Usual biographical details,' Batchelor told him. 'Born in a place called Steubenville, Ohio, in 1814, so that makes him fifty-four.'

'Old enough to know better,' Grand nodded. The brandy was burning his tonsils.

'Became a lawyer.'

'Somebody has to.'

'Got to Washington in Fifty-Six. Made Attorney General under President Buchanan.' Batchelor paused. 'President Buchanan? Not sure I've ever heard of him . . . where was I? Oh, yes, opposed secession and Lincoln made him Secretary of War – that was January Sixty-Two. You'd have been in the thick of things by then.'

'I would,' Grand remembered. 'I was.'

'So he switched sides,' Batchelor was trying to make sense of American politics. 'Party-wise, I mean. Became a Republican.'

'I always remember Lincoln's comment on him,' Grand said. He cleared his throat and struck a declamatory attitude. '"He is the rock on the beach of our national ocean against which the breakers dash and roar . . . without him, I should be destroyed."'

Batchelor looked at Grand. It was great rhetoric, but both men knew that Lincoln *had* been destroyed, shot dead by a maniac at Ford's Theatre the same night that Grand had gone to see a play. Where was Stanton then?

'You see, what I don't understand is why, if Luther Baker has a man in the frame for his cousin's death, he's sent for us.'

'He needs evidence,' Grand told him. 'Stanton's not in office any more, but neither is Luther Baker. He can't pull the strings he used to and Stanton is angling for a job on the bench of the Supreme Court. Mars outgunned the Bakers during the war and he's still doing it now.'

'Mars?' Batchelor frowned.

'Stanton's nickname. He's a little feller, but he packs a mighty punch.'

'Oh, the god of war. Yes, I see. But why couldn't Baker have brought the police in? Or the Pinkertons?'

Grand raised an eyebrow. 'The war made us all jump at shadows,' he said. 'If we trusted each other before Fort Sumter, we sure as Hell don't now. Laff Baker made a lot of enemies here in Washington, Stanton among them. Cousin Luther wants an independent, impartial enquiry – that's our job. All very laudable in a way.' He caught the look on Batchelor's face. 'James, my boy, you look perplexed.'

'If Lafayette Baker made a lot of enemies, how can we be sure Stanton's our man?'

Grand nodded. 'I was thinking much the same thing myself. But, for the moment, Luther's the piper, so we'll dance to his tune. How are you with medical matters?'

'Dr Rickards?'

The man with the grey dundrearies looked up and adjusted his pince-nez. 'That's entirely possible, young man. What can I do for you?'

'My name is Batchelor,' Batchelor said. 'I write for the *Telegraph*.' James Batchelor was always a little vague with his tenses.

'The *Baltimore Telegraph*?' No one could accuse Dr Rickards of not being parochial.

'No, sir,' Batchelor explained. 'The London *Telegraph*.'

'London, England?'

Batchelor nodded.

'I thought I caught that foreign accent. If this is about antiseptics . . .'

'No, sir, it's about the late Colonel Lafayette Baker. I'm writing a piece on him. You were his physician, I understand.'

'I was.' It was noticeable that the doctor, at first open and affable, had suddenly become morose, careful.

'His death was a tragedy.' Batchelor sat opposite Rickards with pencil and notepad in hand. He didn't think 'enquiry agent' would get him very far in Washington's medical circles; as a journalist, he might do better.

'It was.' Dr Rickards had become monosyllabic.

'I understand he is buried in Philadelphia.'

'He is.'

'What was the cause of his death, doctor?'

Rickards pointedly took his half-hunter from his waistcoat pocket. 'I am a very busy man, Mr . . . er . . .'

'Batchelor. For my readers, though, for the record.'

'For the record,' Rickards sighed, 'it was dropsy of the brain. If that is all, sir?'

'Well, I . . .'

But it *was* all. Dr Rickards had gone.

Batchelor had learned almost nothing. Except perhaps that American doctors were as tight-lipped and self-protective as their British counterparts. Grand was out renewing old acquaintances, so it would not be until the evening that the pair of them could decide what to do next. Batchelor boarded a streetcar of the Washington and Georgetown Railroad Company at Seventh Street and took his seat, trying to remember his way back to the Willard. These straight streets and right-angled junctions were all very well and good, but the lack of character, of *geography*, was really turning his sense of direction upside down all right. He had almost worked it out when, suddenly, a burly guard barked in his ear.

'What the hell are you doin' there?' Batchelor had been miles away – just approaching the junction of Twelfth and Constitution Avenue to be totally precise – and jumped, before looking up at the man with startled eyes. But the guard wasn't looking at him; he was looking at a sedate old black lady at his elbow. Batchelor had tipped his hat to her already before he had taken his seat, and the woman's smile had surprised him; there seemed hidden depths to it.

'I'm talking to you, girl,' the guard snapped.

The old lady turned slowly, her smile gone, her face composed. 'I'm not your girl, mister,' she said.

'No, and you ain't my passenger, neither. Get out!'

'I've paid my fare,' the woman said.

'For the *outside*,' the guard reminded her, 'not in here.'

He lunged across and grabbed the woman by the shawl. She was not only old, she was tiny, and the guard lifted her off her feet.

'What the hell do you think you're doing?' Batchelor was on his feet, knocking the guard's arm away, 'treating a lady like that.'

'*Lady?*' The guard's eyes bulged. 'Mister, where the hell you been for the last thirty years?'

'London, mostly,' Batchelor told him. 'And over there, bus conductors don't manhandle passengers, especially ladies.'

'Well, we got laws over here,' the guard persisted as the streetcar rattled on, the horses lathered in the heat of the day. 'Blacks ain't allowed to ride inside the cars.' He scowled at the woman. 'And she knows that damn well.'

'I thought you people just fought a war over slavery,' Batchelor said.

'What's that got to do with it?' The guard seemed genuinely confused. 'The war was over state rights, mister, whatever some bleeding hearts will try and tell you.'

The old woman touched Batchelor's sleeve. 'It's very kind of you, sir,' she said, 'but . . .'

'Out!' The guard grabbed her again and Batchelor had had enough. He knocked the man's arm away with one fist and brought the other hard into the pit of his stomach. The guard jack-knifed, but a sudden lurch of the streetcar made Batchelor lose his balance and both of them were sprawled on the dusty floor, gouging and punching in the confined space between the seats. The other passengers did what passers-by will always do in situations such as this; some moved to the end of the car, others jeered and whistled, cheering on the guard or the pint-sized Limey, depending on their preferences. The little black lady kept demurely and sensibly out of it, but the brawlers were up on their feet again, trading punches. What had Grand said? Use your boots and any furniture that comes to hand? Well, on the Washington and Georgetown Railroad Company's streetcars, there wasn't much furniture, so boots it had to be.

It was as though the guard had read Batchelor's mind, because as the boot came up towards his groin, he caught it and pushed the Englishman back. Batchelor steadied himself along each seat as he passed it, but he was moving backwards and all the momentum was with the guard. They reached the open door just as the driver, aware of the commotion, hauled on the reins, and the pair somersaulted off the car and into the dust of Pennsylvania Avenue, right into the arms of the law.

Matthew Grand had not sent Batchelor off on his medical journey to get rid of him – or at least, not *just* to get rid of him. He needed to spend some time in this town of his, to reacquaint himself with it, to breathe its air, to feel his home back in his lungs and his blood. He hadn't realized how homesick for Washington he had been until he had stepped down from the train. But now he leaned against a wall, warm with the sun, and turned his face up into the shade-dappling of a walnut tree, overhanging from the garden on the other side of the wall. He was oblivious of the snick of the wicket and would have happily dreamed the day away had he not had a sudden buffet in the ribs and heard a shrill voice in his ear.

'Matthew Grand!' That voice had once had him dancing attention, but it had no such powers now. He opened his eyes and stood up slowly, looking down at the woman by his side, squaring up for another poke at his ribs.

'Arlette. How lovely to see you again.' Matthew Grand had never been a very good liar, but for Arlette he would make an exception.

'Why are you lurking outside my house?' she hissed.

Now, Grand was on his dignity. 'I was certainly not lurking, ma'am. And I had no idea it was your house.' He looked over his shoulder at the substantial pile which was visible over the sun-warmed wall. 'Although, if it is, you seem to have done well for yourself.'

'No thanks to you,' she said, drawing herself up and tucking her parasol under her arm. He was glad to see her do this – that last jab had been quite painful. 'I was the laughing stock of Washington for months.'

'But not any longer,' he observed.

'Well, no.' She allowed herself a smirk. 'I did marry well as a matter of fact. The gentleman is a little older than me, but . . . the war left us so short of men.'

'How thoughtless.'

She narrowed his eyes at him. 'You were always cold, Matthew Grand. Cold as ice. Trust you not to think of all us women left behind.'

There was, quite literally, no response that he felt it safe to give. A smack upside the head would have served, but he felt that may be inappropriate. After a silence, he said, 'But you're happy, Letty, are you?' He touched her forearm gently. She couldn't help it if she had but one thought in her pretty, empty head.

She looked frantically from side to side. 'Don't touch me,' she hissed. 'If Madison should see . . .'

'Madison?'

'My husband. He was born on the day James Madison became President.'

Grand looked at the sky while he did some simple subtraction. 'My land, Letty,' he said, all sophistication gone. 'He certainly is a little older than you, isn't he? By . . . thirty-six years!'

'He's very vigorous,' she asserted, with perhaps a little too much fervour. 'Look.' She parted the front of her duster coat and showed him a swollen belly.

'Well done, both of you,' Grand said, smiling. He was genuinely happy for Arlette. She would finally have someone she could dominate well and truly. 'When do you expect the happy event?' To Grand's untutored eye, it could be any minute.

'My midwife says it will be in the next week,' Arlette said, covering herself back up. 'Apparently, you can work it by counting forty weeks from the day . . . well, from the day.'

'Not that vigorous, then,' Grand remarked.

'What?' Arlette almost spat the word.

'Well, if you can work it out from The Day. What vigorous man with a hot little bride in his bed gives her the chance to know what The Day was?'

'How do you know?' she said, coming closer and tipping her face up to his. 'Married, are you? Have a hot little bride, do you?'

He put her at arm's length. 'What I am and what I have is no longer any of your business, Arlette,' he said and tipped his hat.

'I see marriage hasn't changed you. That's nice. Goodbye,' and he stepped around her and walked jauntily down the street.

'Matthew Grand, come back here this minute!' He heard her little steel-tipped boot smack down on the pavement. Always a good little stamper, was Arlette. He waved an arm in the air. 'I said goodbye, Arlette.'

That was a close one, he thought as he made his way along G, heading west. He realized with a jolt that he was missing the twisting alleys of London; as he looked ahead, he could see for what seemed like miles, without a twist or a turn to be had. He could hear running feet and decided to ignore them. Then he remembered the little Arlette or Madison, waiting to be born forty weeks from the day, and he relented. Arlette stood there, panting, hat awry.

'What are you doing, Arlette?' he said, but didn't take her arm or ameliorate his tone. He had realized long ago he didn't really like this woman, let alone love her. But he was a human being when all was said and done. 'Would you like to sit down?' There was a coffee shop just a few doors down and he steered her towards it. She was too out of breath to complain, but contented herself with swivelling her eyes from side to side, which he took to convey she was afraid that Madison might spot them.

He gestured to the bus boy and sat Arlette at a quiet table away from the window. 'Take your time,' he said to her. He could treat her like a client; that would be the best.

'Madison . . .'

'Yes, I know. Madison would be furious, madly jealous; he'll tan my hide. I can manage.' He just stopped himself from adding that a man over twice his age would give him no trouble, but didn't when he saw her face. 'Arlette? Are you afraid of your husband?'

A hot tear coursed down her cheek and dripped off her chin. Arlette had never been an attractive crier and marriage and incipient motherhood had not changed that. He handed her a handkerchief and she blew her nose gratefully. 'Clara Rathbone's husband has tried to kill her, you know,' she said, apparently out of nowhere.

'Poor Clara. Poor Henry. I gather he had reason . . .' Clara had always been a little loose around the stays as he recalled.

Perhaps she hadn't changed on marriage, any more than Arlette had.

'No, no reason. Poor Clara had . . . well, she had stopped doing what she had done through the war. She was only cheering up those poor boys, you know.'

Grand settled for a smile.

'So, anyway, he tried to poison her first; then, when that didn't work, he tried to drown her. In the Potomac.'

'It makes sense. Big body of water like that, pointless really to go elsewhere . . .' He looked up at her. 'Henry really tried to drown her?' he asked, more gently.

'When the poison didn't work, yes.'

'That's dreadful. I suppose it was the shock . . . Ford's Theatre and so on.'

'He never really recovered,' she said, wiping her eyes.

Henry Rathbone hadn't. He had been Lincoln's guest in the Presidential Box that fateful night and the madman John Wilkes Booth had slashed his arm with his knife, having sent a Derringer slug into Lincoln's brain. Over the months that had followed, the memory of it had never left him and as months became years, his fears had crystallized into a certainty of his wife's infidelity.

'But you? Why are you frightened, Arlette? Rathbone has nothing to do with you, surely?'

'No, but Madison is so jealous. You know what Washington society's like, Matthew. Clara is clinging to Henry for better or worse – for appearances' sake. I suppose I'll have to do the same.' There was a silence. 'My food sometimes tastes funny . . .' she added in a whisper. 'I think he's trying to kill me, like Henry's trying to kill Clara.'

Grand leaned forward. 'He wouldn't kill you when you are . . .' he gestured vaguely.

'He has children,' she whispered, 'from his first wives.'

'*Wives?*'

'Five of them. They all had one child, before they . . . died.' Her eyes were huge in her white face. 'I heard you were a policeman, something like that. In London.' She grabbed his hand and pressed it into the crisp white cloth. 'Please, Matthew. Help me.'

He looked at her sitting there – pretty still, but so afraid. 'I'm here on other business, Arlette,' he began.

'But not every hour,' she said, another tear spilling from her eye. 'He'll kill me, Matthew. Please. Don't desert me.' And then, because she was Arlette and couldn't help it, 'Again.'

Despite himself, Grand patted her hand with his free one and nodded. 'Of course, Arlette. Of course I'll help you.'

Into the middle of the scene, the bus boy was suddenly at his elbow. 'Tea?' he said, slamming down the pot. He looked Arlette up and down. 'I guess you get to be mother.'

'Name?' The inspector of the Metropolitan Police looked and sounded weary. It had been a long day and the last thing he wanted to do at the end of his twelve-hour shift was to have to sort out an altercation on a streetcar.

'Sojourner Truth,' the little old black lady said, her back ramrod straight, her little poke bonnet straightened again after her struggles – first with the streetcar guard, then with one of Washington's finest.

'*Real* name,' the inspector yawned. 'Come on, Sojourner, you know the drill as well as I do.'

'And you know my real name as well as I do,' she came back at him, quick as a rattler.

'I sure do.' The inspector dipped his pen into the inkwell and wrote it down in his ledger. 'Isabella Baumfree. What are you now? Eighty?'

Sojourner stood even more erect, if that were possible. 'I'm seventy-one,' she said, 'and if you were a gentleman, you wouldn't even ask that question.'

'If I was a gentleman, lady, I wouldn't be listening to the likes of you every third day. Do you want to pay the fine or go see the judge?'

'You know the answer to that too,' she told him.

The inspector sighed and made various scribbled notes in the ledger's margin. Then his eyes fell on Batchelor.

'Who are you?' he asked.

'James Batchelor.'

'Where you from, Mr Batchelor?'

'London – England,' he was already learning to add.

'With them vowels, I didn't take you for a native of Virginia. What brings you to Washington, Mr Batchelor?'

'Sightseeing,' Batchelor lied. 'We've read so much about your country at home. You know . . . the war.'

'Yeah,' the inspector nodded slowly. 'I know. "Though with the North we sympathise, it must not be forgotten that with the South we've stronger ties that are composed of cotton."'

'The *London Charivari!*' Batchelor recognized the quotation and he was impressed.

'I can quote you from Mrs Beecher Stowe too, if you like. No doubt Sojourner here would enjoy that. Instead, though, I'm going to quote from Officer Ruggles' testimony.' He cleared his throat and shuffled through the papers on his high desk. '"I was patrolling on the corner of Pennsylvania Avenue this morning when a streetcar pulled up in front of me. Two gentlemen alighted from said vehicle" – got a good line, ain't he, Ruggles? – "and they were engaging in fisticuffs. I had reason to separate them and had to summon assistance." . . . It gets kinda graphic then with injuries done to the said Ruggles by you, Mr Batchelor and, I blush to admit it, some rather choice language we seldom hear on Pennsylvania Avenue.'

'Yes.' Batchelor shifted a little. 'I have already apologized to Miss Truth . . .'

'Mrs,' she corrected him.

'Mrs. I was a little provoked.'

'Why was that, Mr Batchelor?'

'I was merely trying to protect this lady,' the Englishman explained.

The inspector leaned back in his chair and clasped his hands over his waistcoat. 'I'm not sure Sojourner needs much protection. Tell him what happened back in Fifty-Eight, Sojourner.'

'Busy year,' she muttered.

He cocked an eyebrow at her.

'You mean the speech?' She wanted clarification.

'You know I do.'

'I was making a speech, Mr Batchelor, a reprise, I'm embarrassed to say, of my "Ain't I a Woman?" oratory, when one of the rowdies in the crowd called out that I was a man.'

'And what did you do, Sojourner, by way of witty repartee?' the inspector asked.

Sojourner looked a little shamefaced. 'I exposed my breasts,' she said, suddenly defiant.

The inspector shook his head. 'Just got them titties right out,' he chuckled. 'So, you see, Mr Batchelor, a woman who can do that can certainly hold her own, so to speak, on a streetcar.'

'Why aren't black passengers allowed to ride inside the car?' Batchelor wanted to know.

'Amen, brother,' Sojourner murmured.

'Go ask President Johnson,' the inspector shrugged. 'All my boys and I do is apply the law as it stands, not as we'd like it to be.'

'But Lincoln set the slaves free,' Batchelor persisted.

'That he did,' the inspector said, 'and there are a few folks across the Potomac, not to say this side of it, who are still mightily displeased about that. You can fight City Hall if you want to, but if you do, I'll have to arrest you. Again.'

Silence fell on the precinct station house and apart from the ticking of the station clock, all was still.

'You've got a choice,' the inspector said. 'You pay a fine plus costs for damage done to the car guard and Officer Ruggles, and for uttering lewd words in a public thorofare. Or you can go before the judge. It's up to you.'

It was and Batchelor dithered.

'I should point out that Sojourner here does this kinda thing a couple of times a week. She's making a point, Mr Batchelor. By electing to go before a judge, she draws attention to herself – and her cause. What's that this week, Sojourner, black rights or women's rights? I declare, I can't keep up with you.'

'A little bit of both,' she said, smiling at him.

'You got a cause, Mr Batchelor? One worth being deported for?'

That made Batchelor's mind up for him. The last thing he wanted at that moment was unwelcome publicity. 'I'll pay the fine,' he said.

The inspector smiled. 'Where you working now, Sojourner?'

'The Freedmen's Hospital,' she said, 'with Dr Augusta.'

'I know it,' the inspector nodded. 'That place at Thirteenth and R. They do good work there, I'm told.'

'With the help of the Lord,' Sojourner added.

'Always,' the inspector beamed. 'I don't suppose you're considering retiring any time soon?' he asked hopefully.

'Not until my work's done.' She looked him squarely in the face.

'That's what I thought you'd say,' he sighed.

# FIVE

B y that evening, James Batchelor was beginning to remember
every detail of his altercation aboard the streetcar, largely
because his cheek was purple, his left eye half closed and
there was a gaping hole in his wallet.

'Seemed a reasonable chap, Inspector Haynes.' He was working
his jaw semi-independently from his words. 'Not unlike dear old
Tanner at the Yard.'

Matthew Grand was less impressed with Inspector John Tanner
than his colleague. The man was sweetness itself but there was
an inner core of steel it was difficult to miss. And Tanner didn't
suffer enquiry agents gladly. Haynes didn't have to confront that
problem; as far as he knew, James Batchelor was a hapless
tourist in Washington who had got on the wrong streetcar at the
wrong time.

The lamps flickered at the Willard that night. Both men had
had quite a day of it and Grand was ready to call it quits when he
noticed that Batchelor had his nose in a book again.

'Don't tell me you're still in the clutches of the Siren of the
Shenandoah,' he said, swilling the brandy in his glass.

'No, this is even better,' Batchelor enthused. '*The Narrative
of Sojourner Truth: A Northern Slave*, privately printed by
William Lloyd Garrison.'

'The woman's a celebrity all right,' Grand nodded, 'and like
all people with a mission, she's quite capable of taking you or
anyone for a ride – no pun intended.'

'There's a quiet dignity about her,' Batchelor went on. 'Listen
to this. It's about her escape from slavery – "I did not run off,
for I thought that wicked, but I walked off, believing that to be
right." Marvellous stuff. Deathless.'

'Yes,' Grand thought it best to bring Batchelor to the here and
now, 'but it's not deathlessness we've come to find, James. It's
death itself.'

\*     \*     \*

The train rattled northeast that Friday, courtesy of the Philadelphia and Baltimore Central Railroad. The green of Maryland had turned yellow this hot August, and Grand and Batchelor had shed their topcoats. Batchelor had bought himself a natty little straw boater, while Grand stuck to the shady canopy of his wideawake. The car jolted behind the steaming, snorting locomotive, bouncing over the points as the waiter ignored the movement and expertly poured their coffees.

'You know, I'm still not happy about this, Matthew.'

'No more am I, James,' the American said, 'but we have to start somewhere. Luther says Lafayette was poisoned. The doctor says palsy of the brain. Where else can we go?'

Batchelor looked across the table at him. 'To the body in question,' he shrugged.

There was a time in both these men's countries when the robbing of graves was big business. The thriving medical schools in Batchelor's London were crying out for subjects, cadavers on which the students could practise their dissection. The law then only provided such corpses from the list of the hanged and the damned. Enterprising businessmen like Ben Crouch had set up a watch on the churchyards and cemeteries, waiting for a funeral, even mingling with the mourners, draped in deepest black and expressing every sympathy. Then, at night, Crouch's men would ram their spades into the freshly turned earth and prise open the coffin lid. Two or three quick tugs and the shrouded subject would be into a fly and away, ready for old Ben to claim his prize money by providing 'something for the surgeon'.

Grand and Batchelor strolled in Philadelphia's Mutual Family cemetery that afternoon. Philadelphia was a city of graveyards, but Luther Baker had been most specific. They had checked in to a hotel and caught a cab to where Passyunk Avenue crossed Federal Street – when Batchelor saw the strange angle where the streets met, he felt a little less homesick for his rookeries. It was peaceful here; dark yews standing dumb in the heat of the day, the sun kissing the rows of crosses, angels and broken columns that marked the last resting place of the great and the good in this city of brotherly love.

They checked the gates and Grand chatted casually to the keeper. Those gates would be locked at ten sharp; there was an element in Philadelphia that was not above robbing the dead for their gold trinkets – even their teeth. Admittedly, the keeper told them, all that was a while ago, but the cemetery company were taking no chances. Grand was careful not to ask for the grave of Lafayette Baker and Batchelor was careful not to open his mouth at all. If things went wrong tonight, the last thing either of them wanted was for the keeper to remember a tall American in a wideawake and a Limey with a funny accent.

It was nearly sunset by the time the pair found the grave they were after. They noted its position then drifted five tombs away and solemnly removed their hats over the resting place of a complete stranger. A mournful angel, her face buried in her arms, slumped over the slab. A nice clear landmark, even by moonlight. They put their hats back on and left.

Passyunk and Federal looked very different after dark. There was no moon after all and the scudding clouds flew high and thin in the Pennsylvania night. Both men carried spades under the flaps of their Ulsters and they walked slowly. One of Philadelphia's finest was crossing the street ahead, his bullseye sending shafts of light darting at weird angles into the darkness. Both men held their breath. If this precinct was as dozy as C Division back in London, all would be well. They hadn't reckoned on the fact that this particular officer was a sparrow cop. He'd crossed somebody in the corridors of power and had been relegated to guarding the grass in the city's parks. He also wanted to get back in favour, so he missed nothing.

'Evening, gentlemen,' he said, touching his peaked cap with extended fingers. His own lantern flashed briefly on the badge on his left breast and the double row of buttons that marked his calling.

'Officer,' Grand said, smiled and nodded. Batchelor just smiled and nodded – it was still better if he said nothing.

They waited until his boots had clattered away along the uneven sidewalk of Federal, then doubled back and shinned over the wrought iron with its chains and padlocks. The gate was higher than Batchelor had remembered and, for one long and agonizing moment, he got stuck at the top. Then he hit the ground too hard and his boots crunched on the gravel.

'Shit!' he hissed, dropping his spade to add to the noise.

'Don't fret yourself, James,' Grand said. 'Folks around here aren't likely to be disturbed any time soon. Well, only one of them anyway.'

They retraced the steps they had taken during the day and found Baker's grave, a wooden marker until they erected a headstone. Grand slid the bullseye from his coat and lit it, placing it on the graveside.

'God forgive us,' Batchelor muttered. He had never been a particularly religious man, but this, by anybody's reckoning, was sacrilege, and it bothered him even more now than it had bothered him when they had hit upon the plan in the first place. And it was a plan, they both acknowledged, born of desperation. His spade crunched into the earth. The summer sun had baked the ground iron hard and this would be heavy going. By the time they had cut down to the colder clay, both men were in their shirtsleeves, praying that the white of the linen didn't show from the street. They were breathing hard and sweating by the time Grand's spade hit something solid. They had found Lafayette Baker.

'Damn it to Hell,' Grand muttered.

'What?'

'It's a Gravenstine.'

'A what?' Batchelor was no further forward.

'What I've just hit isn't the casket.'

'It isn't?'

Grand shook his head. 'It's an icebox, on top of the casket. Designed by John Gravenstine to keep bodies fresh.'

'Lovely,' Batchelor murmured.

'Could work for our purposes, though, James, my boy. Give me a hand, here.'

Together, they freed the icebox from its housings and surrounding earth. Grand brushed the soil from the casket lid to reveal the face of the deceased through the glass. Batchelor dropped his spade. He hadn't expected this. Glass-topped caskets were not customary in Britain and it threw him. Grand reached the bullseye down, its shafts filling the grave. Batchelor caught his breath. For a moment it looked as though Baker's eyelids flickered, as though he was outraged by those disturbing his sleep. It was a trick of the light, of course, Batchelor kept telling himself as his heart descended from his mouth.

'Say hello to Laff Baker,' Grand said. 'Dead or no, the old bastard looks just like he did when I saw him last. And that was in the Old Capitol Prison three and a half years ago.'

'Really?' Batchelor steeled himself to look closer. The colonel's nose was disintegrating and his closed eyes were hollows in the gaunt sockets. But his hair still curled and his beard looked freshly combed. Batchelor pointed and mimed a full beard. 'Isn't that—'

'A sign of arsenic poisoning?' Grand finished the sentence for him. 'Yes, it is. What colour is that?' He was pointing to globules of a substance that coated the dead man's lips.

'Difficult to see in this light. I think . . . is it . . . yellow?'

'I think it is,' Grand nodded, 'and I've seen it before.'

'You have?'

'Comrade of mine, back in the Wilderness,' Grand told him. 'Lost his nerve and went to pieces. Oh, we all tried in our various ways to help him through it, but in the end he killed himself. With what the army doctor called arsenious acid. It leaves yellow traces like that.'

'And preserves the body,' Batchelor said. 'God, it's as though he's just gone to sleep.'

'Nobody moves!' The gravediggers froze at the voice above them. The sparrow cop was standing there, a pistol in his hand. 'You'll oblige me by putting that spade down, sir.' Batchelor did. This was going to be awkward.

'Just paying our respects, officer,' Grand bluffed, but that wasn't going to work.

'The Hell you say,' the cop grunted. 'Now, you both come out of there. We'll have a little stroll to the precinct house.'

'I'm not sure that's necessary,' Grand said, climbing out of the hole he had just helped to dig. 'Know what this is?' he fished a brass disc from his pocket and it flashed in the sparrow cop's bullseye.

'Looks like . . . some kind of cypher,' he said, reading the letters on it.

'That's right,' Grand said. 'I shouldn't be showing you, still less explaining. Who's our next president, officer?'

Politics was not the strong suit of the lower ranks of the Philadelphia Police. 'Er . . . Seymour?'

'That old blowhard? Never.' Grand closed to the man, as far as the pointing pistol would let him. 'Ulysses S. Grant.'

'Could be,' the cop agreed, nodding sagely.

'That's his personal cypher. The one he used with the Army of the Potomac. We're Pinkertons.'

'Detectives?'

Grand nodded. 'I can't, of course, be precise about all this,' he waved to the open grave as if it were the most natural thing in the world. 'You'll just have to take it on trust that we have our reasons.'

For a moment, the sparrow cop hesitated and his life flashed before him. Batchelor could read the signs – he had seen it often in C Division along the Haymarket. He fumbled in his wallet, considerably slimmer these days, and pulled out a few crumpled notes. 'Have a drink on General Grant,' he said, holding the money out.

'You gotta funny accent, mister,' the cop said, and made no attempt to accept the bribe.

'Pinkertons,' Batchelor reminded him, 'International Branch.'

He wasn't ready for what happened next. Neither was the cop. Grand's spade hit him squarely upside the head and he went down, poleaxed on the edge of the grave. He didn't move.

'God, Grand, you've killed him.' Batchelor knelt beside the man, feeling for a pulse.

'Well, he's in the right place,' Grand murmured, collecting his bullseye and shovelling the earth back over the dead face of Lafayette Baker.

'It's all right,' Batchelor said, 'he's still breathing.'

'He'll just have a bit of a headache in the morning, James; trust me, I've knocked out men before.'

'Why are you filling that in?' Batchelor asked.

'Because I'd rather the authorities didn't know whose grave we've disturbed. We'll drag Philadelphia's finest here a few aisles away and chances are he won't remember whose grave he found us in. And James . . .'

'Yes?'

'The next time you want to bribe an American peace officer, check with me first, won't you? You're not at home now, you know.'

Luther Baker proved difficult to find. He had told Grand and Batchelor he could always be found at the National Hotel now that the place had been cleared of Southerners, but nobody there had seen him for days. Came and went, did Mr Baker, the clerk confided after Grand's paper money came his way across the counter. Philadelphia police officers might be above such things, but Washington clerks had their price.

So it wasn't easy to find Jane Curry Baker, relict of the late colonel, and the pair had to use all their sleuthing skills to track her down. Her rooms at the Kirkwood House, on Pennsylvania and Twelfth, left a little to be desired, but generally speaking she was better off than most of the widows the war had made.

'I've been expecting you,' she said, inviting her visitors to sit. 'Will you take tea, gentlemen?'

'Thank you, no, ma'am,' Grand said, looking for somewhere to put his hat.

'Please accept our condolences,' Batchelor nodded. The face of the woman's dead husband still haunted his dreams.

'Thank you.' Jane Baker was a beautiful woman with hair that was raven black and skin like marble. In all, she looked the perfect picture of dignified widowhood.

'You know that Luther has employed us to look into the colonel's death?' Grand checked.

Jane nodded. 'I do,' she said, 'and that's brigadier general, by the way. Lafayette was promoted because of his excellent work in tracking down the murderers of the late President.'

'You were with him, Mrs Baker,' Batchelor began, 'when he . . .?'

'Died? No, sir, I was not. You know that Lafayette was fired by Mr Stanton – the second time, I mean.'

'So we believe,' Grand said. 'Something to do with—'

'He was put in the frame, Mr Grand,' she interrupted, 'as the policemen say. It's a ghastly phrase I've picked up from my brother. He's a detective in the War Department.'

'So,' Batchelor was wrestling with the details, 'when the . . . brigadier was dismissed, he—'

'Went home to Philadelphia.' She finished the sentence for him. 'We both did, to our house in Coates Street.' She stood up suddenly, circling the room so that the only sound was the swish of her satin. She turned to look at the men. 'In his last months,' she said, 'he became dependent upon alcohol. A bitter man, worn out by the war and all it stood for. I did my best. I tried to nurse him through it, but . . . in the end, I had to let him go. He took to staying away from home, spending his nights in hotels, rooming houses. Even then, I had no idea . . .' Her voice faded and she touched her eyes with a delicate handkerchief.

'What exactly was the cause of your husband's death, Mrs Baker?' Batchelor asked.

'Dropsy of the brain,' she said, mechanically repeating the official version.

'Except that Luther doesn't believe that,' Grand reminded her.

She looked into his eyes. 'My husband was a complex man, Mr Grand,' she said. 'Cousin Luther sees everything in black and white. I cannot help you further. Except, perhaps . . .' She crossed to a sideboard and lifted a book from its surface. 'You might find this useful.'

She held it out and it was Batchelor, the writer of penny dreadfuls who took it from her, reading aloud the gilt letters on the spine. '*The United States Secret Service in the Late War* by General Lafayette C. Baker.'

'The dedication,' Jane said, stony-faced, 'is "to the people of this great nation, to the brave boys in blue and their heroic leaders who lifted the dark pall of slavery from our national escutcheon, restoring, with new lustre, a brightness that can never again be shadowed".' Batchelor, who had opened the book at its first page, mouthed silently along with her. 'Read that book, Mr Batchelor, and you'll see shadows aplenty.'

'Like to buy you a drink, gentlemen.'

It was a generous man who made that kind of offer in the Willard, considering their prices. He was short, spectacled, and with a severe centre parting separating hair of the salt and pepper persuasion. 'My card.'

Batchelor took it. 'Thomas Durham, *Washington Evening Star*,' he read aloud.

'So you see, we're . . . sort of . . . ink brothers, Mr Batchelor, you and I.'

'You know who I am?'

'Of course.' Durham clicked his fingers and a flunkey hurried over. 'I'm a journalist.' He caught the bewilderment on the faces of Grand and Batchelor and laughed. 'Sojourner Truth,' he explained, 'told me all about you.'

'You know Mrs Truth?'

'She's like part of the furniture at the *Star* offices. I am an ardent abolitionist, Mr Batchelor – and I use the present tense intentionally, in that slavery has still not been eradicated. I help Sojourner's cause whenever I can. Er . . . bourbon, gentlemen?'

They nodded and the flunkey disappeared.

'You were more difficult, Captain Grand.' Durham leaned back in the leather comfort of the East Thirteenth Street Corridor, the hotel's most exclusive bar.

'I was? And that's just "Mr" these days.'

'That's a pity.' Durham lit a cigar and offered one to his new friends. 'You were in the Third Cavalry, Army of the Potomac, with George Custer.'

'I wouldn't say "with" exactly,' Grand said. He remembered Autie Custer from West Point, and a more over-promoted idiot never walked God's earth.

'From what I hear, Custer's chasing glory again.' Durham blew smoke rings to the ceiling. 'He's trailing the Cheyenne along the Washita.'

Grand knew that couldn't end well, but he didn't say so in front of a journalist with who-knew-what connections and allegiances.

'How's old George Sala?' Durham asked Batchelor.

'You know George?'

'Why, sure. The old cigar-sucker made his second home here at the Willard when he was covering the war. Must've had a pretty generous editor, huh?'

Batchelor thought of crumbly, petulant old Leigh Hunt, and couldn't imagine that Durham could be wider of the mark.

'So, what's the London *Telegraph* doing here again? War's over, you know.'

'Er . . . I'm covering various key people for my readers,' Batchelor lied. 'You know, the President, Mr Stanton . . .'

'Brigadier General Baker,' Durham finished the list.

'Er . . . yes,' Batchelor agreed, as though Baker was so far down his list he had forgotten all about him.

'Let's see now, two of the men you've mentioned are on the rails. One's out of office and one's dead. So, when you say "key people"?'

'Two are on the rails,' Grand repeated. 'Stanton would be one, the other would be the President.'

The bourbon arrived and Durham clicked his fingers at Grand in realization. 'Of course, you guys weren't here, were you? Missed all the fun.'

'Us "guys"?' Grand raised an eyebrow. This wasn't a term he knew.

'God, you really have been away. It's the coming phrase, believe me. Cuss.'

Grand understood.

'Cuss?' Batchelor didn't.

'Man,' Grand and Durham chorused.

'Johnson fired Stanton,' Durham explained, breathing in the fumes from his glass and closing his eyes in pleasure.

'Why?' Batchelor asked.

Durham's chuckle sounded like a death rattle. 'Maybe he knows where a few too many bodies are buried,' he said. 'After Lincoln's murder, Mars turned into Attila the Hun. Habeas corpus was suspended; there was martial law here in Washington. I looked into the arrests he ordered. Stopped counting at just past twenty thousand – and, believe me, that was small potatoes. I won't bore you with the complexities of the Constitution, Mr Batchelor, but not even a President can fire a Secretary of War just like that. He had to tweak the rules a tad and Congress impeached him. Or tried to.'

'We read about that,' Grand said. 'Not long before we came away.'

'Did you read that Stanton barricaded himself in his office? Refused to come out. If it happened in the schoolyard, you wouldn't believe it, but when the players are statesmen – or so called, at least – then, believe me, the writing's on the wall.'

He raised his glass and they all drank. After a short silence, Durham closed to the enquiry agents. 'When it comes to Lafayette Baker, now – that's a horse of a different colour.'

'In what way?' Batchelor tried to sound as casual as he could. Durham tapped the side of his nose. 'Why don't we get a bottle of this stuff, gentlemen, and retire to your rooms? There may not be any Confederate spies at the Willard any more, but you can't take chances.'

# SIX

Arlette Mitchells sat by the window, her sewing forgotten, her hands loose in what remained of her lap. The baby had been kicking like crazy all day but now, suddenly, it was still. She hated her life. She hated being poor little Letty, left in the lurch by that handsome Captain Grand, forced to settle for a man old enough to be her grandfather, almost. When she was alone, she let herself think about his old man's legs, the veins standing out like purple ropes, his old, dry hands all over her. She carried her thoughts on her face and so when she thought of Grand's comment about The Day, she frowned and then burst into tears. If only what Grand had suggested was really true, that there had only been one day. But there had been hundreds. The disgusting old goat had more vim than many a man half his age. Oh, God . . . she threw her head back and let the tears stream down her cheeks. Even now, with the baby kicking and bouncing.

But . . . she put her hand on her swollen stomach, under her soft house dress. There was no sign of the kicking and shifting she had lived with so long. Everything had gone quiet and still. Her heart skipped a beat. Although she had cursed this child through the heat of the summer, she needed it so desperately. Someone to love her, no matter what Washington society might say. Someone to be just hers, hers alone. She knew that Madison would take no notice of it. His other five children were farmed out to relatives along the eastern seaboard. They came to see them once in a while, the younger ones at least. As soon as they reached their majority, they never came again. When Madison had first come calling, Arlette had felt sorry for the poor man, widowed so sadly and so often. But now, she completely saw their point. The odious old . . .

From over her shoulder, on a gust of the old-man smell of damp biscuit and cobweb, a veined hand grabbed her wrist and pulled her caressing hand away.

'What are you doing, madam?' Madison Mitchells snarled. 'What would the servants say, seeing their mistress stroking herself in such a way? Only a husband's hand is allowed to do such a thing.'

There was a pause, during which Arlette held her breath. Then, when he didn't speak, she ventured to fill the silence. 'The baby . . . it has gone so still.'

'Stupid girl,' her husband said, dropping her hand. 'Don't you know that's because it is its time. Did it turn?'

'Turn?'

'Yes. Turn head down. Mary . . . no, forgive me, Susan, it was. She was out walking when her child . . . John, that would be, I think . . . turned and she fainted clean away, stupid woman. In any event, he was born that night.'

Arlette sprang up, her eyes wide. 'You mean . . . the baby could come soon. Now?' All this childbirth talk was all very fine and well, but he didn't have to do it.

'Stupid woman,' he said, turning away. 'Not now, no. Unless you are having cramps. *Are* you?'

She shook her head.

'Then not now. But soon.' He looked her up and down and clearly disliked what he saw. 'I'm going out to the Willard for dinner. I must say I can't really bear to be in the house when birthing is going on. I'll send Bessie. Perhaps you ought to think about going upstairs while you can do it on your own.' He turned and was halfway out of the room when she spoke.

'I'll send word when it's born, shall I? Let you know what it is and that we are well.'

Without looking back, he stopped. 'As you wish,' he said, and the next thing she heard was a door slamming. And the next thing she felt was a mule kick her in the belly.

'Bessie!' she screamed. 'Bessie!'

Night had long since fallen over the Willard and three men were engrossed in conversation on the third floor overlooking Pennsylvania Avenue.

'That's an interesting book you've got there, Mr Batchelor.' Tom Durham tapped the dark green leather. It was Brigadier General Baker's opus. ''Course, I wouldn't believe everything between its covers.'

'No?' Batchelor raised an eyebrow. That was more or less what Grand had told him about Belle Boyd's book too.

'First, he didn't write it. And second, Lafayette Curry Baker was the biggest liar north or south of the Rappahannock.'

Grand and Batchelor looked at him and then at each other.

'Even so,' Durham was topping up his glass, 'I'm not sure lying – except under oath, of course – is an offence worth dying for.'

'You think—' Batchelor began, but Durham cut in.

'I think somebody wanted dear old Laff dead. Hell, yes.'

'We understood it was natural causes,' Grand said.

Durham laughed. 'You've been talking to Rickards, haven't you? Laff's doctor?'

Grand nodded.

'Did he tell you he and Laff went way back?'

'No,' Grand frowned.

'They weren't just doctor and patient. They were friends of nearly twenty years standing. The man was a saint as far as Rickards was concerned. I doubt you'll do better with Laura Duvall.'

'Who?' Batchelor asked.

Durham remembered to close his mouth before he looked hard at the younger man. George Sala must be tearing out what little hair he had left if this was the calibre of his junior colleagues.

'Laff's "lifelong friend" – and I'm quoting from his will here.'

'You've seen his will?' Grand checked.

'Look, boys,' Durham reached for a refill of the bourbon. 'I'll come clean with you. I think Lafayette Baker was murdered and that's why you're both here.'

'Is it?' Grand refilled his own glass and leaned back, brazening the situation out.

Durham sighed and put down his glass. Then he fished in his vest pocket and produced a card. He cleared his throat and read aloud, 'Grand and Batchelor, Enquiry Agents, 41, The Strand, London.'

'Where did you get that?' Batchelor was half out of his seat.

'Journalist shall speak unto journalist.' Durham tapped the side of his nose.

Batchelor subsided. 'George Sala,' he said.

'George Sala and the miracles of modern telegraphy,' Durham

nodded. 'I've been watching you two since you hit town. My turn to let you into a little secret, gentlemen. I started looking into Baker's death almost before the vicious bastard hit the floor. The official version stinks to high heaven.'

'Who have you talked to?' Grand asked.

'Who haven't I talked to?' Durham shrugged. 'Washington is full of wise monkeys, Captain. They're all blind, deaf or dumb.'

'Luther Baker?' Batchelor thought it was safe to mention the name, especially as he was paying for the bourbon.

'You'd like to think so, wouldn't you? But no, Luther and I aren't exactly on friendly terms, seeing as how he threatened to horsewhip me if he ever saw me again. *The Star* is a pro-Union paper, gentlemen; always has been. But it's all about mending fences under Reconstruction. Are we ever going to be a nation again? I don't know, but stirring up old scores won't help.'

'You think the South killed Baker?' Batchelor asked.

'It's the safest bet. Read the book, Mr Batchelor.' Durham pointed to it. '*Some* of it is true. In the meantime, gentlemen,' the *Star*'s man slipped the half-empty bottle into his pocket as he got to his feet, 'let's keep in touch. You two do what I hope you're good at – sleuthing. I'll check with you regularly, and provide whatever you need. Officially, I can't do anything.'

'We understand,' Batchelor said.

'One thing,' Durham paused on his way to the door. 'I get the exclusive. I don't want to read this second-hand in the London *Telegraph*.'

'You have my word,' Batchelor told him.

'One other thing,' Grand said. 'Where will we find Laura Duvall?'

'Laura Duvall's the least of your worries. One gentleman you're bound to run into sooner or later in this business is Wesley Jericho. But don't tell him I sent you.'

Laura Duvall lived along O Street just before it became Hell's Bottom, where no self-respecting lady would be seen, let alone live. Her apartments were set back from the sidewalk in a tenement shared by three families and if she had ever had a servant, there was no room for one now.

Grand and Batchelor explained to the nervous little woman

who peered at them over a chain-lock fitted inside her door that Thomas Durham of the *Star* had sent them. For a long moment, she hesitated, then she let them in.

'We are investigating the death of Brigadier General Baker,' Grand told her. No point in standing on ceremony now.

'I see.' Like Jane Baker, Laura Duvall had a quiet dignity. Grand couldn't imagine either woman being drawn to Laff Baker. But then, at the time, Grand, along with half Washington, was assumed to be a conspirator in Lincoln's death. It wasn't likely that Baker would have shown *him* his charming side. 'Won't you sit down?'

'We are looking into the possibility,' Batchelor said, choosing his words carefully, 'that Brigadier Baker was murdered.'

For the briefest of moments, Laura Duvall's eyelids flickered. The rest of her pale face was unreadable, her eyes a clear blue, her hair, once mouse, now streaked with grey. Batchelor tried to guess her age. Grand tried to guess what she knew.

'That,' she said quietly, 'is entirely possible.'

'You were . . . a friend?' Batchelor wanted to establish the parameters.

'I was his lover,' she said blandly, betraying no emotion. 'I hate the term "mistress", "kept woman" even more so. And before you ask, yes, Jane Baker knew about me.' She laughed, brittle and brief. 'And I'm sure that every night the woman offers up prayers for my demise.'

'We are talking about her husband's demise,' Grand reminded her. 'How did you meet the brigadier general?'

'During the war,' she said, 'I was one of a number of ladies employed by the Treasury Department. We wrote letters and made copies. I had . . . we all had . . . some trouble with one of the supervisors.'

'Trouble?' Batchelor raised an eyebrow.

'Mr Spencer Clark,' Laura told him. 'A beast in the guise of a man. He took liberties with us, ogled us in the offices on the Hill. Without wishing to be too graphic, he placed his hands in inappropriate places. Lafayette Baker stopped him.'

'How?' Grand asked.

'With his fists, I believe. He found me crying one day following a revolting incident I will not trouble you with, and I mentioned

Clark's name. I did not witness what followed, of course; Lafayette was too discreet for that.'

Grand nodded. *That* was the Laff Baker he remembered, a man who would rearrange a reprobate's face in the darkness. He hadn't expected the chivalry that went with it.

'Did Clark keep his job?' he asked.

'No,' Laura said, 'but he lost it for other reasons. Let's just say while groping us girls he was also lining his pockets from Treasury funds.'

Grand and Batchelor both made a mental note. *Another* name in the long list of those who had cause to hate Lafayette Baker.

'When did you see the brigadier last?' Batchelor asked.

'It must have been three days before he died,' she told them, without emotion. 'When possible I visited him at his home in Coates Street, brought him flowers. He loved roses – white ones. In the end, Lafayette took to moving away from home, spending nights in hotels and rooming houses.'

'Why?' Batchelor asked.

For the first time, tears glinted in the eyes of Laura Duvall. 'He became convinced that someone wanted him dead,' she said, 'and he came to trust no one. Not even me.'

'Did he say who that someone was?' Grand asked.

'Judas,' she said loudly, sniffing back the tears. 'Or Brutus. Take your pick.'

Grand and Batchelor looked at each other. Laura got up suddenly and crossed the little room. She opened a cupboard and produced a box. 'Have you talked to Jane?' she asked.

'We have,' Batchelor told her.

'And I assume she was as helpful as a brick wall?'

Batchelor smiled.

'Talk to Bridget McBane,' she said. 'She nursed Lafayette towards the end as his illness worsened. And to Kathleen Hawks – she was Jane's maid until recently. I happen to know that both women are in Washington at the moment. Why they left Philadelphia is anybody's guess. In the meantime,' she selected a small key from the bunch on her chatelaine and opened the box, 'you may be able to make something of this.' She handed Batchelor a book – solid, heavy and well-thumbed. He read the title – *Colburn's United Service Magazine, 1864.*

'What's this, Miss Duvall?' he asked.

'A collection of volumes bound into one,' she said, 'where the earlier part of Sixty-Four is, I couldn't say, but Lafayette's will was most careful about this edition.'

'It was?' Grand took the book that Batchelor passed to him.

'A codicil,' she said, locking the box again. '"To my lifelong friend, Laura Duvall". I think he meant that we were friends from the moment we met; it had to be that, because I hadn't known him all that long. I can't imagine why that particular set of volumes should be so important to him; why he would leave them in my charge.'

'We'll take great care of it, Miss Duvall,' Batchelor promised.

'The book itself is not important to me,' she said. 'Not as long as you nail the heartless son of a bitch who killed my Lafayette.'

There was a knock on the door of Apartment Sixty-Three at the Willard that night. Batchelor was engrossed in reading Baker's book under the light of an oil lamp, so it was Grand who answered the call.

'Message for Mr Batchelor.' The bellhop passed Grand a note and stood expectantly, smiling broadly and waiting for his tip.

'I'm not Mr Batchelor,' Grand beamed back and closed the door in the lad's face. He could hear him knocking on a door further down the corridor, and his muffled voice sharing some news. 'This is intriguing, James.'

'Hmm?' Batchelor was deep in the skulduggery of the Civil War.

'You have a visitor in the foyer. A Miss Julep.'

'Mint?' Batchelor was jerked away from the tome. He was on his feet already.

'Are you sure about this?' Grand asked him.

Batchelor looked at the card. 'Foyer. Important. Julep', he read. The back was blank. 'What can happen?' he chuckled, hauling on his jacket. 'This *is* the Willard, Matthew.'

Grand whirled and presented Batchelor with his Derringer, gleaming dully in his hand. 'At least take this.'

'My dear boy, we've had this conversation. I'd shoot my own foot off. Look, I'm a big boy now; I can handle myself. And no

shadow, all right? You stay here and see if you can make head
or tail of Baker's book.' And he was gone.

The clerk in the foyer was less than happy. It was unusual for
a woman to be unescorted at the Willard, and one glance at the
gorgeous black girl asking for Mr Batchelor had convinced him
of her calling. She wore a velvet cloak that reached nearly to the
ground, but her jewellery and her make-up betrayed her street
origins. He had told her to move on several times, but she threatened a scene unless her note was delivered to the English guest,
so he had reluctantly complied.

Batchelor tipped his hat to her as he reached the bottom of
the stairs, and she crossed to him, linking her arm with his and
sweeping past the clerk's counter. At the door she stopped, opened
her cloak to reveal her tight scarlet bodice and delicious breasts
and shouted, 'See you at the Wolf's Den later, honey!' She
laughed as the clerk's jaw hit the carpet and there was a disgusted
inrush of breath from the hotel residents. She turned to Batchelor.
'On the other hand, the miserable cock-sucker couldn't afford
the Den. Looks more like a Blue Goose man to me.'

'Miss Julep,' Batchelor said, as the muggy night air of
Pennsylvania Avenue hit him, 'where are we going?'

A cab was waiting alongside the kerb. 'The Division, sugar,'
she purred. 'My second home.'

For a girl who rarely stopped talking, Julep was singularly quiet
as the cab rattled west over the hard-rutted roads towards Murder
Bay and the Division. She kept her eyes focused ahead as the
dark shanties of the Contraband Shacks swept by and the broken
skyline of the nation's capital jutted black against the purple of
the night. The gigs and cabs became more frequent as they
reached Marble Alley, and the place was alive with riffraff of
every colour and persuasion. Julep called out to the cabbie to
pull up outside a large, ramshackle building with railings around
it. By the dim street light, Batchelor could make out a brass
shingle that read 'Madam Wilton's Private Residence for Ladies'.
Julep hadn't left her seat. 'You're here, sweetness,' she purred.
'Room Nineteen. The major's expecting you.' And the cab was
gone into the night, leaving just a faint trail of her scent; heavy,
musky, but not, strangely, minty at all.

Room Nineteen. Batchelor had heard that before somewhere, but for the life of him he couldn't remember where. An urgent meeting was all Julep had told him, where he would learn something to his advantage in the case of Brigadier-General Lafayette Baker. The front door swung wide and a broad staircase curved up to his right ahead of him. The walls were hung with photographs of coy young ladies in prim, all-covering pelisses and elaborate bonnets. The middle-aged lady, who was presumably Madam Wilton, sat in the middle of them. The hall to left and right was lined with bookcases, heavy with leather-spined tomes that reminded Batchelor of the British Museum Reading Room, where he had spent many a happy hour researching stories for the *Telegraph*. Room Nineteen, a sign told him, was on the first floor, and he took the stairs, gazing above him into the gloom. It was eerily quiet on the treads, his own footfalls muffled by thick carpet as he padded along the corridor.

He knocked on the door. Nothing. There were no fancy codes here, no quotations from Luther and Byron, just a long, melancholy squeal of hinges as the door opened under his fist. He could see a lamp on a table and the gleam of a pistol, cocked and pointing at him.

'You alone?' a gravel voice asked him.

'I am.' Batchelor stayed in the doorway. He was unarmed and had seen no sign of Matthew Grand trailing him. He was, indeed, on his own.

'Come in. Sit.'

There was only one chair that Batchelor could see and he took it, having closed the door behind him. Now that he was on a level with the gun, he felt he could relax a little. The gun owner had other ideas. 'Keep your hands on the table, Mr Batchelor. Julep.'

The black girl was suddenly there, sweeping out of the shadows. How she had doubled back from the cab and reached Room Nineteen before Batchelor he couldn't understand. But then, there was a lot about Washington, and especially Murder Bay, that James Batchelor didn't understand. With his hands firmly on the velvet of the tablecloth, he could hardly stop the girl from going through his pockets. It may have just been his fancy that she lingered a little in his trousers, but within a moment she had straightened up and nodded to the man with the gun. 'He's clean.' And she was gone again.

'Are you the major?' Batchelor asked.

The muzzle of the pistol came up and its owner eased the hammer back. He slid the weapon out of Batchelor's reach but kept it on the table. 'Caleb Tice.' A firm hand that moments ago had been tight on the gun's butt, snaked out and Batchelor caught it. 'First District of Columbia Cavalry. Course, that was a time ago.'

'Major Tice,' Batchelor nodded. 'You clearly know who I am. Why this summons? We could have met at our hotel – it's very pleasant and . . . not at all threatening.'

Tice chuckled. He leaned back and poured two glasses from a table next to his own. 'Hardly a summons,' he said. 'I just wanted to see the man who's hunting Laff Baker's killer face to face. I figured a plain old telegram wouldn't do it. Julep now, that's different. Quite a looker, isn't she?'

Batchelor had to concede that she was.

'Most expensive message-boy in DC.' Tice raised his glass. 'To absent friends.'

'Absent friends.' Batchelor raised his too. Tice's bourbon made the Willard's seem like velvet and Batchelor felt his eyes start to water.

'So, you're working for Luther?'

'Before this conversation continues, Major,' Batchelor said, 'I need to know why you want to know.'

'Of course you do,' Tice smiled. 'I would expect that. In the dark days of our late war,' he said, watching the lamplight sparkle in the facets of his cut glass, 'I was Lafayette Baker's right-hand man. We ran this city like a warship, everything tied down and ready. Gambling hells, we closed them. Liquor halls? Gone. Bordellos? A thing of the past. Sodom became Jerusalem.' Tice broke off to laugh. 'It's all back now, of course. Did you ever meet Laff Baker, Mr Batchelor?'

The Englishman shook his head.

'He was the hardest bastard I ever met. When Lincoln was killed, Stanton ordered him to get his murderers – Booth, Herold, Atzerodt, the others. The four of us were there when Booth was killed – Laff and Luther, Colonel Conger and me. When all the hoo-ha was over, the trial and the hangings, Laff went to work on the city. I won't pretend we did things by the book. But you don't get to make omelettes without breaking a few eggs. We all made enemies. And without Laff's hand, I am ashamed to say the rest of us sort of lost our directions. So the liquor dens are back, and the bordellos – you know that, you're sitting in one now, albeit of a genteel nature, catering only for the highest of society; you know, clergymen, Congressmen, that sort of cuss.'

Batchelor knew. There were such establishments along the Haymarket too.

But Tice's fond reminiscences were over. 'Then some bastard killed him and that was that.'

'Are you still working with Luther, Major Tice?' Batchelor asked.

The major spat viciously towards an ornate brass spittoon, but missed, to the serious detriment of the carpet. 'Let's just say he and I had a falling out,' he said. 'That's why I asked to see you.'

Batchelor rather liked his definition of 'asked' – to be invited into a room at gunpoint seemed to be stretching it almost to breaking point.

'I know you and Grand are snooping on Luther's behalf and I know he's fingered Stanton. All I'm missing are the details.'

'Why did you ask for me and not Grand?' Batchelor wanted to know.

Tice laughed. 'I remember Grand's reputation when the son of a bitch lived here,' he said. 'He's a by-the-book soldier and a pain in the ass. People like that don't get the job done. I can see you need him, you being a foreigner and all, but I'm hoping you can cut through this here Gordian knot of Washington politics. I'm guessing most people you've talked to have been as tight as clams.'

There was a crash on the ground floor and a series of screams.

'Shit!' Tice hissed through gritted teeth and backed out of the lamplight. Before he could leave his seat, the door of Room Nineteen crashed back and three huge Metropolitan policemen stood there, the copper buttons gleaming on their tunics, night sticks in their hands. Batchelor felt himself being hauled to his feet and his arm forced painfully up behind his back. As they frogmarched him along the corridor, Julep was being led just as roughly in the opposite direction, kicking out at the policemen and swearing in a French patois that Batchelor had never heard before.

'Well, well, well.' Batchelor turned to see who had stopped his rapid progress to the staircase.

'Inspector Haynes,' he said. 'I can explain . . .'

# SEVEN

The precinct station house was crowded that night and it was early morning before James Batchelor found himself face to face with the inspector.

'You see,' Haynes said, yawning after countless hours beyond the end of his shift, 'what bothers me is that twice now in the past few days, you seem to be at the centre of trouble. And you a foreigner and all.'

'Well, that's what *he* said,' Batchelor spread his arms, all innocence. 'Almost word for word.'

'Who?'

'Er . . . the gentleman I spoke to at Madam Wilton's.'

'Yes, and that's another funny thing,' Haynes nodded. 'Most people I know who go to Madam Wilton's don't go for the male conversation. Tell me, Mr Batchelor, is the Division part of your sightseeing in our fair city?'

'Well, you know,' Batchelor bluffed. 'Men of the world as we are . . . Should you ever venture to London, Inspector, I would readily take you on a tour of the dives of the Haymarket.'

'I'll take you up on that offer,' Haynes smiled genially at the Englishman, 'if ever I get enough time off to make a journey like that. I assume you know what Madam Wilton's is.'

'Well, I guessed,' Batchelor said.

Haynes got up and crossed to a wall map of Washington. 'Here,' he jabbed his finger into the complex criss-cross of streets, 'is Hooker's Division. As a sightseer you'll appreciate this. In the late war, General Hooker – Fighting Joe, as we knew him – had the daunting task of defending Washington; gun emplacements on Arlington Heights and so on. Most of his boys were whiling away their spare time – and their Yankee dollars – with various ladies of the night, so Joe decided, if you can't beat 'em, join 'em.'

'He visited brothels?'

'No, Mr Batchelor, he had all the street girls in the city rounded up and he dumped 'em in Murder Bay – not literally, of course. That way, if the Rebs tried to cross the Potomac, he'd know pretty much where his boys were.'

'Sounds logical,' Batchelor nodded.

Haynes went back to his seat. 'Does, doesn't it? Now, I guess the law in your country is pretty much the same as here. We can arrest the girls at Madam Wilton's for solicitation, but the clients . . . well, Democrat or Republican, it's all the same to me.'

'I believe – and this is hearsay, you understand – that most clients go free in my country, even after police raids like yours.'

Haynes laughed. 'Tell me it ain't so!'

'I haven't been quite honest with you, Inspector.'

'Oh?'

'I'm not here as a sightseer. I'm a journalist, writing a piece on espionage during the late war. Naturally, I'm interested in the equally late Brigadier Baker.'

'Naturally,' Haynes nodded, his face as blank as the wall behind him.

'My enquiries took me to Madam Wilton's because a former colleague of his was there.'

'Oh? Who was that?' Haynes asked.

'A former member of Baker's National Detective Force, Caleb Tice.'

'Tice?' Haynes frowned. 'You spoke to Tice?'

'Yes.'

'What did he say?'

'Not a lot, actually, before your boys broke the door down.'

Haynes leaned back in his chair with a frown on his face. He moved a ledger on his desk towards him and flipped it open. He ran his finger down the list of names written there. 'Would you like to reconsider your statement, Mr Batchelor?' he asked.

'Er . . . no. Why?'

'Well, this here,' he tapped the ledger, 'is a list my boys have compiled of Madam Wilton's girls and guests from tonight. There's no Caleb Tice here.'

'Perhaps he got away,' Batchelor suggested. 'Or possibly . . . and I'm sure you've come across this before, Inspector . . . used an assumed name, an alias.'

'Hmm, that's possible,' Haynes conceded. 'But I'm afraid there's a bigger problem.'

'Oh?'

The inspector leaned forward, looking at his man closely. 'You see, we fished the body of Caleb Tice out of the Potomac over a year ago. He was as dead as a nit.'

Matthew Grand would have said that he knew Washington like the back of his hand, but he had a little trouble finding the new home of Kathleen Hawks. Jane Baker had implied, when asked, that she had come down in the world when she left her employment, but this wasn't in fact the case. This was the excuse Grand made to himself when he realized that he had actually walked past the house three times whilst looking for it. Knocking on the door, he had expected to have the door opened to him by the woman he sought – but no; a butler stood there, all white gloves and haughty demeanour.

Grand was glad he had come and not Batchelor. The ex-journalist had been known to be more than a little cowed by butlers; they hadn't featured very much in his life thus far. The enquiry agent smiled his best Washington Quality smile.

'Good morning,' he said. 'Could I speak with Mrs Hawks?'

The butler looked him up and down. 'No,' he said, and made to close the door.

Grand whipped out his card and handed it to the man. 'I am here—'

'We don't buy at the door,' the butler said, in fruity tones. 'Go round back and Cook will see you then.' The man's face was impassive.

'No,' Grand said, stepping forward, 'I want—'

'I know what you want,' the butler said, 'you want to see Kathleen Hawks and I'm telling you, if you go round back, Cook will see you.' He leaned forward and spoke distinctly but much more quietly. 'Get what I mean, fella?'

Grand stepped back, the penny dropping with an almost deafening clang. 'Oh, I *see*. If I go round back . . . yes, I believe I will.'

The butler shut the door and the last thing Grand saw was the man shaking his head, eyes cast up for heavenly guidance.

Going round the back was not as easy these days, Grand found almost at once. Houses were going up all over the city and this one had been built squeezed in between two others, leaving a space which would have challenged a piece of paper. Grand was not an enquiry agent for nothing – he walked along, took a left, then another left, and counted the steps back to the other side of where he had begun and there, sure enough, was a woman who was so clearly a cook she might as well have worn a placard, waiting for him in the yard.

He opened the gate in the picket fence and called out, 'Mrs Hawks?'

She stepped forward, her finger to her lips. 'Hush, sir,' she said. 'The missus is a rare one for gentlemen callers.'

This sounded a tad ambiguous, but Grand decided to let it pass. The cook was not badly preserved but, even so, would not be his first choice had he the time to come calling in that guise. He smiled and touched his hat. 'I won't keep you long, Mrs Hawks. No doubt you have meals to prepare, things of that nature.' Despite eating most meals in his kitchen back in Alsatia, Grand was still essentially ignorant of how food stopped being a selection of raw ingredients and ended up on his plate.

'Midday meal is on the hob,' she said, complacently. 'Dinner tonight is all prepared. Just the broiling to do – this is a simple house.'

It might be simple, but it was big. Much bigger than any establishment the Bakers would have kept. The question must have shown in Grand's eyes.

'I was lucky to get this place, sir,' the woman said. 'I have always been a good, plain cook but I wouldn't have dreamed I would ever have this position. But the missus . . . that's the missus now, you understand . . . used to visit the missus . . . that's Mrs Baker . . . and one day I had made some hush puppies . . . well, Mrs Baker was that low . . . and . . .'

'Yes, I see.' Grand could see he would have to keep this conversation on somewhat of a short leash. 'Everyone loves a good hush puppy.' He was surprised they had ventured as far north as Washington, however, being more at home in the bayous than the banks of the Potomac. 'I would like to talk to you about the Baker household, if I may, Mrs Hawks.'

'Oooh,' she pursed her lips and shook her head, her cap strings flying like whips. 'I don't like to talk about the missus . . .'

'More the master, really,' Grand suggested.

The woman's eyes filled with tears. 'A saint,' she said.

Grand was surprised. He had heard Lafayette Baker called many things, but saint was the phrase used only by Dr Rickards – and surely, *that* didn't count. He cocked his head in an attitude of attention and waited.

'I know people do say that Mr Baker had lost his mind, but he was as sane as you and me,' she said, folding her arms and leaning back to add emphasis to the statement.

'Really? I understood he thought someone was trying to kill him,' Grand ventured.

'They were,' she said, nodding. 'I saw them with my own eyes. One time, someone tried to shoot him. Through the front window, it was. I'd opened the casement, though it was but February, to air the room. I was beating the rugs and the dust did make Mr Baker sneeze so.' The memory flooded her eyes and she wiped them on the corner of her apron. 'He started to feel the cold, and stood up to close the window when, suddenly, a bullet whizzed past him . . .'

'You heard the bullet?'

She nodded fiercely. 'Indeed I did, sir. It went through the rug I was shaking. Fair made me jump, it did.' She looked at him with big eyes. 'I could have been killed. Master too. He hung out of the window and shouted, but the man ran off. Master wasn't well enough to chase him, sir, so we had to let him go.'

'Did anyone else see this?' Grand seemed to have hit on a different side to Baker's story.

'No, sir, just me and the master.'

'What did you do then?'

'I just carried on with the rugs, sir. Otherwise, the rats would get in them, you see.'

'Rats?' Grand knew there were such things in all houses near a river, but living under the rugs was bold, even for city rodents.

'Yes, sir,' she said. 'You have to watch them. Anyways, the master told me that there were men wanted him dead, because of the papers he had.'

'Papers? What did they say, do you know?'

'No, sir. Only that they would send the people to prison, the people who wanted the master dead.'

'I see. Did he say who they were, the people?' Grand was dropping into Kathleen Hawks's speech patterns and was finding the whole experience strangely calming.

'Only one as I saw sometimes, sir. A Mr Cobb, who would come sometimes, of an evening usually, after the master and missus had had their dinner.'

'Can you describe him?' Grand wished he had Batchelor's habit of jotting down notes.

The cook shrugged. 'Just a man, sir. Middling high. Middling wide.'

'Hair?' Grand was leaning forward in his excitement and the cook took a step backwards.

'Not too close, sir. The missus doesn't like gentlemen callers, don't forget.'

Grand put a few paces between them and held up an apologetic hand. 'What colour was his hair?' he asked again.

'Middling.'

He decided to leave descriptions of nose, mouth, eyes . . . he thought he probably knew the answers anyway. 'Did you hear him speak? Did he have an accent at all?'

She shook her head, her mouth set in a line. 'I wouldn't know about that, sir,' she said. 'But I did hear him, once, as he left. I was on the stairs, on my way to bed, and he was at the door. He turned to the master and he said . . .' She screwed up her eyes and tilted her chin, '"Our patience is running short, Baker. You haven't much time."'

Grand was dumbfounded. He had set off to interview this woman having drawn straws with Batchelor. Batchelor had drawn the nurse – surely a better source of information than a simple maid? And yet, Grand seemed to have hit the mother lode. He hardly dare ask, but he did, nevertheless. 'Is there anything else?'

'Oh, yes, sir. The master had a fortune in gold in the attic. It was in a strongbox, with gold chains and all sorts wrapped around it. Stolen Cherokee gold, it was.' She leaned nearer, worries over, followers forgotten. 'That's another reason why people wanted him dead, I expect. Sometimes you could hardly move in their garden for scalps, left there to frighten him into handing it over.'

She gave a knowing nod and again folded her arms and leaned back, the attitude of a woman whose work here is done.

Grand took a deep breath and conjured up a smile. 'Well, thank you, Mrs Hawks,' he said. 'You've been most helpful. I'll let you return to your duties. Thank you again.' And he doffed his hat and turned to go.

The cook held on to his arm. 'You're welcome,' she said, foraging in her bodice with her free hand. Finding what she was looking for, she held it out to him with a friendly smile. 'Hush puppy?'

James Batchelor didn't know Washington at all, but he didn't let that faze him. He set out for Bridget McBane's new place of employment and found it easily – not that it was that hard, as all he had to do was walk down Pennsylvania Avenue and push open the doors of the Naval Hospital. The porter in his booth just inside the door stopped him with a laconic arm.

'Help yuh?' he muttered.

'I'm here to see Bridget McBane,' Batchelor said, through the grille. 'She is a nurse here.'

'Sailor, are yuh?' the porter said, spitting tobacco juice into what Batchelor could only hope was a hidden spittoon.

'Um . . . no,' Batchelor said. He fell back on the old story. 'I'm a journalist. For the London *Telegraph*.'

'London, Tennessee?'

'No, London, England.' Batchelor had forgotten to add the vital word.

'Only, you ain't from round here.' The porter was nothing if not tenacious.

'No, I'm from London. England. May I see Mrs McBane, please?'

'We don't have no women here. Just sailors, see. It's the Naval Hospital.'

Batchelor sighed. 'She's a nurse here,' he said. 'I just need to have a word with her.'

The porter had lost interest. 'You could go find her, I suppose,' he suggested.

'Could I?' Batchelor's acid tone was lost on the man, who was busily cutting another wedge of tobacco.

'You do that,' he said, and began to chew. He gestured up the stairs and Batchelor began his search. Not knowing what the woman looked like was clearly going to be a disadvantage, but after a few false starts – and some grisly sights he would rather not have seen – he found her, in the sluice, washing out porcelain bedpans by the simple expedient of running a cursory cloth around the inside.

'Mrs McBane?' he said as he put his head around the door, recoiling slightly from the smell.

'Yes. Who're you?' The woman was stocky without being fat, with arms like a navvy. Batchelor felt it in his bones that it would be important not to cross her.

He introduced himself with a raise of his boater. He hoped she wouldn't want to shake his hand, but he needn't have worried.

'An enquiry agent?' she asked, her Irish lilt still winning over the American twang. 'What would you be enquiring into?'

'I understand you nursed Lafayette Baker in his last illness,' Batchelor began.

'I nursed him, yes, but only as you'd nurse a viper in your bosom. At arm's length and never turning your back. The man was evil, I tell you. And daft as a brush, so he was.'

'Well,' Batchelor felt it incumbent on him to put the record straight, 'he did run an enormous police force . . .'

'Ah, that may be so,' she said, wielding her cloth viciously. 'But he was obsessed, the man was. Always talking about people wanting to kill him. There was no such thing, although, for the life of me, I don't know why not. Sure, I was up for killing him meself often enough.'

'So . . . you didn't enjoy working for the Baker family?' Batchelor wanted confirmation.

'*She* was all right. Not that she was there much. And that other trollop, that Laura Duvall; no better than she should be and always sniffing around. Not that we saw much of her once the codicil was signed. Thought she'd have a bit of that hidden fortune he was always on about . . . hidden fortune, with me still owed two weeks' pay!' She spat with the same enthusiasm as the porter on a particularly recalcitrant stain and rubbed it with her cloth.

'You never saw or heard anyone threaten him?'

'No. And before you ask, that poisoning thing was years ago and they could never prove it. Them Pettingills was no better than they should be, neither; they ate bad clams and that's an end to it.' She looked at him. 'You don't know about the Pettingills? Where d'you say you're from?'

'London.' Batchelor was startled by her sudden change of tack. His journalist's nose was twitching; there was a story here and no mistake. He took out his notebook and pencil to make a note.

She dashed it from his hand and, bearing in mind what task she was employed in, Batchelor decided to let it lie where it landed. 'No writing,' she said. 'I said there was nothing in it.'

'No, indeed,' he said. 'Nothing at all. So . . .' There must be another question he could ask her without setting her off. 'Thank you, Mrs McBane, you've been very helpful.'

She took a step or two closer and Batchelor kept a weather eye on her cloth. 'Did you say London, England?'

'Yes.'

'How long you been in Washington?'

'A while.' Somehow, the tables had been turned.

'Were you in London when they hanged Mickeleen?'

'Who?'

'Michael Barrett. The sainted man, sent to his doom by that bastard Calcraft, may he rot in Hell.'

Batchelor looked at the brawny arms, at the cloth, and made up his mind in seconds. 'No. I did hear of it, but . . . no. I wasn't there. In London. No, not in London or even near.'

She narrowed her eyes at him. 'I heard he went to his death like a saint, with the heavenly light around his head and flights of angels to transport his soul.'

'So I understand, yes. Indeed, I heard he died a martyr's death.'

She looked at him, eyes sparkling with tears. 'Oh, he did, he did indeed.' She took a step towards him, arms wide for a Fenian hug, bursting into song as she did so.

But with a swing of the sluice door, Batchelor had gone, her singing following him down the corridor as he quickened his pace.

# EIGHT

'*Cui bono?*' James Batchelor had enjoyed a classical education of a rudimentary kind and, even though he had long since lost his grasp on declensions, his awareness of Cicero remained as sharp as ever. Matthew Grand looked at him from his position sprawled on the bed. They hadn't taught Latin at West Point, so the raised eyebrow was as far as he intended to go in confessing ignorance. 'Who benefits?' Batchelor translated.

'In the case of the late Mr Baker?' Grand raised himself so that his head was against the board. 'Who didn't?'

'We've got to break it down somehow, Matthew, or we'll get nowhere. Newshound Durham thinks it was the South. Luther thinks it was Stanton. What if they're both wrong?'

'Say on.'

'Who did Baker cross, apart from Stanton and the South, I mean?'

'The President,' Grand suggested. 'From what we've learned, Baker was intercepting Johnson's mail, tampering with telegrams.'

'So the Congressional committee fired him, yes. What about Johnson? Is he the vengeful type?'

'He's a Southerner with a liking for the bottle and he didn't behave well at the time of Lincoln's assassination but, other than that, I don't know. What can you tell me about Mr Disraeli?'

'Point taken,' Batchelor nodded.

'If it's Johnson,' Grand ran with the idea, 'we'll have even more problems tracing it back to him than we will with Stanton. Unless, of course, Johnson is *au fait* with arsenic himself.'

There was a silence. Both men realized how futile this line of enquiry was.

'What about the city's criminal elements?' Batchelor said, riffling through the notes he had amassed so far. 'Didn't Baker close down every whorehouse and gambling hell north of the Potomac when he ran the National Police?'

'He did,' Grand conceded, 'but if any of that outfit got him, why wait? Why not kill the son of a bitch when he was most active, not wait until he was powerless?'

'But that's the point, isn't it?' Batchelor said. 'While he was at the height of his powers, surrounded by men armed to the teeth led by Cousin Luther, he must have been difficult to reach. Once Stanton fired him, that was it; Lafayette Baker against the rest of the world. And, anyway, who's to say he wasn't a target before this?'

'All right.' Grand sat up, warming to the theme. 'The criminal elements. Cousin Luther himself frequents the Wolf's Den. So that's the whorehouse element in the Division.'

'We may be able to make some headway there with Julep,' Batchelor enthused, until an old-fashioned look from Grand made him change his direction. 'What about gambling?'

'Hell's Bottom,' the local man told him. 'That's where you'll find most saloons.'

'Alcohol,' Batchelor was leaving no stone unturned.

'Virtually everywhere,' Grand shrugged, 'but again – Hell's Bottom, the Division, Bloodfield, Swampoodle. We'd need Haynes's boys and then some to enquire there.'

'What was that name?' Batchelor was turning his pages trying to find it. 'The name Tom Durham gave us? Ah, here it is. Wesley Jericho. Think he may be able to help?'

'Wesley who?' The fat man with the glittering vest peered at them over the rims of his pince-nez.

'The man you work for, croupier,' Grand said, staying the man's blubbery hand on his pack of cards. 'The one who's going to fire you for dealing from the bottom.'

'Are you saying I'm crooked?' The fat man was outraged.

'No, I'm saying you're sloppy.' Grand took the cards from him and shuffled them neatly. 'I'm sure Mr Jericho won't approve of a man with careless card skills. Tell him we want to see him.'

The fat man hesitated and licked his lips. Then he beckoned over a large black bouncer whose fists were heavy with rings. The bouncer nodded and disappeared. The Golden Bowl was alive tonight, well-dressed gentlemen in their top hats rubbing shoulders with the riffraff whose home Hell's Bottom was. Painted girls swished past in short skirts, their buttoned boots clattering on the sawdust-strewn floor. Lamps glowed seductively in corners and the wine and whiskey flowed. Over it all, through the cackling laughter and the bad French of the croupiers, rang the rattle of coin and the whisper of notes.

The bouncer was back in an instant, inviting the guests who had asked to see the manager to follow him upstairs. The hall was dark and dingy and Matthew Grand kept his hand on the butt of his pistol as they reached a glass-fronted door on the third storey. As far as Batchelor was concerned, this was the second floor, but he recognized the type who sat on what could only be called a throne beyond the frosted glass of the door.

'Mr Jericho?' Grand asked.

'I'm Wes Jericho,' the man agreed. He wore a centre parting and a moustache, immaculately waxed and curled. His elegant frock coat was velvet and gold chains criss-crossed his embroidered vest. 'I understand you caught one of my people cheating.'

'That's not why we're here,' Batchelor said.

'Even so.' Jericho glanced at the bouncer. 'Iago,' he said quietly, 'tell Mr Henshaw his services are no longer required.'

'Week's wages, boss?' the bouncer asked.

Jericho screwed up his face, thinking. 'No. This is a serious offence. No, wait – he's got a widowed mamma, though. Make it a day. Now, gentlemen, how can I make your day?'

'You can tell us who killed Lafayette Baker.' Batchelor looked at the man, whose features remained as impassive as the portrait of George Washington on the wall behind him.

'Well,' Jericho smiled at last, 'you just come right out with it, don't you? Is that how you folks do it in England?'

'Needs must,' Batchelor told him, quietly impressed that Jericho recognized the accent.

'Gentlemen,' Jericho got up. 'Let me show you something.' He crossed to a heavy velvet curtain that shrouded one wall and pulled it aside. Beyond it lay a room twice the size of the one they stood in, with a pair of balcony windows at the far end. 'I'd open the windows,' Jericho said, 'but the damned mosquitoes would suck the lifeblood out of you. Even so – you see what I see?'

'The Capitol,' Grand said. He was right. The great black dome jutted into the night sky that lay pocked with stars over the seat of government.

'Oh, there's malaria in these here marshes,' Jericho said, 'and you can't spit for vagrants, contraband, scarlet sisters and pimps, but this is the city of tomorrow, gentlemen. Trust me, one day the United States of America will rule the world.'

'It will?' Batchelor raised a doubting eyebrow.

'It will, brother,' Jericho promised. 'But for now, I'm content to rule Washington. I have an amusing little claret here. Won't you join me?'

They took the proffered chairs and accepted the man's wine. Batchelor was impressed anew, but a man who had lived on a journalist's wages and then on the occasional commission of a private enquiry agent wasn't much of a connoisseur.

'Who sent you to me?' Jericho wanted to know.

'A man who rules Washington hardly needs an introduction,' Grand said, sipping the claret.

'Touché,' Jericho chuckled, 'but I'm not easy to find. Let's see. You've visited . . . eight . . . saloons tonight, looking for me?'

'Nine,' Batchelor corrected him. 'Nobody seemed to know who you were. Until now.'

'Now, I wanted to be found,' Jericho said.

'Why?' Batchelor asked.

'Call it natural curiosity,' Jericho said. 'I know it's killed more cats than the Washington canal, but it's never done me no harm. I wanted to know why you fellas were so keen to meet me.'

'Now you know,' Grand said.

'You seriously think *I* killed Laff Baker?'

'You had a motive,' Batchelor said.

'I did?'

'Certainly.' Grand took up the challenge. 'I assume all nine of the gambling hells we visited tonight belong to you.'

'They do,' Jericho assured him.

'And I guess that's how it was until Baker closed you down?'

Jericho laughed. 'That's about the size of it. Laff and I had an arrangement, though. He closed down every whorehouse and gambling den and liquor establishment north of the Potomac, except mine.'

'He was on the take from you?' Grand was not surprised.

'It's the way the world turns, mister,' Jericho said. 'By the way, you haven't introduced yourselves.'

'Grand and Batchelor,' Grand said. 'Enquiry agents.' He pointed with his thumb to the appropriate chests as he spoke.

'And who are you working for, exactly?'

'Luther Baker,' Batchelor said.

'Hah,' Jericho scoffed. 'That dumb son of a bitch. I had him in my sights once. Should've pulled the trigger.'

'Like you did for his cousin?' Grand asked.

'Laff?' Jericho was suddenly serious. 'No. Like I told you, we had an arrangement. I actually quite liked the slippery bastard. My money's on Stanton.'

'So is Luther's,' Batchelor said. 'So,' he looked into the cold eyes of the entrepreneur, 'we have your word that you didn't shoot Lafayette Baker?'

James Batchelor had never seen a man move so quickly. Before he knew it, Jericho had hauled him upright, the glass and its contents flying over the plush carpet. The Englishman felt his shoulder click and he was on his knees, facing Grand and with Jericho's knife blade glinting at his throat. Grand was on his feet, pistol in hand, hammer back.

'Let him go,' he said between gritted teeth.

'I'm just making a point here,' Jericho said, pressing the blade infinitesimally closer to Batchelor's jugular. 'If I'd wanted Lafayette Baker dead, I'd have done it years ago. And with my Arkansas toothpick here. I don't hold with firearms, Mr Grand; they're so messy.' He sheathed the knife in a swift movement and pushed Batchelor forward with his knees. Grand's pistol muzzle hadn't moved.

'You can cross me off your list,' Jericho said, adjusting the sit of the sheath at his waist, tucking it behind the swing of his coat. 'Now, get the hell out of my place and go talk to Stanton.'

Batchelor got to his feet and made for the door, rubbing the prickly area just above his collar where Jericho's blade-tip had broken the skin. Grand walked backwards, gun still in hand, until they'd reached the head of the stairs.

'You all right, James?' he murmured.

'Tolerably.' Batchelor was still waiting for his heart to

descend from his mouth. 'At least we know one thing – Wesley Jericho doesn't have a clue as to how Lafayette Baker *actually* died.'

'Either that,' Grand said, 'or he's altogether a cleverer son of a bitch than either of us took him for.'

The Washington Memorial was still unfinished, its granite half walls gleaming in the sun. Ladies in parasols strolled beside it, arm in arm with straw-hatted gentlemen taking the air. The park vendors cried their wares – lemonade and chilled tea with twisted candy canes for the children.

Luther Baker rarely ventured out into the sunshine. His cousin was dead – murdered, he was sure, by persons unknown, all of whom worked for Edwin McMasters Stanton. The name of Baker was hated throughout the South, and who knew who was lurking in the bushes in the park, a rifle trained on the man who had been Lafayette's second in command? As soon as the moment permitted, he ducked under an overhanging cedar branch and waited for the men he had arranged to meet.

Grand and Batchelor made their way from the weeds along the river and sat themselves down with their backs to the cedar trunk, as instructed.

'You boys making progress?' they heard Baker ask through gritted teeth. 'Don't turn around. It's best that no one knows I'm here.'

'We found Wesley Jericho,' Batchelor said.

'That asshole? Where does he figure in this?'

'Probably nowhere,' Batchelor went on. 'We gave him the false impression that Lafayette was shot and he seemed to go along with that.'

'And we've talked to the ladies,' Grand told him, looking steadily ahead to the cattle slaughterhouses that still dotted the park from the dark days of the war. 'The nurse, Bridget McBane, and the maid, Kathleen Hawks.'

'And?'

'Hawks left Lafayette's employ over a month before he died.'

'No help, then?'

Grand was inclined to turn but thought better of it. He was becoming as edgy as Luther, imagining every little flicker of a leaf to be an assassin's movement, every noise the click of a gun. 'I'd say Kathleen Hawks is a few cents short of a dollar.'

'So would I,' Luther grunted, scanning the crowds walking in the sunshine, 'but no stone unturned, huh? That's something you fellas should have printed on your calling cards. What about McBane?'

Batchelor took up the tale. 'Mrs McBane is a Fenian,' he said solemnly, as though that explained it all.

'I don't care if she's a goddamned blockade runner; what did she tell you?'

'She said,' Batchelor murmured, 'and I quote, "I think he was daft as a brush". Then she changed the subject and started singing about Ireland being a nation once again.'

'"They're hanging men and women there for wearing of the green",' Grand carolled.

'Close,' Batchelor said, 'and may I say, you sing rather more tunefully than Nurse McBane. But, to sum up the ladies' views for a moment, it seems to me that although they have different opinions about it, the common denominator is that there *were* threats against Lafayette, real or imagined.'

'Which is exactly where you boys were when you first got off the ship,' Baker felt obliged to point out.

'Not exactly,' Batchelor said. 'We . . . or rather *I* . . . have met Major Tice since then.'

There was a silence. The cedar wasn't talking.

'Tice?' Baker said eventually.

'Caleb Tice,' Batchelor went on, 'claims he was there when you and Lafayette caught John Wilkes Booth.'

Baker spat. 'Yeah, and it was because of Tice that we nearly lost him. But you're confused, Batchelor. Caleb Tice is dead.'

'That's what Inspector Haynes said,' Batchelor agreed. He took a cigar out of its case and passed one to Grand. The little boy rolling his hoop through the scythed grass thought it odd that that man with a funny accent was offering another cigar to a tree, but that was probably because he wasn't from these parts.

'I'll stick to the Scotch snuff,' Baker muttered. 'Who's Haynes?'

'Inspector of the Metropolitan Police,' Batchelor told him.

'Oh, that misfit. I remember that son of a bitch looking for a job not so long ago. Laff sent him to the Pinkertons. How does he know about Tice?'

Grand smiled. Since there was no explanation forthcoming from his colleague, he did the honours. 'Young James here was caught talking to Major Tice at Madam Wilton's. James is a trustworthy cuss, though. I can vouch for his intentions.'

'What you fellas do in your spare time is up to you.' Baker took a snort of his snuff and shook his head. 'Just don't charge it to expenses, that's all I ask. This Tice – what did he look like?'

'Er . . . forties, I suppose,' Batchelor said. 'Long hair. Goatee. Not very trusting. Pulled a pistol on me.'

'Politeness isn't what it once was in DC,' Baker said. 'How did you find him?'

'He sent word he wanted to talk,' Batchelor explained. 'Better ask Julep about that.'

'Julep?' Baker frowned. '*My* Julep?'

'How many are there?' Batchelor felt that question should be delivered face to face, and turned to the tree before Baker's boot prompted him to face forward again. 'She turned up at the Willard and took me to Tice at Madam Wilton's.'

'What did he tell you?' Baker wanted to know.

'Nothing.' Batchelor blew smoke rings to the cloudless blue. 'There was a police raid.'

'Why should you and Haynes think that Tice is dead?' Grand asked.

'Don't rightly know,' Baker murmured, 'unless it's something to do with the fact that I put a bullet in the bastard and he fell in the river.'

Both men turned at that, cedar subterfuge or not.

'Affair of honour,' Baker said. 'I don't want to talk about it.'

'Talk about something else, then.' Grand was happy to change the subject. 'What does the name Munson mean to you?'

'Munson?' Baker was dredging his memory. 'It was an alias Laff used during the war. When he was caught by Beauregard's cavalry, he was interrogated by the general and then by Jeff Davis himself. He invented the name.'

'And the place,' Grand added.

'What place?'

'I've read your cousin's book, Mr Baker,' Batchelor said. '"Samuel Munson" hailed from Knoxville in Tennessee.'

Luther Baker laughed, softly so that no one beyond the cedar's boughs heard. 'Well, that's as maybe,' he said, 'I had my hands kind of full back in the day. Cousin Laff, he got around more than I did.'

'So that's our next port of call,' Grand said. 'We've just about run out of options in Washington. We're going south, to Knoxville.'

'Well, good luck with that,' Baker said. 'And when you get back, I expect a full report. Maybe then, you'll get some dirt on Stanton. Contact me at the Wolf's Den.'

'Via Julep?' Batchelor asked.

'*Via con Dios*,' Baker replied.

The paddle wheels of the riverboat *City of Knoxville* churned the brown waters of the French Broad into a foaming mass. Black smoke was belching from her twin stacks and the captain was shouting incomprehensible commands to his crew.

Grand and Batchelor had travelled via the East Tennessee Railroad until they reached the river, then whiled away a few hours playing poker in the *Knoxville*'s saloon. Batchelor was not exactly adept at the game, but was keen to try. Grand had tried and failed many times to introduce him to pinochle; this looked much simpler and the company was friendly, so what could possibly go wrong?

Their travelling companions were drummers in ladies' under-garments – always a job strictly reserved for married men in order to spare everybody's blushes – and they both knew the river well.

'Yessir,' one of them said, peering through a pair of bottle-bottom pince-nez, 'battle of Fort Sanders. I was there. Must've been end of November, Sixty-Three. Snow. Fog. We had it all. Rebs tried a frontal assault – you can't tell me Jim Longstreet didn't have guts; blood was ankle deep. Lee called him his old warhorse and I can see why.'

'I met Ambrose Burnside once,' his companion said. 'You know, the Union general. He was a good man. Bald as an eagle. Had more hair on his cheeks than on his head. Talk to Schleier, the photographer in Gay Street – he took his likeness several times. I'll raise you, Mr Batchelor.'

There was something about the flow of speech, the slap of the paddles and the gentle rock of the river that served to hypnotize the two enquiry agents. That, anyway, was the excuse they gave for being completely cleaned out by two men in ladies' undergarments. Grand, patting his empty wallet tucked inside his coat, hoped that there was a sizeable bank in Knoxville so that he could wire Boston to top up his spending money. He could hardly put in a chit for gambling losses to Luther Baker.

The posters on board claimed that Knoxville lay in the Switzerland of America and, once he had come to grips with that rather odd concept, Batchelor could see why. At all points of the compass, majestic mountains stood snow-capped, even in a late summer as hot as this. At Deery and Co.'s wharf, the *Knoxville* dropped her anchor chains and her passengers waited until the gangplank was secured. Deery's catered for the world, it seemed, selling everything from Baltimore Rio coffee to chocolate, blasting powder and La India cigars. In fact, Grand was just refilling his case with six of the last when he grabbed Batchelor and pushed him round a corner, out of sight of the street.

'Good God, Matthew!' Batchelor shouted. 'What the—'

'Sshh!' the American quieted him. 'There, on the sidewalk. In green.'

Batchelor followed the man's pointing finger. An attractive lady with a parasol was chatting to two others. A black woman stood at her elbow, holding the hand of a little girl, who was the image of the lady in green. 'Enchanting,' Batchelor agreed.

'And that's not all it is,' Grand muttered.

'I don't understand,' Batchelor admitted. It was a phrase he had used rather a lot in recent weeks.

'The lady with the parasol,' Grand said. 'It's my guess she's carrying a Derringer in that purse. You are looking, James, my boy, at the Cleopatra of Secession, the Siren of the Shenandoah. That's Belle Boyd, confederate spy. And killer.'

The Lamar House was the best hotel in town and, once Grand had sorted his business at the bank (Batchelor, unknown to Belle Boyd, was keeping watch for her outside), the pair checked in. It wasn't exactly the Willard, but it was comfortable enough.

Their room overlooked the broad expanse of Gay Street and bunting of red, white and blue flapped in the warm breeze from the river.

'But she did tell you she planned to return,' Batchelor reminded Grand. He was hanging his spare shirts in the wardrobe.

'To the States, yes, but – as I am sure you have noticed, James – this is a big country. What are the odds of Belle Boyd being here?'

'You didn't spot her in Washington? Or Philadelphia? She's very striking,' Batchelor mused. 'She would be quite hard to miss. And she has her little girl with her; perhaps she's just on holiday.'

Grand looked at him quizzically. 'That soft heart of yours will get you into serious trouble one of these days, James,' he said. 'I haven't seen her until today, but I get the impression that Miss Boyd is only seen when she wants to be seen.'

'Why don't we find out?' Batchelor suggested.

'How?' Grand really didn't like the look in his colleague's eye.

'Trust me, Matthew,' Batchelor slapped his friend's shoulder, 'I'm an enquiry agent.' And he was gone, thundering down the Lamar's stairs, two at a time.

'Can I help you, sir?' The desk clerk didn't like rowdy elements at the Lamar; it lowered the tone.

'Yes,' Batchelor beamed. 'I'm a journalist, from London . . . England. I'm doing a story on Miss Belle Boyd.'

'Who?'

'Stonewall's ADC,' Batchelor said, bubbling with mock enthusiasm. 'My readers are huge fans of the late General Jackson. As am I. I understand Miss Boyd lives hereabouts.'

The clerk almost shuddered. 'During the recent unpleasantness,' he said, closing his eyes, 'I supported the North.'

'Ah.'

'However . . .' Batchelor knew the portent of that pregnant pause and fished his last few dollars out of his wallet. When he glanced back inside it, it was completely empty. The clerk took the notes and they disappeared with a speed Batchelor had never seen before.

'Hm?'

'Dr John Mason Boyd is Miss Belle's uncle. He's a fine man,

even though he was surgeon to the CSA at Bull Run. He may know something.'

'And where can I find him?'

'Well . . .'

Batchelor was down to coins now and he passed them over.

'The Blount Mansion. You can't miss it.'

'Many thanks,' Batchelor called, and made for the stairs, before he was expected to spend any more.

'I could tell you about the Mabrys,' the clerk called, 'or the McClungs? And don't even get me started on Parson Brownlow, the mad cuss.'

'How about Samuel Munson?' Batchelor had paused on the bottom stair.

The clerk stared at him, then became unaccountably deaf and bent his head, intent, it appeared, on other duties.

It may be that the Tennessee sunshine blinded him; it may be that he was too busy wiping the sweat from his forehead – for whatever reason, James Batchelor didn't see her until it was too late. She, however, saw Matthew Grand.

'Why, Captain Grand, now just Mister, are you following me?' Belle Boyd looked alluring that morning in a gingham day dress, her wide bonnet shading her eyes. The black servant and little Grace had gone.

'Mrs Hardinge.' Grand tipped his wideawake, as annoyed with himself as with Batchelor for allowing this meeting to happen. On the other hand, Knoxville was a small town; it was unlikely they could have avoided each other for long.

'Who is this?' Belle asked, smiling at Batchelor, who fell in love on the spot.

'My associate,' Grand said, 'James Batchelor. Allow me to introduce Isabella Hardinge – Belle Boyd.'

'Mrs Hardinge,' Batchelor tipped his hat too, trying to look sophisticated and soigné. 'What a pleasure. I've read your book. Fascinating.'

'Mr Batchelor was a journalist by trade,' Grand explained.

'Then I consider that praise indeed, Mr Batchelor, thank you. So, if you're not following me, Mr Grand,' she turned her warmest smile on the man who was once her enemy, 'why *are* you in Knoxville?'

'Chasing shadows,' Grand said.

'One shadow in particular,' Batchelor said. 'Samuel Munson.'

For the briefest of moments, Belle Boyd's concentration slipped. When she had talked to Grand back in London, the name Munson had not cropped up. Goddamn! This man and his sidekick were better at the investigation game than she'd expected. Then, she was herself again, composed, relaxed. 'Do you have time to eat in this shadow chase?' she asked.

Grand and Batchelor looked at each other.

'You must come to dinner,' she said. 'Tomorrow night. Six sharp at Blount Mansion. On the way out of town. You can't miss it. Uncle John and Aunt Sue will be delighted to meet you.' She took a step closer to Grand and placed a soft hand on his lapel. 'And, please don't worry, Mr Grand; you won't need your pocket Colt. And Mr Batchelor,' she turned her head to him, but kept her hand lightly on Grand, flashing the ex-journalist her most dazzling smile, 'I look forward to hearing all about your exploits with the *Telegraph*. Until tomorrow night, then.'

There were smiles and hat-tipping all round and Grand and Batchelor wandered away.

'*Telegraph*?' Batchelor muttered out of the corner of his mouth. 'I didn't mention the *Telegraph*. *You* didn't mention the *Telegraph*. What's going on, Matthew?'

Grand sighed. 'Believe me, James,' he muttered back, 'when I figure it out, you're the first person I shall tell.'

# NINE

The Blount Mansion had been built years before when the town of Knoxville was the state capital and it had been the home of the governor. Nashville had that honour now and the governor was Parson Brownlow. If you were for the North in those days, William Brownlow was a saint. If you were for the South, he was a deranged bastard with the sunken eyes and grim mouth of a ghoul. Whichever side you were on, everybody agreed that Knoxville without Parson Brownlow was altogether a calmer place.

Dr John Boyd was a gentleman of the Old South. Grand had met his type before; honest, upright, a model of rectitude. But the war had destroyed such men; left some broken, some bitter. Boyd was neither of them, but there was an all-pervading sadness about him, a longing for what once was and what might have been.

His wife, Susan, was a charming Southern lady, and what else could she possibly be? Grand and Batchelor were charmed; she was Belle, but without the edge, and seemed delighted to welcome two strangers to her home. If one was a Billy Yank and one was a Limey, no one would ever guess from her demeanour, which was talc and perfume and Southern hospitality in equal measure.

The dining room of Blount Mansion was a blaze of candles, silverware and mahogany, polished by loving hands over the years and trotted out for the visitors. Belle slipped a cool hand into Batchelor's arm and led him to the seat next to hers.

'Belle,' her aunt admonished gently, 'don't keep Mr Batchelor to yourself, now. I want to speak with him of London; my great-grandpa was from there.'

'Now, Aunt Susan,' Belle said back, her hand still firmly in the crook of Batchelor's elbow, 'you can have Mr Batchelor to yourself once we've eaten. You can have Mr Grand for now – how does that sound?'

Before her aunt could reply, the door of the dining room had crashed back and a little bundle of fury barrelled in, a nurse in hot pursuit. 'What's going on, John Boyd? Who's this you've got sitting at your table? If he's not a Yankee then I'm a yellow-belly racer!'

Boyd stepped forward politely, but Grand guessed, from the gleam in his eye, that instead of propelling the old girl forward to make the introductions, he wanted to wring her neck. 'Grandma,' he smiled down at the top of her crisp cotton cap, 'these gentlemen are friends of Belle's, from London.'

The old lady narrowed her eyes and set her toothless jaws. 'No better'n she should be, that one,' she said. 'Bringing all and sundry to your table, John Boyd. Where is she?' She peered round, dazzled by the candlelight.

'I'm here, Great-Grandma,' Belle said, letting go of Batchelor's arm. It felt warm where her hand had rested and he could hardly resist stroking the place, but Grand was eyeing him and he knew it was unwise. 'Be nice, now. Come and join us, why don't you?'

Susan Boyd stepped forward, aghast. Grandma hadn't dined with the family for years, not since that last incident.

The old lady hung back, looking at Belle from beneath malevolent eyebrows. 'There's no place set for me,' she said.

'Please,' Grand stepped forward. 'Take mine. I can sit here, look, on the end; I'm tall, this stool will be fine for me.'

The old woman looked him up and down and, for a moment, the enquiry agent thought she was going to spit at him. But after a moment, her face broke into a grin. She poked him in the solar plexus with a gnarled finger. 'You may be a Yankee, young fella,' she said, 'but you're mighty easy on the eye. I'll sit here next to you. That weaselly Limey can sit down yonder on the end.' She tugged Grand nearer and whispered in his ear. 'Time was, I could have taken two your size and still had the strength to hogtie a gator or two. These days, I'd have to leave the gator till tomorrow.' Sadly for Grand's eardrums, Grandma hadn't managed a whisper for some time, so everyone had the pleasure of the mental picture she had so charmingly conjured up. Still chuckling and waving the nurse away, the old lady hutched her chair up to the table and picked up a knife and fork. She smiled round at everyone.

'What we having?' she demanded. 'It's a good while since I had a nice roast armadiller.'

Susan Boyd sighed and settled the old lady nearer to the table and swathed her front in a snow-white napkin. 'It's not armadillo, Grandma,' she said, keeping her voice level. 'We've got company, don't forget.'

Grandma looked with gimlet eyes at Batchelor, who was trying to keep out of it at the end of the table. 'Limey!' she said. 'Don't appreciate good Southern cooking.'

The conversation was broken up by the arrival of the soup and, despite the ear-splitting slurping of Grandma, it was eaten in silence. The fish was a whole river perch and although Batchelor had a natural aversion to being served anything that could still look at him, it was delicious, smoky and delicate, and he did it good justice. His troubles began with the roast and, although the Boyd family were delightful company, refined and cultured, they did have a skittish streak when it came to pranks. His slices of pork – 'From our own hogs,' Mrs Boyd told him proudly – were recognizable enough, and if the accompaniments were not as clear to him, being mainly composed of beans and corn, he was still doing them justice when Grandma piped up, 'Here, Limey. How's the food? How's the chitterlings?'

'Hush, Grandma,' Dr Boyd said. 'You know there are no chitterlings tonight.' He smiled at Batchelor. 'Take no notice, sir,' he said. 'Grandma is just joking, aren't you, Grandma?'

The old lady glowered at her grandson, but said nothing, choosing instead to slather her pork with some sauce from a sticky bottle. Then, politely, she smiled at Batchelor. 'Would you like some sauce, Limey?' she said. 'Put a bit of poke in your pork?'

Belle put up a warning hand, but she was too late. Batchelor reached out a hand for the bottle and it was passed over with some meaningful looks between Dr and Mrs Boyd. Grand thought he detected a twinkle, but decided to ride it out and see where the joke went. After all, the old lady was mopping the stuff up with her bread; it couldn't be poisonous, at least.

Batchelor sprinkled the sauce over his meat and set the bottle down. Still smiling, he piled some unknown vegetable onto a piece of meat and popped it into his mouth, chewed and swallowed.

After that, as he later told Grand in their hotel room, his mouth caught fire. His gums seemed to sizzle, his throat constricted, and his lips felt as though they had grown to four times their normal size. He tried to speak, but couldn't; nothing in his mouth, from his tonsils out, seemed to work any more. He reached for his water, but Belle halted him.

'Not water, James,' she said. 'That just makes it worse. Auntie Susan, ring the bell for some milk.' She looked at the old woman, convulsed in her chair with laughter. 'That was cruel, Great-Grandma,' she said. 'You must know that Mr Batchelor wouldn't have come across your grannie's special recipe tabasco-pepper sauce before. You have to be born to it.' She got up and went and stood behind Batchelor, who was breathing as though each breath was his last, and she rubbed his back in a way that didn't help him as much as she thought it might; having a back rub from Belle Boyd would interfere with most men's breathing.

The door opened and the butler arrived, with a glass of milk on a tray. Batchelor grabbed it and drank it down in one go. In London, he would have been on the alert for the usual milk inclusions such as mouse droppings and hairs, but this looked cool and good and, anyway, he would have drunk anything to put the fire out in his mouth. And, slowly, the feeling returned to his tongue.

His enquiry agent's mind was whirring. 'How did he know to bring milk?' he slurred. 'Is there a code?'

Belle laughed and sat back down. 'No,' she said. 'The kitchen always has a glass of milk ready when Great-Grandma and her sauce are at the table with a stranger.' She wagged her finger at her aunt and uncle. 'That was very naughty of you,' she said. 'Poor Mr Batchelor could have died.'

Dr Boyd laughed too and wagged his finger back. 'No one's died at my table . . .'

'. . . not since that one time,' his wife added, her eyes twinkling.

The butler took Batchelor's empty glass and left the room.

'Poor Mr Batchelor,' Belle said. 'You've had hardly any dinner. Would you like a new plate?'

Batchelor, whose mouth was no longer flaming, having settled to a mild sizzle, shook his head. All he wanted was a nice cool ice for dessert and five minutes alone in a room with the mad old besom down the table. He looked past the candles, the flowers and the silverware to where Grand sat, smiling with the rest, and vowed to get even. He had never introduced the American to jellied eels, being too polite. But, when they got back to London, his time would come and then he would be sorry.

The table fell quiet again as everyone ate – Southern manners didn't exclude talk, but the Boyds were trenchermen to the last and believed in the maxim that every time you speak, you miss a mouthful. When the much-wanted ices had been eaten, Belle turned to her aunt.

'Auntie Susan,' she said, 'will you sing to us?'

The woman looked down modestly and shook her head, making the flowers in her cap rustle. 'No, Belle,' she said, quietly. 'You should—'

'No, Auntie Susan,' the woman said. 'It's so long since I heard you sing. Please . . . just one. "Lorena"; just for me.'

Dr Boyd patted his wife's hand. 'Yes, Susan. Mr Batchelor won't have heard the old songs. And you play so beautifully.'

Twittering and fluttering, Mrs Boyd went to the piano in the corner of the room and opened the lid. The music was already on the stand and this was clearly her party-piece. Her voice was clear and pleasant, her fingers flew over the keys and if the song wasn't the happiest Batchelor had ever heard, it was certainly among the most tuneful. He was still humming it under his breath as the gentlemen retired to Dr Boyd's study, leaving poor Susan trying manfully to induce Grandma to return to her room upstairs. Batchelor was rather disconcerted to find that Belle joined them in the study, sipping her uncle's best brandy along with the guests. Would this country ever stop delivering surprises?

'You find us in turmoil, Mr Batchelor,' John Boyd said. 'We are a community still coming to terms with what has happened. As a doctor, I know something about the healing of wounds. It takes time.'

'Now, Uncle John,' Belle scolded the man gently. 'You promised you wouldn't talk about politics.'

'I've been away,' Grand said, 'and James here has never set foot on American soil until now. We'd like to understand what's happening.'

Dr Boyd smiled. Belle knew when she was beaten and lit cigars for the men. 'You had a civil war, Mr Batchelor, back in the old country,' he said.

'Two, if you include the Wars of the Roses.'

'You killed your King.'

'Charles I, yes.' Batchelor was impressed – there was many an Englishman he knew who had less grasp.

'And we killed our President,' Boyd nodded, 'and God knows how many boys along with him. Blue or gray, it doesn't make much difference. The problem is what to do about it now. What happened in England, Mr Batchelor, after the execution of the King?'

'That was all a long time ago, sir,' Batchelor shrugged. 'Times change.'

'They do,' Boyd conceded. 'All the same, humour me.'

'Parliament ruled,' Batchelor said.

'Congress.'

Batchelor nodded. 'They squabbled among themselves, of course. Without the King, they couldn't decide how to govern.'

Boyd chuckled. 'It's uncanny,' he said. 'History repeating itself. There are those in Congress who want the secession states punished for the war, keep us out of government entirely.'

'That can't work, surely?' Batchelor said.

'Maybe not.' Boyd winced as the brandy hit his tonsils, 'but it's happening already. You weren't here, Mr Grand; Belle, neither were you. The Carpetbaggers moved in.'

'I've read that word somewhere,' Batchelor said.

'Some of them are genuinely concerned with improvements for the blacks,' Boyd said, 'but most have jumped on the band-wagon. They're confidence tricksters out of the North, making money out of the ex-Contraband they're supposed to be helping. Poor white farmers are losing their land, their livelihood. The scalawags help them.'

'Scalawags?' That wasn't a term that Batchelor had ever heard.

'Southern trash who've joined the Carpetbaggers. They're tearing the heart out of their own country. It's tragic.'

'Can't the President—' Batchelor began.

'Johnson?' Boyd sneered. 'He's the worst of them. A Southerner by birth, but he's got no balls – saving your presence, Belle.

He's just survived impeachment by one vote. He can't go to the bathroom without checking with Congress. And Congress is dominated by hardliners.'

'So what *can* be done?' Batchelor may not have been a reporter any more, but he could espouse a cause as well as the next man.

'Ask the Klan.' Boyd blew smoke rings to the ceiling.

'The Klan?' Grand leaned forward.

Dr Boyd exchanged glances with his niece. 'The Invisible Empire,' the doctor said. 'A bunch of rednecks from Pulaski, along Richland Creek. They formed a social club, they said, on Christmas Eve 1865. Set up stupid rules and called themselves the Ku Klux, from Kuklos, a circle in ancient Greek.'

'They were university men?' Grand asked. 'I don't see many natives of Pulaski knowing the Greek for circle from a hole in the ground.'

Boyd chuckled. 'You're right; some of them had attended university and something must have stuck, I suppose. They got their mothers to cut up old bed sheets and they wrapped themselves up in them, riding around the countryside putting the fear of the Lord into the black folks. They called themselves Grand Cyclops, Grand Turk, Grand Scribe. Their meeting place is the Den. It's all ritual and make-believe.'

'Overgrown schoolboys playing childish games,' Batchelor said.

'Don't underestimate these people, Mr Batchelor,' Boyd warned. 'They burn crosses and hang blacks they call Uppity Niggers. The same goes for any white man deemed to be speaking on behalf of said blacks.'

'Lynch law,' Grand said, simply.

'The West is built on it,' Belle murmured. 'This is all a far cry from London, Mr Batchelor.'

'It is,' he had to agree, 'but we hang people there, too.'

'Who's their leader?' Grand asked.

Dr Boyd shrugged his shoulders. 'Nobody knows, but the rumour runs it's Nathan Bedford Forrest himself.'

Batchelor looked at Grand. 'Sounds like a football team,' he said.

'Confederate general,' the ex-Union man explained. 'One of the best.'

'Have the Klan caused trouble around here, Dr Boyd?' Batchelor asked.

'Round Knoxville? No, thank God. The fact is, Mr Batchelor, we lost the war. The miracle was that we kept going for as long as we did. The knights of the Klan, with their pseudo-Greek claptrap, can't accept that. For them, the war isn't over. It'll never be over.'

A silence descended on the Blount Mansion and the cigar smoke hung heavy in the atmosphere. It was Belle who broke it.

'That's enough gloom for one night,' she said. 'Tomorrow, I have an appointment at Mr Schleier's photographic studio. Won't you join me, Mr Batchelor?'

Batchelor's heart lurched in his chest, but before he could answer, she continued speaking.

'Mr Grand, you can come too, if you like.'

The men nodded politely and ground out their cigars. This seemed to be a sign the evening was over and they took their leave, dodging out into the hall furtively, listening for signs of distant grandmothers.

'I didn't hold with Mathew Brady, no sir.' The voice was coming from under a black hood and just above a pair of legs, bent at odd angles behind the tripod. 'Bad enough the war was fought at all, but photographs of corpses – there's no call for that.'

The enquiry agents knew the work of Mathew Brady. Most photographers – Schleier included – chose living subjects. Their men in uniform sat in studios with martial expressions on their faces. Brady's subjects lay in foxholes, bled to death or strewn over some desolate field. The man had a point to make.

'Not that you can call me partisan either.' Henry Schleier popped his head out of the hood, sliding plates and fussing with his equipment. 'Look at the examples around you, gentlemen. You'll see the blue and the gray equally represented. That's George Stoneman in the corner, Mr Batchelor. See how he has placed his hand under his coat? In imitation of Napoleon Bonaparte – though, I fear, that's where any similarity ends. That – and there's the hand in the coat again – is William Tecumseh Sherman. I was lucky to get that one. Sherman didn't care for Knoxville, no sir. Too anxious to march to the sea, I guess. Ah, now, that's my favourite you're looking at there, sir; General Ambrose Burnside to a tee. Wet collodion process, of course. I confess I am something of a master of the daguerreotype.'

Belle Boyd shifted slightly on the high stool.

'I'm going to have to ask you not to fidget now, Miss Boyd,' Schleier said. The little man with the wild hair and crooked teeth was normally a timid creature, but once behind his camera, he became a martinet. And, in his studio, *nobody* moved. He had been known to tie down recalcitrant children; he saw no problem with others suffering for his art. 'Are you thinking *carte de visite* for this?'

'I am, Mr Schleier,' she said, tilting her head to one side again. 'And perhaps these gentlemen would care to be next?'

Grand shook his head absently, answering for both. His attention had been drawn to a particular photograph on the wall, to the left of the aspidistra, and he nudged Batchelor to examine it too. Three men had sat for Schleier, two standing to either side of a seated officer wearing gray.

'Who's this?' Batchelor asked.

'Ah,' Schleier beamed, 'that there's a special piece of work. That is General Nathan Bedford Forrest. He doesn't like having his portrait took. Come to think of it, neither did the other two. But I can be pretty insistent.'

Grand and Batchelor didn't doubt it.

They had luncheon with the mercurial Mrs Hardinge, who everybody in Knoxville still called Miss Boyd, and saw her back home. It was while they were walking back that Batchelor said, thoughtfully, 'You know who that was in the photograph, don't you? The one with Forrest.'

'I do,' Grand nodded, checking that they were alone on the road, 'and how odd that he should be photographed standing with the enemy.'

'So, what do you make of it?'

'Well, I suppose as Samuel Munson he had to play the part to the full. Whatever he was doing here, he had to make people believe he was a Rebel.'

'Samuel Munson?' Batchelor had stopped walking, so he could concentrate better. Grand's longer legs always made keeping pace with him a trial for the Londoner and he needed all his faculties. 'Matthew, what are you talking about?'

Grand stopped too. 'What are *you* talking about?' he countered.

'The man standing next to Forrest in Schleier's photograph.'

'To Forrest's right or his left?'

Batchelor closed his eyes and pointed. Opening them, he said, 'To his right.'

'I was talking about the man on his left.'

'Who's the man on the left?'

'You saw him in his coffin,' Grand said, 'and I remembered how little he had changed in death. That was Lafayette Baker, known in these parts, and for his own purposes, as Samuel Munson.'

'I see,' Batchelor murmured, walking on.

Grand stopped him. 'So . . . who was the man on the right?'

'That,' Batchelor was striding for the hotel, for once setting the pace, 'that was Baker's right-hand man, Caleb Tice.'

'So,' James Batchelor was sampling his third Early Times whisky, just to make sure he still liked it. 'Let me see if I've got this straight. Mr Schleier, the photographer, has – among the many examples of his work – a study of the former chief of the National Detective Force and his number two, sitting cosily with a Confederate general whose head you would, not so long ago, have wanted to see on a plate.'

'That's about the size of it.' Matthew Grand already knew he liked Early Times, but even without needing reassurance, he was also on his third glass. 'Pity we don't know exactly when that was taken.'

'It didn't seem appropriate to ask him,' Batchelor said, 'what with Belle there.'

'Belle, is it, now?' Grand was good at nuance.

'We *have* been to her uncle's house for dinner, Matthew,' the Englishman reminded him, his tongue tingling at the memory, '*and* accompanied her to the photographer's. "Mrs Hardinge" seems a little formal, don't you think?'

'Well, get as informal as you like,' Grand said. 'Belle may or may not have been in Knoxville when this photograph was taken, but it's clear she knows more than she's telling.'

'What makes you say that?'

Grand sighed. There was a sucker born every minute and, when it came to the ladies, that sucker was James Batchelor. 'Who told us about Mr Munson?' he asked.

'Er . . . Judah Benjamin.'

'And Knoxville?'

'The same.'

'And yet Belle Boyd, who has relatives here and was arrested and interrogated by "Mr Munson" made no mention of the connection. And when you raised the name in the street the day before yesterday, she changed the subject.'

'Well, I expect—'

'It slipped her mind? Come on, James. We're talking about the Siren of the Shenandoah here, remember – a woman even Laff Baker couldn't crack. Take her on a picnic.'

'What? Oh, I couldn't.'

'This isn't some goddamned tea party run by an English vicar,' Grand snapped. 'We've got a murderer to catch.'

'Oh, all right. What'll you be doing?'

'Me?' An odd light shone in Matthew Grand's eyes. 'I'll be polishing up my ancient Greek. Specifically, the word Kuklos; a circle.'

# TEN

Grand sat with his back to the Forty-Niner's door. At the Coal Hole in the Strand, or any of London's watering holes, he wouldn't have bothered, but this was Pulaski, Tennessee, home of the Klan. Here, men carried guns and their tempers were short. The man who had fought so many battles wondered again that day what had it all been for.

The saloon itself had clearly once had pretensions. It had etched-glass windows, brass fittings to the bar and a honky-tonk piano in the corner. The waitresses, if there had ever been any, had long gone, and the only service came from the bar, where the Red Eye was cheap and the cigar smoke lingered. Forty-Niner was an odd name and as Grand sat in a shadowed corner, his hat on the beer-ringed table in front of him, he realized that the clientele wouldn't know a gold nugget from a hole in the head. They came in all shapes and sizes, but they were all men, some still wearing Confederate gray, their jackets torn and patched. One man had lost an arm. Another swung on crutches, his progress to the bar slow and painful. Yet another still had the parchment-yellow skin and sunken eyes of a prisoner of war, from the hellhole that was Camp Douglas.

But it was none of these that Grand targeted. He was watching the boy in the fancy vest with a derby hat perched on the back of his head and a shabby frock coat that fitted him nowhere. Grand was playing solitaire, flicking the cards from one hand to another, tossing them in the air and catching them again. When he had done this a few times, the object of his attention wandered over.

'You play poker, mister?' the boy asked.

Grand looked up at him. He was no more than twenty, which would have made him seventeen when the war ended. Old enough, Grand knew. The bloody ground from Richmond to Shiloh was strewn with the bodies of seventeen year olds. 'Poker?' he said in impeccable Arkansas, 'Satan's game, son. My granpappy, the minister, wouldn't allow playing cards in the house. Said they were the devil's picture book.'

'All right,' the boy shrugged, backing away. 'My mistake.'

Grand let him get halfway across the room before he said, 'Twenty-One, now; that's different.'

The boy smiled and came back, scraping a chair from the table and extending a grubby hand. 'Lester Merkel,' he said.

'Matthew Granger,' Grand said, shaking it. 'You from these parts, Lester?'

'Yessir. Born and bred right here in Pulaski. You?'

'All over.' Grand called the barman over. 'A bottle of your best bourbon,' he said, 'and a glass for my friend here.'

'That's mighty white of you,' Merkel said, and watched in a daze as Grand shuffled the cards.

'What do you say, Lester?' the man who was not from all over asked. 'Dollar a point?'

Merkel blinked. He worked the warehouses on the creek. A dollar was a day's wage for him.

'Just joshing you, son,' Grand smiled. 'I'd play for the pleasure of your company.'

Lester Merkel had never crossed the state line out of Tennessee, but even so, he had heard of men who liked the company of other, younger men. He decided to be very wary of this stranger. But that was a decision he made at half past two by the Forty-Niner's clock. By half past three, after more bourbon than was good for him and more wins at Twenty-One than were likely by the law of averages, Lester Merkel was more than a little relaxed. His wins became more numerous still and his tongue ever looser.

'Any action round here, Lester?' Grand asked, having gone bust for the umpteenth time.

'Action?' Merkel was slurring and Matthew Granger appeared to be blurring at the edges.

'I hear there's some Contraband in these parts getting above their station.'

'Don't get me started on uppity niggers,' Merkel shook his head. 'Anyhow, we've got that covered.'

'You have?'

The boy waited until Grand had refilled his glass, then leaned forward, the queen and ace in his hand yet again temporarily forgotten. 'There's a fella not far north of here,' he whispered, 'name of Peters.'

'What about him?'

'The black bastard owns a coupla acres and a mule.'

Grand frowned. 'How did he manage that?'

'That's Tennessee for you.' Merkel leaned back and closed his eyes; then, regretting it immediately when the room spun round, opened them wide and tried to focus. 'Mason-Dixon line gets a mite hazy this far west. We've got more free Contraband than they got in Africa, I shouldn't wonder. And we're fixing to do something about that.'

'Who's we?' Grand asked.

Merkel's mouth opened; then he checked himself. 'No,' he said. 'It's a basic rule. I can't tell nobody; not even a gentleman like yourself.'

'I understand,' Grand nodded solemnly, topping up the boy's bourbon. 'The colonel always said the same thing back in the day.'

'The colonel?'

'Mosby.' Grand dropped the name as casually as many men dropped their aitches.

Merkel's jaw dropped too. 'You . . . you know Mosby?' There was sheer, unadulterated awe in his voice. 'The gray ghost?'

'I had the honour to ride with him,' Grand lied. To be fair, it was not *that* far from the truth. He had ridden *after* the Rebel renegade on many an occasion. And had never caught him once.

'What about . . .?' Merkel began, but Grand's hand was in the air.

'Like I said, son,' he said, 'I can't tell you a goddamned thing.'

'Yeah, sure, sure.' It was Merkel's turn to reach for the bottle, topping up Grand's glass. It wasn't easy and he slopped most of it onto the table. 'No, I understand. Sure.'

For a moment, there was a silence as each man drank and looked at the other. In a contest like that, the green boy from Pulaski was no match for a man who had ridden with Mosby.

'Say what,' Merkel had a proposition in mind. 'You tell me all about your time with Mosby. And I'll tell you about Nathan Forrest.'

Grand screwed up his face. 'I don't know,' he said. 'All respect to General Forrest, but that's a bit like swapping a knave for an ace.'

'All right.' Merkel took Grand's point. 'How about I *introduce* you to General Forrest?'

Grand looked at the boy, his eyes sparkling with the heady mix of bourbon and enthusiasm. 'I don't know . . .' he said.

'Look, we've got some business tonight, me and the boys, with that son of a bitch Peters I told you about.'

'You have?'

'Sure. Put a rattler up his ass, pay a call, you know. But tomorrow night . . . Well, that'll be a night to remember.'

'It will?'

'I'll have to talk to the Grand Cyclops.'

'Who?'

'Better you don't know for now,' Merkel assured him, 'but as soon as he knows you rode with Mosby, it'll be fine. You can come to the Den and meet the Grand Wizard himself.'

'The Grand Wizard?' To Grand, this sounded ever more ludicrous.

'General Forrest.'

'I see.' Grand sipped his bourbon and laid down his pathetic hand of cards. 'All right,' he said. 'I'll see if I can make it. Now,' he leaned back, 'I first set eyes on Colonel Mosby on . . .'

At first they were white shapes in the darkness, moving slowly and without noise. Ghosts, men said, of dead Rebels whose souls could not rest because the South was still bleeding. Grand lay flat on a tree-lined ridge, hoping the sound of his horse cropping the lush grass wouldn't attract too much attention.

Batchelor had suggested, in that rather oblique way of his, that he should come along too, but Grand had firmly turned him down. On the hard-pounded streets of London, James Batchelor was a good man to have at your side; but out here, in what to him was a wilderness, he would be out of his depth. The man wasn't even much of a rider and it felt good for Grand, the ex-cavalryman, to be back in a McClellan saddle again. Trotting round St James's Park really hadn't filled the void in his soul; this was the real thing.

So here he was, with rations for three days and a Sharps rifle bought from Deery's, watching a surreal scene unfold. The white shapes had sharpened now and he counted eight men in tall, hideous hoods, their masks like the scarecrows he remembered as a child in the fields beyond Washington City. One of them carried what appeared to be lengths of timber. So did another. They made no sound; said nothing. Grand looked closer. Even their horses' hooves were wrapped in sacking so that they padded over the grass flitches, fanning out to right and left as silent as a dream.

The men with the timbers dismounted and silently went to work. Beyond them, Grand could see the black silhouette of a lonely farmhouse. Two more dismounted and sneaked beyond the barn. Alert as he was, Grand heard every tiny sound. He heard what he fancied was the rattle of a chain and the sudden yelp of a dog, shrill and sharp. Then silence. The two men came back, carrying something between them.

Before his eyes, Grand saw the timbers hauled skywards, lashed together in the shape of a cross. As the horses shifted under the weight of their riders, the two men still on the ground tossed a rope over an arm of the cross and tugged on it. At the noose end, a dead dog, still bleeding from its cut throat, twisted in the night air. At a signal from the leading horseman, a firebrand flashed from nowhere, the flame glinting on the dog's chain and the blood on his matted fur. They applied the brand to the timbers and the whole thing burst into light, the smell of pitch rising with the sparks and the flames.

There was a crash from the farmhouse and the roar of a shotgun. The horsemen recoiled, steadying their mounts.

'You people go to Hell, now, y'hear?' the man with the shotgun shouted, but he had fired both barrels and would have to reload.

'Behold,' the leading horseman called back, his voice deep and muffled by the hood, 'the light of Christ!' and he pointed with his horsewhip to the crackling flames. Grand was in a dilemma. The man with the shotgun on his porch was out of ammunition, at least for now, and no one else was coming out to help. The horsemen, on the other hand, had eight guns at least. And those odds seemed less than reasonable. The last thing Grand wanted to do, however, was to tip his hand. He could bring down one, perhaps more with the Sharps, but that wasn't going to get him anywhere near General Nathan Forrest. On the other hand, he couldn't stand by and watch a man killed by these lunatics in fancy dress.

A moment, later, his problem was solved. Silently, the riders turned their horses' heads as the farmer screamed at them and the cross blazed. A moment after that, the Klan and their horses were billowing white shapes again and Grand eased his thumb off the rifle's hammer. The Invisible Empire had vanished completely.

They came in ones and twos on their cloth-foot horses, the Klansmen of Pulaski, walking the animals up the twisted paths that led to the ruined house. This had been a fine home once, with children running and laughing on the lawns. Ladies in lace and crinolines had danced with their beaux on the warmth of a summer evening, and all had seemed right with the world.

It was different now. The war and the weather had torn it down and ivy crawled its crumbling walls. There was no rocking chair on the porch now, and the storm-torn oaks stood like ghostly sentinels, watching the horsemen who rode in from the south. Two of these rode away from the others and only one wore the pointed hood of this Klavern. The other was Matthew Grand.

A solitary horseman, a cross stitched in silver on his hood, sat in his saddle by the roadside. Lester Merkel saluted him and the horseman waited. He was studying Grand closely, taking in the man's bearing, his horse, his clothes, trying to gauge his worth. Then he slipped a silver whistle from his robes and blew three shrill blasts. While Grand and Merkel waited, three answering whistles echoed back from the direction of the old house.

Merkel had told Grand the gist of what would happen and he let his reins fall, holding out his arms in the form of a cross. Merkel dismounted and led his own horse and Grand's up the hill. The house looked dark and foreboding ahead, and Grand knew that the men inside were those who had burned the cross in Peters' front yard the night before. They had not drawn their guns then, content to let the black man run with sweat. But what would they do tonight with an ex-Billy Yank cavalryman in their midst?

Two Klansmen emerged from the old house. Grand swung out
of the saddle, his arms still out to his side, and let them tie his
wrists behind his back before blindfolding him. In total darkness,
he felt himself prodded across a yard and he stumbled across the
hard-baked, foot-rutted mud, turned to iron by the long Tennessee
summer. He felt the air change. It was cool here and he knew
he was inside. He half fell down the steps suddenly at his feet,
and he counted them as he went down. Six, seven, eight, and he
was on the level again. He heard a bang ahead, then a door swung
open ahead of him, squealing on hinges eaten with rust. Then a
second. And a third. He felt the two Klansmen at his back but
could still see nothing but blackness.

Suddenly, he went down to a thump in the small of his back.
His knees cracked on uneven flagstones; when he tried to get
up, he felt a slap around the head and something hard and wooden
hit him across the shoulders. He was hauled upright and thrown
against a wall by silent assailants. His head was singing and he
tasted blood trickling into his mouth. One of his teeth felt loose
and his left arm was aching.

Just as suddenly as it had begun, the rough-housing stopped
and he was steadied, held upright by strong hands.

'Acolyte,' he heard a stern voice shout and stood to attention.
'I am the Grand Cyclops of the Pulaski Klavern of the Ku Klux
Klan. Who are you?'

'Matthew Granger,' Grand said.

'Where you from, Granger?' the Cyclops asked.

'Van Buren, Crawford County, Arkansas.' Grand hoped he
could keep the lazy accent up and also that Van Buren was small
enough to be just another president as far as these lunatics were
concerned.

'Did you serve in the late war?'

'I did.'

'What outfit?'

'Mosby's Rangers.'

'You were with him at Manassas?' the Cyclops wanted to know.

'Never been to Manassas in my life,' Grand said, 'and neither,
as far as I know, has Colonel Mosby.'

There was a silence, then a roar of laughter, and not just from
the Grand Cyclops.

'Place him before the royal altar, boys,' he said, 'and adorn his head with the regal crown.'

Grand felt himself being led into another room. All sounds here echoed and he knew he was in a vaulted chamber, the cellar – or perhaps the still room – of the old house. He felt something being placed on his head, then his hands were untied and the blindfold came off. He was looking into an oval mirror set on a table hung with black cloth and lit by candles. His crown was a battered old wideawake with ass's ears pinned to it. There were whoops and whistles and stamping from the Klansmen standing around.

'Grand Cyclops.' One of them stepped forward, taking off his hood and extending a hand. 'You can call me Larry.'

'You can call me a mule's ass,' Grand said, wiggling his loose tooth with his tongue.

'Ezra Hammond,' another Klansman swept off his hood. 'Grand Turk.'

'Charmed,' Grand nodded.

'Sorry about the Manassas question,' the Cyclops said. 'Can't be too careful. Young Lester here's not been with us long. Gets a bit carried away. So you rode with Mosby—'

'Cyclops,' the Grand Turk interrupted, 'the Grand Wizard is waiting.'

'Of course.' The Cyclops put his hood back on. 'Where are my manners? Granger, we'll administer the oath later. The Grand Wizard takes precedence over such procedures.'

The Cyclops and the Turk led Grand, still with his donkey's ears, out of the chamber and up some steps to a side room. At a table lit by a single candle, sat a man in the most hideous costume Grand had ever seen. It had horns protruding from each side of the hood and an evil skull grinned in gilt embroidery from the forehead. The man swept the cloth off and Grand recognized the face from Schleier's photograph at once. The steady grey eyes, the square-cut goatee and the long, curled hair.

'General Forrest,' Grand saluted, regretting the move immediately as every muscle he possessed ached from the rough handling he had received.

'Grand Wizard,' the Cyclops reminded him.

'Thank you, gentlemen,' Forrest said, folding the hood neatly on the table. 'Granger, won't you take a seat?'

Grand would and did. The stewards disappeared. Forrest looked up at the floppy ears and gestured. The acolyte was relieved to take them off.

'Sorry about the theatricals,' Forrest said, and passed Grand a handkerchief to mop his bloody temple. 'And about the horse-play. The boys get a little rough sometimes.'

'That they do,' Grand agreed.

'You wanted to meet me.' Forrest unbuttoned his white robe to reveal the frock coat of a Confederate general underneath, glittering with gold lace.

'I've heard so much about you,' Grand said.

'Oh, where was that? The Army of the Potomac?'

Grand felt his heart pounding in his chest and the blood rushing in his ears. They didn't call this man the Wizard of the Saddle for nothing.

'No, I—'

'I don't know whether your name is Granger, whether you're actually from Arkansas or whether you actually want to join the Klan . . .' He paused, then leaned forward, 'but you sure as Hell never rode with Mosby.'

'Didn't I?' Grand dropped the accent and the clipped vowels of Washington came into play. 'How do you know that?'

'The salute,' Forrest smiled. 'Oh, Yank, Reb, blue, gray. Don't make no never mind. But Mosby's boys were a law unto themselves. They didn't salute at all. Not even generals. So . . .' he leaned back again. 'Who are you really and what do you really want? I don't flatter myself you just wanted to see face to face the bastard who ran rings around you Northern trash for so long.'

'My name is Matthew Grand. I was with the Third Cavalry of the Potomac.'

Forrest nodded. 'Good outfit, Grand,' he said. 'I'm impressed.'

'That was then,' Grand said. 'Now I'm an enquiry agent. Looking into the murder of Lafayette Baker.'

Forrest's eyes narrowed. 'I heard the old bastard was dead,' he said. 'Didn't realize it was murder.'

'My enquiries took me to Knoxville,' Grand said, 'and,

surprise, surprise, I saw a photograph of him there, sitting in a studio with you, General.'

'That's right!' Forrest clicked his fingers. 'Goddamn! I've gotta get that picture back.'

'You have?'

Forrest fished out cigars, one for himself and one for Grand. 'Let's just say it wasn't my finest hour. Baker was calling himself Samuel Munson back then, running guns for the South. Quite a few crates of Beecher's Bibles, if I remember right. Wasn't for a few weeks we found out they was about as serviceable as chicken-shit. By that time, of course, "Munson" had long gone. With a lot of Confederate gold in his pocket.'

'What about his second in command?'

'Who?' Forrest asked, drawing on the cigar.

'Caleb Tice.'

'Caleb Tice? You've been misinformed, Grand. Caleb Tice was a member of the American Knights.'

'The . . .?'

Forrest thrust two fingers between his lips and whistled loudly. The door crashed back and the Grand Cyclops stood there, hood gone, pistol gleaming in his hand.

'No call for that, Larry,' Forrest said. 'Granger here has some pressing business. He'll have to go through the ceremony some other time.'

'Er . . . is that acceptable, Grand Wizard?'

Forrest looked levelly at the man. 'It is if I say it is,' he said. 'That boy who brought Granger here, a Ghoul . . .'

'Lester Merkel, Grand Wizard.'

'The barrel, I think.'

'The barrel?' The Grand Cyclops blinked. 'But that's reserved for—'

'Reprobates who don't deserve to be in the Klan; yes, I know. I helped write the rules, remember? What's the first rule of the Klan, Grand Cyclops?'

Larry stood an inch taller. 'Absolute secrecy,' he said.

Forrest nodded. 'Seems that Ghoul Merkel hasn't quite grasped that,' he said, 'seeing as he brought Granger here.'

'But . . .'

'The barrel, Larry,' Forrest insisted quietly.

The Grand Cyclops hesitated, then slid the gun away and closed the door.

'The boy Lester . . .' Grand began.

Forrest shook his head. 'Don't worry, Grand. It's no more than you got. We'll just roll him down the hill a little. And kick him out of the Klavern, of course. His pride'll be hurt more than anything.'

'You were telling me about Caleb Tice,' Grand reminded him.

'I was,' Forrest agreed, 'but I shouldn't have been. Like I reminded Larry and like I'll remind Lester Merkel, the first rule of the Klan is absolute secrecy.'

'But—'

'There aren't no "buts", Grand. Now, you ride away now, y'hear. Because if I see you again, I'll shoot you like the lying dog you undoubtedly are. Do I make myself clear?'

'When you met Lafayette Baker,' Batchelor said, helping himself to more of Belle's lemonade, 'at the Old Capitol Prison; was that the first time you'd met him?'

Belle laughed. 'As a matter of fact, it wasn't. But you know that from his autobiography. I'll give you this, James Batchelor, you're a single-minded man.'

'Humour me,' he smiled.

For a moment, on the gentle hills above the French Broad, their eyes met. Then, she lowered her lashes and looked down at her hands, twisting a sprig of wild thyme in her lap. 'If you remember his narrative,' she said, 'I met him at Manassas in the early months of the war. I was posing as a tract-seller – a colporteur we called them in those days. I lied to his face. I told him I was a Yankee sympathizer, with a sister in New York. I offered to pass any letters he cared to write to his friends for him.'

'And he said?'

She laughed again. 'You know what he said – "I think I shall see my friends before you do." Oh, he was good, was Laff Baker. Saw through me like plate glass.'

'And you next saw him?'

'About a year later.'

'In Washington?'

'That's right.'

'Tell me about that.'

Belle poured herself a lemonade and took off her bonnet, laying it on the ground beside her. 'I told your friend the captain,' she said.

'You did.' Batchelor watched as Belle unpinned her hair and shook it free. The ringlets shone in the high sun and her eyes sparkled. It was difficult to believe that such a lovely girl had led such a chequered life. 'Matthew and I differ in that he isn't a natural communicator. I have been telling tales all my life.'

'Telling tales?' Belle opened her eyes wide and looked at him in mock horror. 'But you were a journalist on the *Telegraph*. Surely, the truth was your watchword, Batchelor?'

'If you say so,' he smiled. 'And perhaps one day you'll tell me how you know about the *Telegraph*. But Matthew has no such upbringing, quite the reverse. He's a Billy Yank to the core. But you know my commission, Belle; *anything* I can learn about the late Brigadier Baker might be of use.'

'The tables were turned,' she said, gazing out over the sluggish waters, low in the banks with the drought. 'I suspect Baker let himself be captured at Manassas to see what he could learn. I had no choice in Washington. I told him nothing, of course, not even in the bastard's Room Nineteen.'

'His torture chamber?'

'You could say that.'

A silence as thick and black as molasses hung in the stifling air. 'Tell me about this book,' Batchelor said, and slid the leather-bound volume from his satchel.

Belle twisted her head to read the title. '*Colburn's United Service Magazine*! Damn, I'd have given my right hand to set eyes on this a few years back.' She flicked open the covers and thumbed through the pages. 'How did you get it?'

'Baker's mistress was left it in his will.'

Belle's eyelids flickered a moment, then she smiled. 'I'm going to enjoy this tale of yours, James, but what do you say to having something to eat first? Eliza has set us up this lovely basket, and neither of us has eaten a morsel. Poor woman, she'll be mortified.'

'I am a bit hungry, now you mention it.' Batchelor was always hungry; he was a tenement child whose mother occasionally lost count of who had had what when it came to feeding her children, so hunger could well have been his middle name. But he was learning to be careful. 'Great-Grandma didn't have a hand in this, did she?' He knew his mouth would always burn in cold weather, for as long as he lived.

Belle laughed. Great-Grandma's sauce could always bring a smile to the table. 'No, just Eliza.' She peered into the basket. 'It's all quite harmless, James, look. Just ham and pickles and biscuits.'

That all sounded very familiar and he took a look. There was a black thing peeking out of a napkin, some jars of beans and some scones, but he knew better than to criticize. 'Looks delicious,' he said, bravely. 'I'll just have a little of each.'

While she sliced slivers off Eliza's famous root-beer baked ham and fished out some pickles from a jar, she got back to the case in hand. 'Was this all Baker left her?' she asked. 'I assume *Mrs* Baker, if there is one, got a tad more?'

'No doubt she did,' Batchelor murmured, 'but isn't this a slightly odd thing to specify in a will? I mean, a whole library, a gold watch, even the man's army sabre, but a single book . . .?'

Belle looked closer. 'What are these?' she asked, 'these pencil marks, circling letters and in the margin?'

'That's where I hoped you could help,' he said. 'Grand and I have racked our brains over it, but if it's a cypher, it's beyond us. Whereas you—'

'I see.' She looked at him coldly. 'So *that*'s what this picnic is all about. You're using me, Batchelor. And that's not kind.' She slammed the book shut.

'No,' he said. 'Please, Belle.' And he reached out to touch her hand. She pulled away and he sighed. 'I'm sorry,' he said. 'In my world you're a suspect; someone who had good reason to want Lafayette Baker dead. Physically, I know that's impossible. You weren't even in the country at the time; but . . . your past . . .'

'Cleopatra of Secession, Siren of the Shenandoah,' she nodded, pursing her lips. 'Yes, I know. Even now there are people north of the Potomac who would cheerfully hang me from a wild oak tree.'

James Batchelor, against all his logic, and ignoring the job he had come to do, reached across again and kissed her full on the lips. The Siren of the Shenandoah's eyes widened in surprise and he felt her lips part slowly. Her hair and skin were warm and soft in the Tennessee sunshine and she went with him as he leaned forward, holding her hands over her head in the tall grass. Then he sat up.

'I'm sorry,' he said again. 'I shouldn't. You are recently widowed and we hardly know each other.'

She lay still, smiling up at him, her lids heavy over sparkling eyes. 'And both those things,' she murmured, 'would have made this impossible a few years ago, at least this side of the Atlantic. But now? Well, now, I don't know . . .'

And he kissed her again.

# ELEVEN

The lamps glowed in the Lamar House late that night and Grand and Batchelor were closeted in their rooms, poring over the treatise that Belle Boyd had worked on.

'It's a code,' Batchelor said, 'as we suspected. It's just that we couldn't crack it.'

'But you've worked it out now?' Grand was impressed. 'How?'

'Oh, you know.' Batchelor grinned sheepishly, tapping the side of his head. 'Application of the old grey matter.'

'Useful, was she? The old grey matter?'

'What?' Batchelor frowned, annoyed that his partner could see straight through him.

'Come on, James,' Grand laughed. 'You spend the day – or was it more? – with an ex-Confederate spy and coincidentally you become an expert code-breaker. I don't buy it.'

'Oh, very well,' Batchelor snapped. 'Belle may have helped.'

'What you do in your spare time is up to you,' Grand said. 'Right now, I'm more interested in this.' He tapped the book.

'All right.' Batchelor climbed down from whatever high horse he had been about to mount. 'I won't trouble you with the sliding substitution, but here, circled letters on page 181, dated 2.5.68.'

'Hmm,' Grand nodded. 'February.'

'February?' Batchelor repeated. 'No . . . oh, yes, of course. You people write your dates backwards for some reason, don't you? Linking these disparate letters together, it says "I am constantly being followed. They are professionals. I cannot fool them."'

Suddenly, Grand was all ears. 'This is dynamite,' he said.

'It gets better – "In New Rome, there walked three men . . ."'

'New Rome,' Grand said. 'Washington.'

Batchelor nodded, translating on. '"Three men, a Judas, a Brutus and a spy."'

The light of remembrance glowed in Grand's eyes, 'Laura Duvall mentioned Judas and Brutus,' he said.

'She did,' Batchelor agreed, and went on, '"Each planned that he should be the king when Abraham should die."'

'Lincoln,' Grand shouted. 'The conspiracy to kill Lincoln.'

'"One trusted not the other",' Batchelor read on, '"but they went on for that day, waiting for that final moment when, with pistol in his hand, one of the sons of Brutus could sneak behind that cursed man and put a bullet in his brain . . ."'

'John Wilkes Booth,' Grand said, the hairs crawling on his neck. 'His father was the actor Junius Brutus Booth.'

'And, if you know your Shakespeare,' Batchelor countered, 'or indeed your classical history, Marcus Junius Brutus was the leader of the conspiracy against Julius Caesar. Baker is talking about the assassination of Lincoln. And it wasn't confined to the men we know about.'

Grand was impressed, but didn't show it. 'What else does it say?'

A sharp knock on the door broke the moment. Grand and Batchelor looked at each other and Batchelor slid the book away under a copy of the Washington *Evening Star*.

'Who is it?' Even in friendly Knoxville, Grand wasn't inclined to take chances. His pocket Colt was in easy reach.

Nothing.

He clicked open the door. There was no one there and he was staring at the flock wallpaper of the Lamar House's landing. On the carpet, however, lay an envelope. Grand snatched it up and closed the door, with a last quick look to left and right. He thumbed open the envelope and unfolded the paper. 'Mother of God,' he muttered as he read the note, 'they've got Belle.'

'Who have?' Batchelor was on his feet, heart pounding, vision blurring with panic. This was no way for an enquiry agent to behave but . . . Belle . . .

'The Klan. The Invisible Empire.'

Batchelor grabbed the letter and read aloud. '"Headquarters of the Invisible Empire, Dismal Era, Last Hour. Sir, because you have violated our sacred order and paid scant regard to the sentiments of the South, we have been obliged to engage the services of Miss Belle Boyd of Front Royal. Rest assured that her life will be forfeit if you do not desist in your enquiries and do not quit Tennessee by . . ."' He looked up, aghast. 'Two days. They've given us two days. This is nonsense, Matthew.'

'It is,' Grand nodded. 'But this is the Klan we're talking about. Are they implying that Belle is working with them?'

'Never!' Batchelor shook his head, certain as only a man in love could be.

'Well,' Grand murmured, 'you know her better than I do, but she *is* a daughter of the Confederacy.'

'Yes, she is, but she decoded Baker's encryptions for me. Why would she do that while working with the other side?'

Grand snorted. 'Maybe you don't know Belle as well as you thought.'

For a moment, Grand expected Batchelor to lash out with his fists, but the Englishman controlled himself. He looked at the note again. 'Headquarters of the Invisible Empire. Is that Pulaski?'

'Two days' ride,' Grand nodded.

'Then we've no time to lose.' Batchelor began circling the room, throwing wardrobe doors wide, then rifling through the drawers.

'Hang on a minute,' Grand counselled. 'The first thing we've got to do is to make sure that Belle has actually gone.'

Batchelor looked at him, confused, heart still pounding. What if their meddling had put the woman in mortal danger?

'You're right,' he said. 'That would be logical. I'll do it.'

'James!' Grand took the man by the shoulders. 'It's gone midnight. If there's an innocent explanation for this, Dr Boyd – and Belle – won't thank you for rousing the house at this hour.'

'So what do you suggest?' Batchelor asked. It didn't seem that he was going to like *any* answer Grand gave him.

'We wait. We get some sleep. Tomorrow, after breakfast, you take yourself over to the Blount Mansion; you're paying your devoirs to Belle.'

'And if she's not there?'

'We quit Tennessee,' Grand shrugged. 'Get back to Washington, pick up the threads there.'

'Go to Hell!' And Batchelor barged past him to wake all Knoxville.

The Blount Mansion looked different in darkness. It must have been nearly one by the time Batchelor reached the front porch. The Boyds' dog was barking long before the Englishman's knuckles hammered on the door. Lamplight exploded in a bedroom and a head popped out below the sash.

'Who the Hell is that?'

'James Batchelor, Dr Boyd. I must see Belle.'

'Do you know what time it is, Mr Batchelor?' the doctor wanted to know.

'Yes and I'm sorry, but it's vital I see her.'

'What's the matter, John?' Aunt Susan's head appeared beside her husband's. 'Why, Mr Batchelor . . .'

'I'm sorry to disturb you, Mrs Boyd, but—'

'I don't know how you do things in London, Mr Batchelor,' Boyd interrupted him, 'but in Knoxville, gentlemen call on ladies during the hours of daylight and then only by arrangement.'

'I realize that . . .' Batchelor toyed for a moment with putting his shoulder to the door but the frame looked stout and he wasn't sure how Dr Boyd would take to having his porch demolished.

'Belle's not here, Mr Batchelor,' Susan said.

'What?' Batchelor was getting a crick in his neck from looking up at them, but his heart was in his boots.

'She's gone to visit her cousin Mary for a day or two. Didn't she tell you?'

'No, she . . .'

A sudden wailing cry came from somewhere in the house, echoed by an eldritch screech from towards the rear. 'Oh, that's little Grace,' Susan said. 'I must go to her. Eliza sleeps like the dead. And now Grandma is awake.' Her head abruptly disappeared and she could be heard calling the house awake. When Grandma had woken, no one would sleep for long.

'Belle hasn't taken Grace with her?' Alarm bells clanged in Batchelor's head.

'No,' Boyd said. 'The poor little mite's got a touch of colic. Better she stays here under my care. Now, really, Mr Batchelor—'

'Where's she gone?' Batchelor persisted. 'Cousin Mary – where does she live?'

'I'm not inclined to tell you, sir,' Boyd said, frowning. 'Not the way you're behaving tonight. Or, should I say, this morning?'

'I'm sorry,' Batchelor persisted. 'I mean no one any harm, Dr Boyd, but I have to see Belle, and quickly. It's a matter of life and death.'

Even in his nightcap and shirt and roused from his sleep, Boyd still had enough bonhomie to chuckle. 'You journalists,' he said, 'even when you have given up the print and ink, you can't help the dramatic phrase, can you? If I tell you, will you go away and stop bothering honest folks?'

'You have my word,' Batchelor promised.

'Pulaski,' Boyd said. 'Cousin Mary lives in Pulaski. It's—'

'Oh, I know where it is,' Batchelor said, and he was gone.

'Pulaski,' Batchelor blurted out. He had hurtled round the corner from the Blount Mansion and bumped straight into Matthew Grand.

'I heard,' his colleague said.

'So, let's go.'

Grand leaned towards him. 'Don't look now, James, but we're being followed.'

'We are?'

'And you have been since you left the Lamar. To my left. Back of the cedar. *Don't* look!'

Batchelor kept his eyes firmly on Grand's.

'Do you know who it is?' he asked.

'Personally, no. But it's my guess it's one of the Klan Ghouls. Now, do you want to get Belle back safely?'

'Of course.' Batchelor was quietly outraged that Grand had felt it necessary to ask that question.

'Right. So, now we do it my way. Are you going to play along?' He waited. No response. 'For Belle's sake?'

'For Belle's sake,' Batchelor repeated.

'Well, they've got her,' Grand said loudly, raising his voice for the first time. 'And we're over a barrel.'

'What do we do now?' Batchelor asked, equally loudly. He would never have made a career on the stage, but it would suffice.

'The only thing we can do,' Grand said, turning back towards the hotel. 'We catch a riverboat tomorrow morning, first thing. Whatever else they are, the Klan are gentlemen of the South. They won't hurt a lady as long as we do what they say.'

'You're right,' Batchelor said lamely. When all he wanted to do was to grab the listening Ghoul by the throat and batter his brains out against the nearest tree.

\*    \*    \*

They checked out the next morning, Grand settling up with the clerk by courtesy of Luther Baker, and they made a great show of leaving. Batchelor couldn't help staring at every man in the foyer, on the stairs, on the sidewalk outside. He even found himself staring at the Negroes until common sense told him that was a rather pointless exercise.

The *City of Knoxville* belched black smoke and Grand was generosity itself in the tips he gave to the porters struggling with the luggage. The anchor chain rumbled clear and the great paddle wheel drove into the waters of the French Broad, sending spray to catch the sunbeams of the morning and turn them to rainbows. From the rail, both men watched the crowd on the levee and they saw one man standing looking at them until he was a speck that turned and left.

'So far,' Grand murmured, 'so good.'

Beyond the telescope range of the Klan, Grand and Batchelor left the riverboat at the next landing stage and doubled back. They had their luggage sent back to Washington, because whatever happened in Pulaski, suitcases would only slow them down and carpetbags had a connotation of their own.

James Batchelor *could* ride. It's just that within the confines of suburban London, there was little call for it. He was not of the social class that rode to hounds; neither did he tip his hat to the elegant ladies who trotted in the Row of a morning. So the sorrel with the hard mouth was a *bit* of a challenge for him that afternoon as he and Grand rode southwest in search of their quarry. It could have been worse, as Grand kept telling him. At least he was riding a hunting saddle, more or less what he would have found at home. The McClellan was a bitch by comparison and, Grand assured him, he didn't want to know about a Western rig. Many was the greenhorn who had kissed his balls goodbye.

It was two days' ride to Pulaski, and Batchelor had to grit his teeth and put up with it. The ride itself, however, was nothing by comparison with the overnight camp. There was no town, no hotel, not even a farmhouse with a barn, and the pair slept under the stars, listening to the crickets and the ripples of the stream that served as their water supply and bubbled over pebbles. By the time Batchelor got up the next morning, he didn't know what ailed him most – the head that had suffered all night with just his saddle for a pillow, or the back which had bounced around all day on a horse. Come to think of it, it was the legs, reduced to jelly by gripping the sorrel's barrel for grim death, and his feet, cramped into the leather flaps of the stirrups. His admiration for Grand, the ex-cavalryman, had turned to envious contempt by midday, especially as the pair hardly rode together; Batchelor was yards behind, desperately playing catch-up when he could.

By mid-afternoon on the second day, the heat was unbearable, the horses skittish and jumpy with the clouds of flies.

'Do you have a plan, Matthew?' Batchelor asked, and not for the first time. 'When we get there, I mean, *if*—' he tried to straighten his legs and stifled a groan as his muscles complained – 'we get there.'

'That depends.' Grand reined in and Batchelor was delighted to do likewise.

'On what?' Batchelor unhooked the canteen and took a swig. It was warm and tasted revolting, but it was wet and that had to be enough.

'On exactly what part Belle is playing in all this.'

Batchelor nodded. Grand was still singing from the same old hymnbook, but Batchelor knew he had to make allowances. The man had fought the South – Belle Boyd's South – for four long years, and had seen his President go down to an assassin's gun. Men weren't always rational after that, and they were hardly ever forgiving. 'We're assuming there's no cousin Mary?' he said.

'I don't know,' Grand shrugged. 'She may be real enough. But let's assume for now that she's not. I only caught a part of what Dr Boyd said to you from his bedroom window. Did he look like a man beside himself with worry? Somebody whose niece had been kidnapped and who has been told to keep his mouth shut?'

Batchelor shook his head. 'I'd say not,' he said. 'He seemed to me to be just like a man whose niece has gone to see her cousin Mary.'

Grand eased himself in the saddle. He was a born rider, but he hadn't done this kind of cross-country work for years and he realized how unfit he had become. He took off his wideawake and brushed the sweat from his eyes. 'Tell you what,' he said. 'This is a long shot, but it may be I know a man who can help us.'

'Who's that?'

'Somebody who I'm guessing is a nice man at the end of his tether. You'll get some good ol' home cooking and a lot of questions,' he nudged his horse forward, 'if you don't get a belly full of buckshot first.'

The only buildings Batchelor had seen like this were the old Contraband shacks in Hell's Bottom. Everything seemed broken down, neglected, from the sloping sod roof to the charred remnants of the barn. A few scrawny hens scratched in the dirt and washing hung limp from a line in the stillness and heat of the early evening.

He saw them before they saw him. He crept around the side of the house, past the old pump, clicking his shotgun hammers as he came. *This* time he was ready for them. *This* time he had spare cartridges in a belt at his waist and a Bowie knife stuffed into his right boot. 'That's far enough!' he called, and the horsemen reined in.

'Mr Peters?' Grand shouted.

The shotgun came up level. 'Who wants to know?'

'My name is Matthew Grand. Third Cavalry of the Potomac.'

'What do you want?'

'To put my arms down.' Grand had them out to his sides, as he had not far from here, days earlier, when he had gone to the Klan bake. 'And not to feel a rifle at my back.'

Batchelor jarred his back with the speed of his turn and he nearly fell off his horse. He had no idea anyone was there but, sure enough, the muzzle of a rifle was poking out from the few uncharred planks of the barn. At the other end of it, scarcely hidden at all now that Batchelor was aware of him, crouched a black boy. He was perhaps twelve, wearing a patched shirt and canvas trousers.

'Throw whatever you're carrying ahead of you,' Peters ordered. 'Now.'

Grand lowered his arms and hauled the Sharps out of the rifle basket on his saddle. He threw it on to the grass. Next – and he did this very slowly – he lifted the Colt from his shoulder-holster by the trigger guard and threw it after the rifle. Finally, he leaned down and flicked the Derringer out of his boot, sending that through the stifling air to join the others.

'Now you,' Peters barked at Batchelor.

'I'm not armed,' Batchelor told him, his hands out to the side too. He was praying fervently the sorrel didn't move or he'd be joining Grand's guns on the ground.

'He's from England,' Grand said, by way of explanation, and the man gave a grunt of understanding. 'I've just come to talk to you, Mr Peters. And, for all our sakes, I thought I'd come in daylight.'

If Batchelor had been bemused by the table at the Boyds' and the picnic with Belle, he was transfixed by the fare that Mrs Peters provided. At least the food on offer before had been vaguely recognizable, but this was . . . clearly food, because of the way the family were tucking in. The vegetables he could manage; he didn't expect cabbage and boiled potatoes when he was away from home. Biscuits he understood now, and although he had reached that stage of homesickness where he would kill for a garibaldi, he had come to expect a kind of scone. But the meat . . . what *was* it? It smelled delicious, he had to admit, but the legs were a little small for even the youngest rabbit. He looked at one of the youngest children, a girl who was sucking the meat off a delicate bone. He raised an eyebrow and she smiled at him, the gap-toothed smile of the seven year old.

'Squ'r'l,' she said, and wiped around the plate with a biscuit.

Batchelor turned wide eyes to Grand. 'Squ'r'l?' he muttered.

Grand leaned over, his fingers greasy with the dripping. 'Squirrel, James,' he said. 'It's delicious. Don't go all squeamish on me now. Where you come from, they pee in the milk or so I understand it, so just eat your squirrel and be quiet.'

'Pee? Squirrel?' Batchelor was aghast. But he was also hungry and took a tiny bite. It really was delicious! Probably it wasn't even squirrel. Squirrel was probably just a Tennessee name for rabbit. Yes, that would be it. He tucked in, grease running down his chin. Grand and the Peters family watched him indulgently. Foreigners! What did they know about the good eating on a squ'r'l?

When the dishes and the children had all been taken to the scullery out back, for a wash down under the pump, Grand passed Peters a cigar, which he turned down politely. 'I guess you've had a few Klan visits,' he said. He had noticed that the man's eyes rarely strayed from the front door, which was left slightly ajar.

'You could say that,' Peters said. The children would all soon be in bed, tucked up safely under the eaves, and he could relax a little then, especially with Virgil, the eldest, who sat on the porch, his rifle cradled across his lap. There had been a lot of questions. Elijah had wanted to know why the Englishman didn't talk properly. Suzannah wanted to know where England was and wondered if she would visit it someday. Little Zachariah, the shy one, asked nothing. Batchelor had let him play with his derby hat and the toddler had spent most of the meal with it resting low over the bridge of his nose. The squirrel grease would defy even the ministrations of Mrs Manciple, and Batchelor was glad she wasn't here to see it. 'They have a pattern, you know. First, they burn a cross near your house. That's their calling card. And they killed the dog, too, just to show they mean business. If that don't scare the Bejesus out of yuh, they call again. Killed my mule that time. Last time, it was the barn. Me and the kids put it out eventually but, as you see, with a summer like this one, we lost most of it.'

'Is there no help for you, Mr Peters?' Batchelor asked. 'The law, for example?'

Their host laughed, but there was no mirth in it. 'I believe Sheriff McGovern calls himself Night Hawk after dark.'

'Another pointy head,' Grand nodded.

'Oh, they're all honourable men, Mr Batchelor,' Peters told them, 'the knights of the Klan. There's Freemasons, Presbyterians, Methodists. Lawyers and doctors.'

'Led by Nathan Forrest,' Grand said.

'So they tell me,' Peters said. 'The irony is, I believe him to be a *really* honourable man.'

'But he calls the tune,' Batchelor said, astonished at the man's magnanimity.

'He's got a wolf by the ears,' Peters told him. 'I'm just a farmer, Mr Batchelor – what do I know? I just get the impression the Wizard of the Saddle's bit off more than he can chew this time. Remember, he's not local. In his absence, God alone knows what the Klaverns get up to.'

'So who do you believe is in charge of these attacks on you?' Grand asked.

Peters leaned back from the table. 'I'd put my money – if only I had any – on the Grand Cyclops; Larry Hogan.'

Grand nodded. 'I've met him. Butter wouldn't melt.'

Peters snorted. 'You wouldn't say that if you'd seen what he done to his slaves.'

'I didn't think Tennessee was plantation country, Mr Peters,' Batchelor said.

'With respect, Mr Batchelor, you've been reading too much Mrs Beecher Stowe. To her – and you'll excuse the pun – the whole issue is black and white. Believe me, it ain't. Hogan's never seen a plantation in his life, any more than Mrs Beecher Stowe had ever seen a slave; but that don't stop him owning slaves and beating them half to death.'

'The Emancipation Proclamation stopped that,' Batchelor reminded him with all the innocence of the ingénue he was.

'Did it, Mr Batchelor? You'd like to think so. Oh, don't misunderstand me. I'll bless Abraham Lincoln until the day I die – although that day may not be too long away now. The problem with the South is that they ain't good losers. Many of 'em figure they lost some battles, but they ain't going to lose the war.'

'Hence the Klan.' Grand blew cigar smoke to the ceiling.

'I'm a free negro, Mr Batchelor,' Peters said. 'But I was born a slave. How I progressed to be a man with a barn, a mule, some chickens and a few acres is one of the miracles of modern America. And it makes the Klan mad as Hell.'

'We're interested in one type of Klan activity,' Grand said. 'Kidnapping.'

Peters frowned. 'That's a new one on me,' he said. 'Black folks ain't worth kidnapping. No ransom value.'

'What about white folks?' Batchelor asked. The phrase sounded strange in an English accent.

'We believe the Pulaski Klavern has kidnapped a white woman,' Grand explained.

'A *white* woman?' Peters frowned. 'Now, why in Hell would they do that?'

'Assuming they did,' Grand persisted, 'where would they keep her?'

'I don't exactly know their addresses,' Peters said. 'I know McGovern's office. And I know where Hogan lives. Other than that, the only other place I know – the Den, they call it – is the old Davies place on the hill north of town.'

Grand knew that too. Knew it blindfold.

'You gonna get her back?' Peters asked. 'This white woman?'

'You can count on it,' Batchelor said.

'Mr Peters,' Grand stood up. 'You and your family have been very kind, but we must be going.'

'It's late,' the farmer said, the oil lamps flickering on the table. 'You're welcome to stretch out here. I can't even offer you the barn.'

Poor and run-down though the Peters' house was, it looked like paradise to James Batchelor. There were even cushions, one hundred times softer than a saddle, even if the covers were sacking. 'We accept, Mr Peters,' he said quickly, before Grand could disagree.

But Grand had grown a little soft and could do with a roof over his head too. 'We certainly do,' he said, 'thank you. I'll sit out on the porch awhile, spell young Virgil out there.' And he waved them goodnight, taking the Sharps with him.

# TWELVE

Sheriff John McGovern was still having his breakfast when Grand and Batchelor walked into his office the next morning. A building more different from a London police station it would be difficult to imagine as far as Batchelor was concerned. The sheriff's desk was cluttered with papers, curled at the edges and stained with the rings of coffee cups, used without benefit of saucers. At the back, a solitary down-and-out was snoring on a bunk behind iron bars. Both men noted the Confederate flag standing alongside the Stars and Stripes.

'Can I help you fellas?' McGovern asked. He was a large man with huge hairy hands and deep-set eyes. His mouth was full of cold chicken.

'We're looking for Mrs Isabella Hardinge,' Batchelor said.

McGovern raised his eyebrows and spread his arms, knocking a pile of hush puppies to the floor.

'You may know her as Miss Belle Boyd.'

There was less bewilderment on the law officer's face now, but he was still ignorance itself, in all senses of the word. 'I don't believe I—'

'Perhaps I should explain.' Batchelor produced his Westminster Library card, which he flashed briefly under the sheriff's nose. 'My name is James Batchelor, British Embassy, Washington. Miss Boyd was recently a resident in London and took out British citizenship. That makes her my responsibility.'

'So?' Officialdom had rarely impinged much on Jack McGovern.

'So,' Batchelor was patience himself; he could have been born for a career in the Diplomatic. 'We have reason to believe that Miss Boyd has been kidnapped by an organization calling themselves the Ku Klux Klan and that she is being held against her will, here in your town.'

McGovern looked at Grand, seeming to see him for the first time. 'And who are you?' he asked.

'I'm with him,' Grand smiled, opening his coat to show the gleaming butt of his revolver.

McGovern teased a bit of chicken from a gap in his teeth and pushed the plate aside, wiping his fingers down the sides of his trousers. 'Belle Boyd, you say?'

'The ex-Confederate spy, yes,' Batchelor agreed. 'No doubt you've heard of her.'

'Well, you know how it is,' McGovern bluffed. 'War was a long time ago, now. Who'd you say's got her?'

Batchelor looked hard at the man with the badge. 'The Ku Klux Klan. No doubt you've heard of them too.'

'Oh, sure,' McGovern said. 'Troublemakers to a man. But this ain't their style.'

'Not?' Batchelor continued to play the out-of-his-depth foreign bureaucrat.

'No, they defend the South,' the sheriff said, leaning back and clasping his fat hands over his large girth. 'Keep out the Carpetbaggers and the scalawags.'

'And the blacks?' Grand asked. 'What's the Klan's take on the Contraband?'

'Well, if there's an uppity nigger . . .' McGovern desperately tried to read the expressionless faces of his visitors. He had no luck. 'Look, I've nothing against the black folks myself. But give them the vote? Hell, that's not natural. It's against God's law, that's what it is.'

'And Miss Boyd?' Batchelor brought the conversation back on track. 'Can you help us?'

'Well, I'd sure as Hell like to,' McGovern said, 'but, as you see, I'm pretty shorthanded. Look, I'll make some enquiries. Don't have too many strangers in town. Where you staying? The Phoenix?'

Grand and Batchelor had passed that as they had ridden in. It appeared to be the only hotel in town.

'We are,' Batchelor said, tipping his hat. 'Thank you, Sheriff. We look forward to hearing from you.'

They saw themselves out and crossed the street to where a boy held their horses. They watched the sheriff's office from that vantage point and then Batchelor flicked out his half-hunter. 'I make that thirteen seconds,' he smiled, as Sheriff McGovern burst out of his front door and trotted off down the street in the direction of what was clearly the town hall.

'Isn't it gratifying,' Grand chuckled, 'that even in Hicksville, our law officers are so wonderful. I bet he finds Miss Boyd before his coffee's brewed for elevenses.'

Grand and Batchelor made themselves obvious during the day. They drank at the Forty-Niner, had lunch at Miss Tushingham's. They sent a meaningless telegram from the telegraph office and inspected the horse sale at Crossman's livery establishment. Grand even expressed an interest in a new gig; the finest in the state, or so Mr Crossman assured him. Everywhere they went, they made small talk about the parlous state of the South. Batchelor even offered to help an old black lady across the street until Grand pointed out that it would have repercussions on the old girl later and it was not a good idea – not everyone was a Sojourner Truth.

As the long summer day drew to a close and the purple clouds of night began to build over the town, a strange hush fell on Pulaski. It prickled the skin like an impending thunderstorm. Horses' ears and tails flicked in the town's stables, and honest folk scuttled to their beds. They knew what was coming and wanted no part of it; what the eye didn't see, the heart didn't need to grieve over. Also, the heart was less likely to attract lead that way.

It was a little before midnight that a note was slipped under Grand and Batchelor's door at the Phoenix. There was no knock, no greeting, and the hallway was as empty as it had been back at the Lamar in Knoxville. Grand read the note aloud. '"What are you doing here? Come to the old house north of town at one o'clock. I have an important message for you. Belle."'

Batchelor looked over Grand's shoulder. 'Is that her handwriting?'

'Don't know,' Grand said. 'Never seen it. It's not the same as the last Klan message.'

'It's a trick, of course.'

'Of course,' Grand agreed.

'You know where this old house is?'

'The Den,' Grand nodded. 'Yes, I do. It's the Klavern headquarters.'

'So we're walking into a trap.'
'That's about the size of it.'
Silence hung heavy in the stifling room. There was no breeze
to waft the drapes and the street lay still and deserted.
'So, what time should we leave?'

All the way to the old house, Grand had tried to persuade
Batchelor to carry a gun. And all the way there, Batchelor had
refused. The place was just as Grand remembered it from the
previous week, black ruins with broken chimneys pointing to
the sky. But there was no Lester Merkel riding with him now,
no cloth-clad Night Hawk waiting with his whistle by the roadside. This time, the night visitors were on foot and Grand wasn't
going to throw down his weapons for anyone. His rifle nestled
under his arm and the duster coat; it was loaded and ready.
'Looks deserted,' Batchelor whispered.
'Oh, there are ghosts here aplenty, James. But it's the flesh
and blood ones we have to be careful of.' Grand led the way to
the front door. It was here he had been blindfolded, but he felt the
uneven floor under his boots and the house was as dark as if his
head had still been wrapped in cloth. Both of them picked up
the smell, an indefinable waft of the grave. Cobwebs shimmered
in the darkness and Batchelor spat them out, wiping his arm
across his face.
'Here,' Grand murmured, his voice echoing strangely in the
hallway. 'Steps to the cellar. Eight of them. There are several
rooms down there. Watch your step, James.'
They had agreed not to bring any matches and certainly no
lamps. Darkness could be their friend as well as their enemy and
they took comfort in it now. Grand's boot nudged the first door
and he let it swing open ahead of him. Batchelor collided with
old, empty wine racks to his right, but steadied himself and went
on. There was a grille high to his left that let in some light from
the starlit sky and this room took on a grey, ghostly appearance.
Rotting furniture lay scattered along one wall and Grand recognized this as the room with the altar where he was to have been
initiated into the Invisible Empire.
'Knew you couldn't keep away,' a voice sneered, and the room
flashed with the sudden light of lanterns as their shutters flew

up. Grand barely had time to breathe, still less bring the Sharps into play. A dozen Ghouls filled the room, padding in on silent feet, their robes a putrid white in the shafts of light, their eyes glittering behind the hideous masks.

'Where is Miss Boyd?' Batchelor asked.

'Shut your mouth, Limey!' a Ghoul ordered – Sheriff McGovern by his voice.

'What say we drop the fancy dress?' Grand suggested.

A pistol hammer clicked. 'You'll see our faces soon enough,' another Ghoul said. 'In fact, they'll be the last things you see before we string you up.'

Another lantern swung into the room and the Grand Cyclops stood there, robed and hooded like the rest. 'I suggest, Mr Grand, that you let the rifle drop. To the ground, please. And no nonsense.'

'Certainly, Larry,' Grand smiled, 'when your boys drop theirs.' He was dazzled by the lights and his chances of getting off a clear shot in that confined space were limited. Besides, Batchelor was defenceless and, in the ricochet of bullets, God alone knew what the outcome would be. He took the only alternative and let the Sharps slide to the ground. As he could have predicted, a Ghoul bent to pick it up and Grand saw his chance. He grabbed the man by the hood and spun him round, holding him across the throat with one arm and pointing the pocket Colt at his temple.

More hammers clicked and the lanterns swung as the Klavern moved forward.

'That's enough!' A female voice rang out, making the echoes shiver.

'Belle!' Batchelor took a step forward, then thought better of it. 'Are you all right?'

'Never better, James,' she said, her skirts sweeping the dust of the cellar floor. 'Captain Grand.'

'Mrs Hardinge,' Grand smiled. If Batchelor was surprised to see Belle, untied and clearly in charge of the situation, he wasn't. The Siren of the Shenandoah hadn't lost her touch.

'What do you want us to do with them, Belle?' the Grand Cyclops asked, muffled through the mask. 'Hang 'em from the old oak?'

'Let them go.'

There was a stunned silence, then the hubbub started.

'Captain Grand.' Belle's was the first coherent voice. 'You'll oblige me by letting young Jem go. He doesn't mean any harm. He's a few cents short on the dollar, if you get my meaning.'

Grand did. Even lunatics could fire guns – he had seen that for himself at Ford's Theatre not that long ago. Even so, he eased his thumb off the hammer and pushed the boy forward to land painfully on his head. Might knock some sense into him. He scrambled up to join the others. Belle walked into the circle of light the lanterns made. She looked at Batchelor. 'Why didn't you leave?' she asked. 'We gave you a way out. We told you to leave Tennessee and you didn't.'

'We thought you were in danger, Belle,' Batchelor said. 'How could we leave you like that?'

'Whereas, in fact, you were never in danger at all, were you?' Grand asked. 'All the time you were playing the dutiful niece and the charming Southern belle, you were playing fast and loose with these excuses for men.'

She spun on her heel and slapped him hard across the face. 'I *am* a dutiful niece,' she said. 'And, before you ask, Uncle John knows nothing about this. As for playing fast and loose, the Grand Cyclops here will tell you women aren't allowed in the Klan. I use the tools at my disposal. I always have, Mr Grand.' She stood in front of him, looking up into his eyes. 'You used to be an officer in the Army of the United States. Will you, as an officer, give me your word that you and Mr Batchelor will now leave Tennessee, like we asked you?'

Grand looked at her, his cheek still stinging from her slap. Then he looked at Batchelor. 'You have it,' he said.

'Just a Goddamned minute,' the Grand Cyclops said, breaking forward from the ranks of his men. 'That can't happen. Not now. They know too much, Belle. Our names. This place. The Grand Wizard—'

'Nathan Forrest's got nothing to do with this, Larry. Kidnapping women's not his style. I'm sorry I let you talk me into it.'

'We're wasting time.' Sheriff McGovern had ripped off his hood and was brandishing a noose, the hemp rough and more than ready. Grand was about to reach for his pistol again, but Belle beat him to it. She thrust her hand inside his coat and the Colt emptied in a flash of powder and flame. McGovern staggered backwards, dark crimson spreading over the white of his robes.

Nobody moved. Nobody breathed, least of all the ex-Sheriff of Pulaski.

'Now, get out!' Belle ordered and threw Grand his pistol.

'Belle . . .' Batchelor moved towards her, but Grand held his sleeve and bundled him away through the darkness.

Neither of them spoke until they had reached the gateway to the old house where the ivy had long ago covered the brickwork as surely as the Klan's white hoods covered murder and madness.

'James.' He heard her whispered voice in the darkness.

'Belle. You must come with us.' He held her arms firmly. 'It isn't safe for you here now.'

'It never has been,' she said. 'Mr Grand, I'm sorry for the slap. Could you give us a moment?' He half bowed and wandered away. 'I'm as safe here as I am anywhere,' Belle said, reading concern in Batchelor's face, even in the dark. 'Anyway, I shan't be staying for long. There'll be some questions to answer, but I can handle the Klan. They're the boys I grew up with. I don't hold with their bloodier activities, but I understand where it comes from. We are a broken people, James, in a way you can't understand. They all think what they're doing is right.'

'But it isn't,' he insisted.

She smiled at him, running her hand along his cheek. 'That's something we'll all have to live with,' she said, 'but you don't. You've got to find Lafayette Baker's murderer and – Mr Munson apart – you won't find him here.'

'Why didn't you tell Grand?' Batchelor asked.

'Tell him what?'

'That Baker, posing as Munson, was in Knoxville during the war. You must have known that. But you didn't say a word.'

'No,' she cast her eyes down. 'No, I didn't. As far as Grand knew – as far as you knew – Lafayette Baker was the Yankee bastard who interrogated me in the Old Capitol prison.'

'But . . .' Batchelor was confused. 'He was more?'

'Much more,' she said softly. 'I met Lafayette Baker when he was selling us down the river as Mr Munson. He was a spy, pure and simple. And I . . . I fell in love with him. That love was rekindled in the Old Capitol. Grace isn't Grace Hardinge, except by name; she is Grace Baker. But, like me, she's still a daughter of the Confederacy.'

Belle Boyd took a deep breath, strangely elated now that she had told the truth. 'Look after yourself, James Batchelor,' she said. 'Leave Tennessee and go catch the son of a bitch who killed my Laff.'

# THIRTEEN

The rains came to Washington that Tuesday and the summer, suddenly, was over. Lightning forked through the darkness, flashing on the dome of the Capitol and outlining the stump of the Washington Memorial. The rain fell vertically, in huge drops that battered the lime leaves along Pennsylvania Avenue and bounced on the sidewalk, bringing down twigs and birds' nests to litter the ground. Swampoodle became a swamp again and the ladies of the night who haunted Marble Alley and the Division sidled indoors if they could or took shelter under awnings, hiding their wares from the weather.

'Empire of King Mud, indeed.' James Batchelor peeled off his boots, caked with a slimy brown. London in the rain was dismal, stinking and grey, but at least the roads were metalled for the most part, and if you couldn't go dry-shod, at least your boots would survive. Looking at his footwear now, thick with clay and misshapen with the wet, he wondered and poked at them disconsolately with his ever-present pencil.

'The Willard has people to do that,' Matthew Grand reminded him. He sometimes forgot that Batchelor had not been born to hotels and boot boys. 'Just leave them outside the door.'

Both men were tired. The trip back from Knoxville, by river-boat and train, had been long and arduous, with rain threatening in the lowering sky, and the time of the year that Grand persisted in calling the Fall creeping over Maryland. The Willard had retained their rooms, as per Grand's request, but neither man felt up to the cold ham and chicken on offer in the kitchens, still less the brandy and bourbon in the East Thirteenth Street Corridor. Batchelor opened the door to place his boots out for the boy and saw an envelope lying there, addressed to them both.

'What is it about this country?' he asked Grand, opening it up. 'Is it a colonial thing, leaving notes outside people's doors?'

'We're a new nation,' Grand said. 'Hell, for a while there we were two nations. One day we'll get round to a postal service that works – we've only had ninety-odd years practice; we'll get it right eventually.' For the briefest of moments, he saw an image of a Wells Fargo Pony Express rider, galloping hell for leather across the open prairielands of Surrey. He shook himself free of it; the journey from Knoxville had been longer than he thought. He looked down at the balled-up stocking in his hand and threw it at Batchelor. 'And that's quite enough of the colonial remarks, if you don't mind, James.'

'It's from Tom Durham,' Batchelor said, ducking automatically so the missile flew past his shoulder to land behind the clothes press. 'The *Star*'s star. It's a list.'

'Of what?'

'People who crossed Lafayette Baker.' Batchelor looked down the column of names. 'Here in Washington. Good of Durham to help us.'

'He said he would,' Grand reminded him, craning across to look at the names, albeit upside down. 'Anybody we know?'

'Well, Edwin Stanton's here, of course. In fact, he's number one.'

'Thought he would be,' Grand nodded, pouring himself an Early Times and another for Batchelor.

'Ah, Wesley Jericho.'

'Yes,' Grand sipped his amber nectar. 'If I remember rightly, Durham was pretty keen to mention him last time we met.'

'But we can rule him out, surely,' Batchelor said. 'He bought our bluff about Baker being shot.'

Grand nodded. 'Unless it's the old double bluff,' he said. 'Jericho feigning ignorance of the actual murder method.'

'Yes,' Batchelor said, 'but I've been thinking. Jericho's a gambling man. Would he give a rat's arse about that? I can still feel the man's blade at my throat. Seems to me he's the kind of man who would say, "Yes, I did it. I killed Laff Baker. What are you going to do about it?"'

'Who else is there?'

Batchelor ran his eyes down the list. 'There are fourteen names here . . . Well, well – Caleb Tice.'

'Really?' Grand sat up. 'It's been crossed out. Durham's put a line through the name – presumably because he's dead. He may have been a threat to Baker once, but not recently enough to be his killer.'

'Except he's not dead, is he? I've met him.'

'So you say,' Grand murmured.

Batchelor chose to let the remark go. It *had* been a long journey.

'All right.' Grand could read a withering look as well as the next man; better, when the withering look came from James Batchelor. 'Let's assume he is alive. What now?'

'We need to find him,' Batchelor said. 'The point is – how?'

'Julep was the go-between last time.'

Batchelor looked less than enchanted. 'It's your turn there,' he said.

'Me?' Grand chuckled. '*You're* the cute one, according to her. Not so long ago you couldn't wait to go spooning with the girl.'

'That was before . . .' but Batchelor didn't finish his sentence.

'Before Belle Boyd,' Grand murmured. 'Take some advice, James, my boy. Let Belle Boyd go.'

Batchelor had not told Grand what Belle had told him, about Lafayette Baker and their child. Like some of the details of their picnic, it seemed an intimacy too close, a truth that could afford to lie hidden – at least for a while; perhaps forever. 'You wouldn't understand,' he said.

'I understand that the Siren of the Shenandoah didn't get that name without a reason,' Grand said. 'If my limited grasp of Greek legend serves, the sirens were cruel murderesses in the guise of beautiful women, luring innocent sailors on to the rocks and killing them.'

'As I said,' Batchelor persisted quietly, 'you wouldn't under-stand. But to get back to the list.' He waved it between them. 'Three names we know about – Stanton, Jericho and Tice – and eleven we don't.'

Grand knew a changed subject when he heard one. He took the sheet of paper from Batchelor. The names meant nothing to him either, until . . . 'My God!' He was on his feet, staring at Durham's copperplate in disbelief.

'What?'

'Madison Mitchells.'

'Who?' Batchelor was none the wiser.

Grand sat down again. 'Look, James, I haven't been entirely honest with you.'

'Oh?' Batchelor was glad to hear that. It meant that Belle Boyd's secret could stay with him like a ghost at the feast, but with less guilt at its shoulder.

'You know when we got here first how I had business to take care of, people to see?'

Batchelor did.

'Well, one I didn't plan on seeing but who I ended up bumping into was my old flame, my fiancée, Arlette McKintyre. She was with me at Ford's the night Booth killed Lincoln.'

'I remember,' Batchelor nodded. There had been a lot of evenings in front of the fire with no work to do between then and now, a lot of confidences exchanged. The death of Lincoln haunted them both.

'Well, Arlette is married now. To Madison Mitchells.'

'My God!'

'That's more or less what I said.'

'Have you met this Mitchells?'

'No. And from what Arlette has told me, I don't want to.'

'What does he do?'

'Some big hat in the Treasury Department.'

'Close to Stanton?' Batchelor was muddling his government departments again, but Grand understood.

'When Stanton was king of America, yes.'

'You don't think cousin Luther's been right all along, do you? Stanton.'

'You're thinking Stanton called in Mitchells to do his dirty work?' Grand asked.

'It's feasible, isn't it?'

'It is,' Grand said. 'According to Arlette, he's an old man. Not the type to go up against Lafayette Baker with a gun or his fists. But arsenic poisoning, now; that's a different matter.'

Batchelor took the list back. 'We need to find out why he's on the list; come to think of it, why any of them are. We know Stanton hated Baker because Baker knew where Stanton's bodies are buried. We know Jericho hated him because he was breathing down his neck in the illegal gaming trade . . .'

'Although Jericho said he and Baker had an arrangement, that the National Detective Police left the man alone.'

'And you believe that?' Batchelor asked.

'Why, Mister Batchelor,' Grand was speaking Arkansas again,

'I do declare this great country of mine has made you a suspicious old cuss.'

'Guy,' Batchelor corrected him. 'That's the new word, according to Tom Durham. What time is it, Matthew?'

'I make it nearly midnight,' Grand said, checking his hunter.

'Durham's a senior man at the *Star*,' Batchelor was thinking aloud. 'He's not likely to be at his desk until nine, perhaps later. That gives us a few hours to catch up on some sleep. Tomorrow, we can get Durham to fill in the details on this list.'

'Tomorrow,' Grand yawned, tossing back the dregs of his drink. 'Yes, tomorrow it'll all make sense. Goodnight, James.'

'The *London Telegraph*?' the boy with the outsize collar was impressed. 'Well, now, just fancy that.'

'I did,' Batchelor said. 'That's why I went to work for them. But now, we'd like to see Thomas Durham.'

'Oh, I'm sorry, gentlemen; Mr Durham's not here right now.'

Around them, the *Star* was humming. Harassed-looking men scurried this way and that, carrying copy, chewing pencil stubs, already on their third coffee of the morning. It made Batchelor feel quite nostalgic.

'When do you expect him?' he asked.

'Well, that's kinda odd, really. Mr Durham's always in by eight sharp, ready for the column.'

'The column?' To Matthew Grand, that was a military formation.

'His regular "From The Hill" column. He writes it Tuesday night and submits it to the editor Wednesday morning. Now, in fact.'

'Do you have his home address?' Batchelor asked.

'Oh, I'm sorry, gentlemen,' the lad said. 'I couldn't give out that kind of information.'

Grand toyed with beating it out of him, but he and Batchelor were still effectively working under cover, and leaving teeth and blood on the floor of the *Star*'s front office was probably the quickest way to expose themselves to all and sundry. Batchelor had a better idea. He quickly read the reporter's name tag, a little idea insisted upon by Edwin Stanton after Lincoln's murder so the Press could be muzzled. He leaned forward. 'Mr A. Cottrell,' he said, smiling. 'What's that? Adam? Abraham?'

'Aloysius.' The lad brightened.

'I'm glad I've had this opportunity to meet you,' Batchelor said.

'You are?'

Batchelor looked perplexed. 'He can't have told him, Matthew,' he said.

Grand was used to playing along. He shook his head and sucked his teeth, hoping that was the appropriate response.

'Told him what?' Aloysius Cottrell prided himself that he was good at sniffing out news stories, reading faces, grasping nuances. 'Who?'

'Tom Durham,' Batchelor explained. 'He hasn't spoken to you?'

'Well,' Cottrell tried to remember. 'He says "Good morning" and "Where the Hell's my coffee", that sort of thing.'

Batchelor threw back his head and laughed. 'Isn't that Tom all over, Matthew?'

'It sure is,' Grand smiled.

'What?' If this was some sort of joke, Aloysius Cottrell wasn't in on it. He looked from Grand to Batchelor for some sort of clue.

'Well,' Batchelor became more confidential, 'I shouldn't be telling you this . . . and when Tom does, you're to express surprise, understand?'

'Er . . . oh, sure.' Cottrell nodded, trying to look like the sort of man who expressed surprise every day of his life. It wasn't difficult.

'He and I have been looking for some time for a special correspondent; somebody to write, on behalf of the *Star*, a column for the *Telegraph*.'

'The *London Telegraph*?'

'Is there any other?' Batchelor asked, fully aware that there was. 'The name that keeps rising to the top, whenever Tom and I discuss the matter, is Aloysius Cottrell. Isn't it, Matthew?' He turned to Grand for confirmation and he dutifully nodded vigorously.

'Oh, my God!' The boy looked as if he were about to faint.

'*But*,' Batchelor was insistent, 'it's vital I contact Tom today, this morning. Time is of the essence.' He tapped the side of his nose. 'You understand.'

'Oh, of course.' Cottrell frowned, in his new capacity as the most famous reporter on either side of the Atlantic, read and adored by all the crowned heads of Europe. 'Sure. Absolutely.' He scribbled an address on a piece of paper and passed it to Batchelor. 'So,' he beamed, 'when should I start writing . . .?'

But Grand and Batchelor had gone.

They caught a streetcar to West Eleventh and M as the sun began to climb again. The torrential rain of the night had left Washington a quagmire, and the horses slipped in the greasy mud, the driver lashing them and extending Batchelor's American vocabulary considerably. Thomas Durham's apartment block compared admirably with the succession of tenements Batchelor had lived in as a London reporter, but then Thomas Durham *was* the *Star*'s star. His equivalent back home would be George Sala, and Batchelor knew that that gentleman, doyen of the penny bloods, had a *very* nice house in Knightsbridge, albeit on the shady side.

'Mr Durham,' Batchelor knocked on the man's door on the first floor. Grand, as far as he was concerned, stood alongside him on the second. There was no reply. It was nearly midday by now. Perhaps the *Star*'s man had had a rough night, what with the storm and all. Perhaps he'd been wrestling with his 'From The Hill' column. Perhaps he'd been out on the tiles or – the most likely possibility – he had been hurtling *Star*-wards as they had headed to West Eleventh and M. On a whim, Batchelor tried the door and it swung open soundlessly under his weight.

Grand held up a hand and slid the Colt from his holster.

'Oh, for God's sake, Matthew,' Batchelor pushed past him, 'there's no need for that. The man's a journalist. Oh . . . oh . . . Jesus!'

Both of them stood looking at what was left of Thomas Durham. The man was still in his nightshirt and it was drenched with his blood. He lay at an awkward angle on the floor, his head thrown back and his mouth open in a silent scream. Instinctively, Grand closed the door, and while Batchelor felt for a pulse in the dead man, he mechanically checked the rooms. The place looked like a battlefield. Drawers were hanging open, their contents all over the floor. Clothes had been ripped from hangers in wardrobes; the mattresses had been dragged from the beds and the pillows slashed, their feathers rising and falling in the breeze of Grand's movements. All the rooms were the same. In the middle of a stormy night, a tornado of fury had swept through the rooms of Thomas Durham, leaving nothing but destruction in its wake.

'What have we got?' Grand asked when he got back to the body.

'Difficult to tell under all this blood.' Batchelor had knelt in the stuff. It clung to his trousers and fingers. 'I'd say he's been hit three or four times with something heavy.' He looked around the room for a suitable weapon and saw nothing. 'A cudgel of some kind.'

'Baseball bat,' Grand suggested. 'Billiard cue at a pinch.'

'Clearly, American sportsmen are a little more violent than the ones I'm used to,' Batchelor said.

'He was hit here,' Grand was following the blood smears. 'See, spattering all over the wall.' He was right. A baseball bat would smash a skull, blood and brain tissue flying in the direction of the swing. 'Two hands, I'd guess.'

'He'd have gone down there.' Batchelor took up the tale the blood told them. 'That puddle on the carpet and skirting board.'

'Then . . . what? He got up? Still had fight in him?'

'It's possible,' Batchelor shrugged. 'It's amazing what we're capable of in our last moments. He wasn't an old man. Strong and mobile despite the drink. He'd have fought back.'

'We have to report this,' Grand said.

'No need for that, mister,' a voice growled behind them. Two of Washington's finest stood there in their broad-brimmed hats, pistols gleaming in their hands. 'You, with the blood on your hands, get up real slow. And you,' the officer pushed Grand back against the wall, 'you make one move for that thumb-breaker I just saw you put away and I'll cover that wall with your brains. Got it?'

Grand got it.

All day, Matthew Grand had been kept waiting at the precinct station house. They brought him something indescribable on a metal plate and left him staring at a wall. As night fell, a policeman had come to light a candle in his cell. He avoided Grand's questions and was gone as quickly as he had arrived.

'Where's James Batchelor?' he asked the next man to arrive, a large, sandy-haired detective with a rather hangdog appearance.

'Mr Batchelor is helping us with our enquiries,' he said. He was leaning against the wall and the metal door had clanked shut behind him. Keys rattled in the lock.

'Who are you?' Grand asked.

'John Haynes,' the man said. 'Inspector of detectives.'

'Why have I been kept here?'

'Two of my boys found you in a ransacked apartment with the body of a very respected Washington journalist. What did you think, that we'd just say, "Don't do it again" and let you go?'

'I haven't done anything.'

'That's not what Batchelor says,' Haynes scowled.

Grand leaned back against the rough bricks of the wall. His bed was an iron frame with a thin, damp mattress crawling with vermin. 'That's an old ploy, Inspector,' he said.

'Ploy?' Haynes folded his arms.

'The he said/he said game. You've kept us apart so that we can't compare notes, concoct the same story . . .'

'So, you do *have* a concocted story?' Haynes checked.

'I have a story,' Grand conceded. 'And it will be the same as Batchelor's, but only because it is the truth.'

'See, there's the problem, right there,' Haynes said. 'This truth business. Your friend Batchelor attracts trouble like a moth to a flame. First he claimed to be a tourist and got himself in the centre of our white supremacy transport issues. Next, turns out he's not a tourist after all. He's a journalist doing research into espionage in our recent bit of unpleasantness and he's in a Murder Bay brothel talking to a dead man. You can understand, I'm sure, why I find your friend Batchelor a *tad* suspect.'

'So, you suspect him of murder?'

'He's got Tom Durham's blood all over his hands and clothes, Captain Grand. But right now, I'm interested in you.'

'Are you?'

'What's an officer and a gentleman doing mixing with lowlife like Batchelor? The man's an enquiry agent. A private detective. And if you don't know what we real detectives think of people like that, I'd be happy to enlighten you.'

'An enquiry agent?' Grand tried to bluff. 'Is he really? I had no idea.'

'Yes, you had, Captain Grand, because *you're* one, too.' Haynes flipped a card from his coat pocket. 'One of the things my boys turned up at Durham's apartment. "Grand and Batchelor",' he read from it. '"Forty-One, The Strand". You boys are in this together.'

'In what, exactly?' Grand asked.

Haynes chuckled. 'Well, now, that's the gold nugget, isn't it? I'm going to let you go, Grand. You'll find Batchelor in the yard, cooling his heels. Don't leave Washington. In fact, don't leave the Willard. We'll need to talk again.'

Grand got up, glad to leave the fleas behind. He brushed past Haynes and made for the stairs that twisted up to street level. Once he'd gone, a plain-clothes figure emerged from the shadows beyond the cell. 'I don't get it, Inspector. You've got enough to hang them both, Grand and the Limey.'

Haynes sighed. 'You'd like to think so, wouldn't you, Sergeant,' he said. 'And if Batchelor wasn't a Limey, I'd throw the book at them. But the fact is, he is, and I'm not about to have the Justice Department breathing down my neck, bleating about international incidents. There are times when being caught red-handed only amounts to circumstantial evidence. In other words, less than a hill of beans.'

It was the early hours before Grand and Batchelor got back to the Willard. They had decided not to talk about the case – or anything at all – in the cab on the way over from the station house. It was only now, in the hushed corridors of the hotel, that they felt it was safe.

'So, what *did* you tell him?' Grand asked.

'As little as possible,' Batchelor murmured. 'I could hardly play the foreign journalist card. He'd found ours – the real one, I mean.'

'I trust when – and if – we get back to London, you'll be giving George Sala a piece of your mind about that. The man's a tad too free with other people's information for my liking.'

'That he is. I gave Haynes some guff about working on behalf of a client who had financial interests during the war.'

'A client whose name you declined to give, naturally?'

'Naturally. I steered away from Baker, as if he was just my cover the last time I spoke to Haynes.'

'You think he fell for it?'

Batchelor sighed, sliding the room key into the lock. 'Never in a month of . . . Mother of God!'

Both men stood in their doorway, blinking. The living room of their suite looked the same as the late Thomas Durham's. It had been ransacked, luggage emptied, furniture strewn about. Even their clothes, newly cleaned and pressed by the hotel, lay discarded and crumpled in various corners. It was the same story in the bedrooms and in the bathroom; both men's razors and toothbrushes lay in the washbasin, Batchelor's Macassar oil broken in the bath.

As if in a dream, they wandered through the place; desolation wherever they looked. Batchelor turned over a chair. There were his gold cufflinks, the most valuable thing he possessed. Grand gathered up a pile of shirts and his double-shot Derringer fell out. It took them moments to realize that nothing had been taken; it was all there.

'Too much of a coincidence,' Grand was muttering, shaking his head. 'Whoever killed Tom Durham has paid us a courtesy call too.'

'To kill us?' Batchelor didn't like the way this case was shaping up.

'No,' Grand was sure. 'They were looking for something. Thank God you've got Durham's list.'

'What?'

'The list. The fourteen names that Durham compiled for us.'

An odd look flitted across James Batchelor's face.

'The would-be killers of Lafayette Baker.' Grand didn't feel he should have to explain all this; the shock of finding Durham must have hit the Englishman harder than he thought. Brain fever could set in so easily and have no symptoms until it was too late.

Batchelor muttered something, but Grand didn't catch it.

'What?'

'I said,' Batchelor stared hard at him, 'I thought you had it.'

'What?' Grand could hardly believe his ears. Perhaps he was the one with incipient brain fever.

'I said—'

The American shook his head angrily. 'I heard what you said,' he snapped. 'I gave it to you. The last time I saw it . . .'

'It was in the cane stand,' Batchelor remembered.

He and Grand collided as they rushed headlong towards the brass cylinder. Grand got there first and turned it upside down. Nothing fell out but a solitary spider. 'I must have a word with the chambermaid,' he said, absently.

'I told you to put it there.' Batchelor was on the defensive. 'I thought I saw you take it before we went to the *Star* offices.'

'And I assumed you did the same,' Grand fumed.

The silence between them was shattering.

'All right.' Grand raised both hands to prevent him from using one of them to loosen a few of James Batchelor's teeth. 'At least we know why Durham died. Whoever killed him was after the list. They couldn't make him talk so they stove in his head and turned his place over. Then they came here.'

'How did they know we wouldn't be here?'

'It's my guess they were watching us.' Grand was working it out. 'Maybe as early as the *Star* offices, but certainly in Durham's tenement block. They saw the cops arrive too. Hell, they may even have sent for them. They'd have known Washington's finest wouldn't be letting us go in a hurry.'

Batchelor checked the door. 'No damage to the lock,' he said. 'No sign of what we call breaking and entering back home. This could be an inside job, Matthew.'

'It could,' Grand agreed. 'But I don't want to tip our hands any more than we have already. Let's get this place put back together. Then we'll mosey on down to the restaurant and make a few casual enquiries among the staff. And in the meantime, James, we'd better put our thinking caps on and try to remember who the Hell was on that list. Because it's my guess that one of them killed Tom Durham. *And* he killed Lafayette Baker.'

If Matthew Grand was right, then another problem had arisen. The murderer had found Thomas Durham's list, but reason would have told him that Grand and Batchelor had read it. That made them targets and they would have to watch their backs *very* carefully from now on.

There was one name on the list that Grand remembered very well, and he insisted on following up on this one on his own. In the meantime, Batchelor stayed put in the hotel, his back to the wall, poring over Baker's edition of Colburn's book, the one that Belle Boyd had helped him with. As he turned the pages, a fugitive waft of her perfume occasionally rewarded his work, but he tried to put the woman out of his mind and bend that mind to the task in hand. Now that he understood Baker's code, he could carry on with the man's hidden message. And it made his scalp crawl.

The Treasury building was sheathed in scaffolding as Matthew Grand's cab creaked and rattled to a halt outside it. He could have walked the short distance from the Willard, but, like Batchelor, he preferred just now to have something relatively solid at his back. The storm had broken the back of the early Fall heat and the workmen, in their overalls and caps, were grateful for that. They had been building this place for over thirty years; in fact Grand remembered as a small boy being taken to see the giant Greek columns in all their gleaming white granite being lifted into place with pulleys, cranes, snorting horses and cursing men. He remembered, too, in the dark days of the war, that this was yet another government building overrun by soldiers. They had thrown up their canvas tents in the south courtyard and sung their marching songs within earshot of the President at the White House.

'I'm afraid the Treasury isn't open to visitors today,' the clerkly looking man called through the open door.

'I'm looking for Madison Mitchells,' Grand said.

The clerkly looking man emerged into the sunlight, squinting to see who had come calling. 'And you are . . .?'

'Matthew Grand,' Grand passed the man his American calling card. It still opened doors in Washington.

'Captain Grand,' the man said. 'Third Cavalry. Glad to make your acquaintance, sir.'

'You are . . .?'

'Oh, I'm sorry.' The clerk took off his glasses and cleaned them on a handkerchief. 'I am Mr Mitchells' secretary. Well, more of a second in command, I could say, really. Wally Pollack.'

'Is he in, Mr Pollack?'

'No, sir, I'm sorry to say he's not. It's a busy life in the Treasury Department. Hub of government, you know. Mr Mitchells is in Philadelphia.'

'Philadelphia?'

'Yes. As you'd expect, we have offices everywhere. What would America be without its dollars, huh?'

'What indeed? Perhaps you can help me, Mr Pollack.'

'I'll try, certainly,' the Treasury man said. 'Come in out of the sun. Not so powerful now the Fall is almost here, but still, hot enough, don't you think? Can I get you a cup of coffee? Or something stronger, maybe? I'm partial to a little imported beer myself. Wenlock Oatmeal Stout. Try some?'

'English beer.' Grand screwed up his face in disgust. 'No, thanks. I'll stick to coffee.'

Pollack went to the door and shouted down the corridor for someone rather lower down the pecking order. He ordered two coffees, make it snappy now and don't forget the good china. Grand eased himself on to the excruciatingly uncomfortable leather furniture; there seemed to be an actual horse somewhere in its construction, not just its hair. He looked about him at the plush fittings, the oak panelling, the fancy etched glass.

'Nice, huh?' Pollack asked, turning back to him. 'This was part of the suite of offices the President used after Lincoln's assassination . . . er . . . President Johnson, that is. Gave poor Mrs Lincoln time to get the Hell out of the White House itself. Well, it was only right. Deranged old besom had more dresses than I've got hairs on my head. Took a wagon train to move 'em. You take sugar?'

'One,' Grand said. 'So, how long have you worked with Madison, Mr Pollack?'

'How did you say you knew him?' Pollack asked.

'I met him at one or two functions,' Grand lied. 'Soon after Lincoln was killed, as a matter of fact.'

There was a tap on the door and a lad with almost unbelievably radiant spots all over his face and disappearing under his grubby collar shouldered it open, carrying a tray with the coffee and a plate of rather dubious-looking cookies, which Pollack waved impatiently away.

'Hmm,' Pollack nodded, and handed Grand his cup of coffee. 'They were terrible times, huh?'

'Terrible indeed,' Grand agreed.

'And what is your business, Captain? With Mr Mitchells, I mean? I notice you use his given name, so I am assuming it's personal. Am I right?'

Grand smiled. 'You ask a lot of questions, Mr Pollack,' he said.

'Sorry.' The Treasury man chuckled. 'Goes with the territory, I guess. Before this, I was with the War Department. You could say I used to be your boss.'

'You *could*,' Grand acknowledged, but he clearly didn't believe it.

'I was a detective then. Still am, I guess.'

'Really?'

'Yessir. Fraud. Misuse of Treasury funds. You know what they say, there's nothing more certain than death and taxation.'

'Do they?' Grand mused. 'Do they really?'

'So . . . er . . . your business with . . .?'

'Is my business, I'm afraid,' Grand said. 'Tell me, is it true the old buzzard has a young wife? *Another* young wife, I should perhaps say. And a new baby? I heard there was a child.'

Pollack looked at him oddly. 'Why, Captain Grand,' he said, the smile suddenly gone. 'I hardly think that's Treasury business. Or yours.'

'Touché, Mr Pollack. Out of the goodness of your heart, however, just tell me one thing.'

'If I can.'

Grand became confidential. 'Tell me that the new Mrs Mitchells – should there be such a person, of course – is not the Clara Harris I remember from my Washington courting days. I carried a bit of a torch, you understand . . .'

'Clara Harris?' Pollack frowned, thinking. 'God, no, she married that over-promoted idiot Henry Rathbone. They were both there, in fact, the night Lincoln was murdered.'

'Get away!'

'In the Presidential box itself,' Pollack said, the proud imparter of information. 'No, if I may say so, Captain Grand, you had a lucky escape there. A real shrew if ever there was one. If I was her husband, I would have swung for her by now. No, Madison – if you don't mind the familiarity, since we're talking of family matters – Madison is married to Arlette McKintyre, as was. Did you know her?' Pollack winked. 'In your Washington courting days?'

'I don't believe I did,' Grand lied.

'I haven't heard there's a baby, though. Mind you, Mr Mitchells can be quite close about his private life. A very private man, yes, indeed.'

Grand swigged back the Treasury coffee like a man and set the cup down on a pile of audits. It had been as he feared; any coffee that appeared that fast had been simmering on some distant hob for many a long hour and had the bitterness to prove it. 'I'll tell you, there are a lot of people I've lost touch with over the past couple of years. Madison is one. Clara, of course. And Henry – I knew him too. Oh, and Laff Baker. Whatever happened to Laff Baker?'

# FOURTEEN

Major Ambrose Richards was the superintendent of the Metropolitan Police and his gout was giving him merry Hell that morning. Mrs Richards was as sympathetic as a blunt razor and he had come to the precinct station house to get some peace.

'Do you want to explain this, Haynes?' he asked the inspector who sat across the cluttered desk from him.

'Sir?'

'This fella Grand and his Limey sidekick. The report says they were arrested at the scene of a murder.'

'That's right, sir.'

'It also says,' Richards looked closely at the spidery handwriting, '"No further action". That's jargon for "we let them go", I assume. You're a lot of things, Jack, but incompetent is not one of them. What the Hell?'

'I'm pretty sure they're involved, sir, right up to their necks. But I'm not sure the District Attorney would see it that way. You know how Gillette likes to have his tees crossed and his eyes dotted.'

'I know he likes us to do his work for him, yes. What do we know about these two?'

'The Limey is James Batchelor. Wouldn't know the truth if it got up and bit him. He's given me three different reasons for being in the city; but actually, he's a private detective.'

Richards spat with ringing accuracy into his spittoon.

'Quite,' Haynes nodded.

'And what's he detecting, exactly?'

'Ah, well, I'm not quite sure about that. The trouble is, sir, that you and I go back aways. This place was so full of spies during the war you could paper the walls with them. We've learned to suspect everybody. Not sure my cat wasn't Secret Secesh back in the day.'

'What about the other one? Grand.'

'Ex-cavalry. A captain in the Third Potomac. Actually, you might know him.'

'Oh?'

'You were in Ford's the night they shot Lincoln.'

'I was.' Richards still had the nightmares.

'So was he – or so I've heard. Cut and run soon afterwards.'

'Cut and run?' The major didn't like the sound of that.

'Left the country. Went to England by all accounts. Hence the Limey.'

'Why'd he leave? I should think the Army's a soft billet in peacetime.'

'Too many soldiers, maybe,' Haynes shrugged. 'Not enough openings. Of course . . .'

Richards and Haynes did indeed go way back, and he knew that look on his subordinate's face. 'Of course . . .?'

'Well, we never did round up all the conspirators, did we?'

'You're thinking that Grand . . .'

Haynes held up his hand. 'I don't want to second-guess any of this, sir, but it could be big.'

'Big enough for Stanton?'

'He was in charge of the operation.'

'And he brought in Baker.'

'Who?'

Richards snapped. Why was everybody being so obtuse this morning? Didn't they know about his leg? 'Lafayette Baker, Haynes. Do try to keep up. Maybe I should have a quiet word with the former War Secretary. Rumour is the man's going for the Supreme Court job. Could be useful to us.'

'Do you believe all those stories about Stanton, sir?' Haynes asked.

Richards looked at him. He was a shrewd man who hadn't risen to the top of the Metropolitan Force by coincidence. Or by sharing his innermost thoughts with subordinates. On the other hand, he could never resist throwing stones at Stanton. 'All of them, no. But some? Well, flies are drawn to shit, aren't they?'

There was no denying that.

'What about this newspaperman?' Richards asked. 'Tom Durham.'

\*   \*   \*

'Thomas Durham was a saint,' Aloysius Cottrell slurred. Grand and Batchelor were very generous with their drinks and the lad was on his third Early Times. Or was it his fourth? Ordinarily, Batchelor would have done this follow-up investigation alone, but because both men felt themselves marked, they followed the precept of safety in numbers.

'You couldn't have known him well, though.' Batchelor played the Devil's journalist. 'Being of the junior persuasion, I mean.'

'I may be young,' Cottrell pointed, trying desperately to focus, 'but I'm going places. You know . . .' he caught Batchelor's lapel on the second attempt. 'You know he had me down for great things. Wanted me to be the *Star*'s special corres . . . cosser . . . writer.'

'Yes,' Batchelor smiled. 'I told you.'

'Well, there we are, then.' Cottrell sat back, hugging himself. 'We can't both be wrong.' He sat upright, stony-faced, almost sober with shock. 'What's going to happen now?' he asked them. 'How am I going to cope without Tom?'

'Did he have any visitors?' Grand asked. 'Recently, I mean. At the *Star*?'

The bar swung and swayed in Cottrell's vision and the lights tumbled on the glasses and the bottles. The place was thick with cigar smoke, and for some reason the sound of the other drinkers, chatting and shouting to each other, seemed to come and go, as though blown by an unfelt wind. Cottrell's eyes suddenly looked shrewd and he leaned forward, finger wagging. 'Ah,' he said, suddenly, 'you're trying to find out who killed him, aren't you? Good. Good. Because you can't leave it to the police, y'know. That cuss Haynes couldn't cross the road by himself. And I can help you there.'

'You can?' Looking at the hapless youth, with his outsize clothes, his tear-stained cheeks and his swivelling eyes, Grand somehow doubted that.

'Mr Batchelor, you're a newspaperman . . . aren't you?' Cottrell suddenly wasn't at all sure.

'Of sorts,' Batchelor agreed.

'Then you'll know. We make enemies, don't we? Cross the odd line. Ruffle some feathers.'

Batchelor nodded again. So many metaphors in so short a

speech. If this was the future of American journalism, the *Telegraph* had nothing to worry about.

Again, Cottrell had him by the lapel. 'Read Durham's "From The Hill" column. He slammed into them all there. Congressmen, senators, even the President. I'll stake my career on the fact that whoever beat poor Tom to death is on that list.'

'Violent lot, are they, Congressmen?' Batchelor asked.

Cottrell's eyes widened. 'Homicidal, most of 'em,' he said. Then he became confidential. 'Even Stanton carries a gun.'

'Does he, now?' Grand murmured. 'That's good to know.'

The *Star* next day carried an obituary of the late Thomas Durham. In that it flowed well and used no metaphors at all, it couldn't have been written by Aloysius Cottrell. The edition was bordered deepest black; the funeral would be held at Arlington the following week. Grand and Batchelor determined to be there but, before that, Grand had business elsewhere. Despite their pledge to investigate from now on as a pair, he again insisted that he do this alone.

Arlette Mitchells' house was even more splendid inside than out, but in a rather dour and outdated way. As Grand waited in the lobby while the butler went to see if madam was At Home, he looked around and felt sorry for the girl he had known, the girl who had never met a shade of pink she didn't like, who had frills on her frills. How lonely she must be in this house of grey and black. Even the tiles on the floor, which in another house would be white or pale rose marble alternating with the glossy black, were here grey alternating with a slightly deeper grey.

Grand wandered over to the stairs and, looking up from the chilly hall, he saw a row of portraits, in dull gilt frames, each one adorned with a black bow in mourning. The identical girls in the pictures could be sisters, but, more chillingly, as Grand correctly identified them as Mitchells' previous brides, now Gone Before, they could be Arlette's sisters. The man may not be a poisoner, but he was certainly as weird as Hell. Grand was straining forward to read the first one's names and dates when he heard a familiar whine from behind him. And even so, he felt sorry for the girl.

'Matthew.' How did she manage to get so many syllables into a simple name, he could never fathom. 'How kind of you to come to see me.'

He turned, pinning a smile on his face. For a moment, he wasn't sure what to say. Was she thinner? Had the baby arrived or not? It was hard to tell, because there was still an awful lot of Arlette under her dark gown. Fortunately for him, she solved his dilemma.

'Come through, into the drawing room. Nurse has brought little Johnson down for his feed.' She leaned forward and cupped a hand around her mouth. 'I feed him myself,' she whispered. 'Madison insists. Only a mother's milk is pure enough for a Mitchells.' She straightened up again and gave a reminiscent tug to the front of her gown. 'But you don't need to worry; it's all done for now. He has some colic, poor little mite, but I rub some laudanum on his gums and he soon sleeps.'

Grand looked into her eyes; something was definitely not quite right there. She didn't seem able to focus on him, even though her smile was amiable enough and she looked well on first glance. He suspected that poor little Johnson's gums were not the only ones to feel the beneficial kiss of the poppy. 'And you, Arlette,' he had to ask, 'how are you?'

'Tired,' she said, nodding. 'Little Johnson, dear little soul, needs to feed very often. He falls asleep at my breast . . .' she put a hand to her mouth but it dropped almost immediately, as though she had forgotten to be shy, '. . . and then nurse has to bring him to me again very soon, because he is hungry. And then, there is Madison . . . did I tell you he is very vigorous?' She looked up anxiously at Grand. 'Should I be talking to you like this? I can't remember . . .'

Grand was no expert when it came to women newly delivered of a child, but several things about her conversation struck him as unusual, even with his limited experience. Firstly, whatever was a woman of her standing doing feeding her own child? He could see that there might be all kinds of advantages to be had, but he had never known a woman give them enough importance to actually do the job – where would the poor women be, if no one used wet nurses any more? Secondly, this child couldn't have been born much more than a month ago? Should Madison, be he never so vigorous, be quite so demanding, so soon? And thirdly – but most importantly – the laudanum. Surely, *that* wasn't Madison's idea? Although it would explain a lot about the rather docile expressions of the women on the stairs.

Grand looked down at the poor creature, still standing in front of him because no one had told her not to. 'Arlette,' he said, firmly. 'I am going to call for your maid and have her take you to bed for a rest. You're ill. I'm going to send for a doctor, for you and little . . . is he really named Johnson?'

She nodded. 'After the Presiden'. All Mitchells babies are named after the Presiden'. 'Cept the girls. They're named after . . . I don' know who they're named after. No girl Presiden's, are there?' She sagged at the knees and Grand caught her expertly and carried her into the drawing room and laid her on the sofa by the window. She lay there, her head lolling to one side and a small bubble growing and diminishing in a corner of her mouth. He looked around and found the bell pull, a poor, ragged piece of rope hanging at the side of the chimneypiece. After a very long pause, he heard raised voices and a slammed door in some distant region of the house, followed by the stump of angry feet.

The door flew open and a furious little woman stood there. She was short and round, her hair flying in wisps from beneath a grimy cap. 'What now?' she snarled, then saw Arlette on the sofa and Grand over by the fireplace. The sweaty face adopted a false smile. 'Oh, madam,' she said, hurrying to Arlette's side, 'whatever is it?' She put a filthy hand on the woman's forehead, making her flinch in her sleep. She looked at Grand. 'Whatever've you been doing to the mistress?' she said.

'Your mistress is ill,' Grand said. 'Can't you see? She is addicted to laudanum would be my best guess, and she is poisoning the baby with it, unawares. What have you all been doing, watching her become so ill? And where is her husband?'

The woman became even more belligerent than she had seemed on entry. 'I don't know who you are, mister,' she said, turning on him like a cornered rat, going for the throat. 'One of them callers the master says we're to watch for. The young 'uns, there's no controlling them, the master says. And he should know.' The woman gave vent to a throaty chuckle, shocking in its obscene intent. 'So, what'd you do to the mistress, I say. Too much for her, whatever it was. Come to ply your wiles on a poor woman weak with childbearin', while her man is out of town.' She looked at him through red-rimmed lids. 'You look no better than you should be, to my way of thinking. You've a look o' that Grand fellow, the one who left the mistress high and dry.' Again, the filthy laugh, ending this time in a hacking cough. 'The talk of Washington she was, poor fool. Anyways,' and she whipped a filthy cloth from her belt and flapped it at him, 'be off with you, before I set the dogs on yuh.'

Throughout the woman's very revealing speech, Grand had not moved, but now he did, walking towards her over the threadbare, dusty carpet, which had certainly seen many of Mitchells' wives' desperate pacing. For a while, she stood her ground, but finally ran off, shrieking, back to the kitchens. While she was gone, Grand looked around for a crib and finally spotted it, tucked in a dark corner behind a chair.

He bent over and peered in. The child inside didn't look very healthy, but Grand, in his years in London, had seen worse. It didn't have the waxy sheen he had so often witnessed in the poorer parts of the East End, but it did lie very still. Although his paternal side had never felt the need to surface, Grand's emotions rose up now and he put forward a gentle finger and stroked the baby's velvet cheek. 'Hello, Johnson,' he said, softly. Then, feeling that Johnson was hardly a name for so small a scrap of life, 'Hello, Jack.' The child opened his eyes and looked briefly at Grand, with the cross-eyed intensity of the very young, then fell asleep again. Another door crashed in the kitchen and Grand felt the baby flinch in his sleep. Afraid, and so young . . . he swore he would rescue Arlette and her little one, if it was the last thing he did.

Grand stepped away from the crib, leaving the youngest Mitchells sleeping fitfully. This time, the door opened more discreetly and the butler stepped in, as though there was nothing wrong with the mistress being unconscious through opium and laid out on the sofa.

'Bessie says there may be a problem, sir,' the butler intoned.

'If Bessie is that unwashed shrew who was in here a moment ago, she's darn right there's a problem,' Grand said, pointing to Arlette, who had begun to snore.

The butler looked at the woman impassively. 'Bessie is my good lady wife,' he remarked, 'but I take your point. The mistress often takes a nap at this time of day, sir,' he added, in a level voice.

'A nap?' Grand was incredulous. 'A *nap?* Man, she is out for the count. Fetch a doctor, at once. She needs medical attention.'

'The master does not hold with doctors, sir,' the butler informed him blandly.

'Well,' Grand played his trump card, 'the master isn't *here*, is he? So, let's get the doctor, eh? You can tell him I insisted. I'll pay, if that's his problem.'

The butler drew himself up to his full height which, Grand was dismayed to notice, was considerable, and in proportion to his shoulders. 'I feel it inappropriate for a stranger to cast aspersions as to the master's pecuniary situation,' he said. 'The master does not hold with doctors because he feels it is better for nature to take its course. This was his practice with his other wives.' The man shut his mouth with a snap, as though the point were proved.

Grand's eyes nearly fell out of his head and he pointed with a quivering finger beyond the butler out into the hall. 'Am I right in thinking,' he said, through gritted teeth, 'that the young ladies on the stairs are the result of nature taking its course?'

The butler's expression became mulish. 'Are you familiar with the work of Mr Charles Darwin?' he asked, loftily.

'Yes. What the Hell has a book about birds' beaks got to do with women dying?'

If the butler thought that a pertinent question, he didn't show it. 'Whatever the case may be, sir,' the butler said, 'I repeat that the master does not hold with doctors.'

'Well,' Grand said, suddenly galvanized into action by the sheer stupidity of the man, 'I do.' He leaned over Arlette and flicked her into a sitting position and then over his shoulder. God, the woman had put on weight; his knees momentarily buckled slightly, but he braced himself and, once balanced, moved with ease over to the crib. He scooped up baby Johnson with his free arm and faced the butler. He knew he was vulnerable, but relied on the fact that not even Madison Mitchells' automaton would attack him when he had an innocent child in his arms. And, indeed, the man stepped back, even going to the lengths of opening the doors that stood between Grand and the street. As the last one shut behind him, Grand was sure he heard the man say, 'And good riddance!'

He was now in the rather unusual situation of standing on the sidewalk of a Washington street, with an unconscious woman over a shoulder and a waking baby in his arms. He was beginning to attract attention, and not of a good kind. If he didn't make his move soon, he would find himself in the precinct house again, and he had a strong feeling that it wouldn't go very well. And, apart from anything else, Arlette was beginning to weigh a bit heavy.

'Honey,' a voice husked in his ear. 'I seen some things in my life, but I declare this takes the biscuit.'

He turned, slowly in view of his burden, and saw the most welcome sight he had ever seen in his life. 'Julep!' he said, handing her the baby and sliding Arlette off his shoulder in the nick of time; ten more seconds and one if not both of them would have hit the deck. 'Where did you spring from? Not that I'm sorry to see you,' he added hurriedly. He would have been grateful to meet the Devil himself if he would have held the baby for a minute. 'As you see, I have a minor problem.'

Julep looked him up and down, then looked closely at the baby. She held him up to her face and sniffed. 'Not so minor, honey,' she said. 'This baby reeks of laudanum. That his momma?'

Grand nodded.

'She the same?'

Again, the nod. 'But worse.'

'Lord! And look at that handsome house. She live there?'

'Yes. It's Madison Mitchells' wife. He works in the Treasury.'

She wrinkled her beautiful nose. 'I don't believe I know him, sugar,' she said. 'But let's get her inside, if she lives here. She needs her bed.' She took a step or two, the baby cradled in her arms.

'No! No, not back inside. We've just come from there. I must take her to her mother. I don't know what the woman has been thinking, letting Arlette get into a state like this.'

Julep peered closer. 'That Arlette McKintyre?' she asked, astonished. 'I wouldn't've known her. Say . . .' she looked at Grand through new eyes. 'You that Billy Yank left her in the lurch?'

Grand was getting a little tired of the label, but wearily nodded his head.

'Well, my opinion, the girl overreacted,' Julep said. 'She couldn't wait for a husband, that one. Do I know this Mitchells? The name sounds kinda familiar.'

Grand shrugged and Arlette moaned softly. He looked at her in exasperation. Whatever had he done? He turned back to Julep. 'You may do. Older man. *Much* older.'

She thought for a moment, then shook her head. She looked down at the baby again and her face softened. 'Let's get these two back to her momma. Marry in haste, repent at leisure, or so they say. Ever been married, hon?' she suddenly asked.

Grand shook his head. 'Married to the job,' he said, with a wry smile.

'You don't mean you and that cute Limey . . .?' Julep's eyes widened.

'No,' Grand disabused her. 'No, not at all. It was just a figure of speech. Now, do cabbies ply around here?'

'They do for Julep, sugar,' she said and, sticking two fingers in her mouth, gave vent to a piercing whistle. Almost as its echo died, a cab clattered to the kerb and Julep held Arlette as Grand climbed in. Then, she handed the woman up the steps and stowed her neatly in the corner, finally giving the baby to Grand. Then, she stepped back on to the sidewalk.

'Are you coming with me?' Grand asked. As so many men had before and would do again, he had happily laid his burden on Julep.

She laughed and swept an expressive hand down from her lovely face to her expensively shod feet. 'I think you have a job to do to explain yourself when you get to the McKintyres' already, don't you, sugar?' she said. 'Without me in tow. Rumour was, old man McKintyre looked for you for three solid weeks, his shotgun under his arm and ready. So, I'll wish you good luck until we meet again.' She reached in and stroked Johnson's cheek. 'And especially you, honey child,' she said. 'Look after your momma. She's gonna need it.'

She stepped back out of the cab again and turned her head to where the cabbie sat on his box. 'Take these good people to the McKintyre house,' she said. 'You know it?'

The cabbie nodded.

She turned to Grand. 'You good for the fare?' He patted his pocket and nodded too. 'Then, off you go,' she said, patting the horse's rump. With a flick of his whip, the cabbie pulled out onto the muddy road and the cab swished away. The woman looked back at the house, where three faces could be seen, the curtain twitching as they ducked from sight. With an expressive and deliciously obscene gesture, Julep wished them heartily all to Hell. Then, she watched as the cab turned the corner at the end of the road.

'Good luck,' she whispered, ignoring the tear on her cheek, 'good luck.'

Washington had seen nothing like it since Lincoln's funeral. The road to Arlington was choked with carriages; some draped in black, like the hearse. Four black mares tossed their ostrich-plumed heads, shaking away the drowsy flies of Fall. There were flowers everywhere – some fresh, some artificial – and black flags fluttered in the afternoon sunshine. The inhabitants of Freedman's Village, on the slope of Arlington Hill, came to pay their respects, the men tugging off their hats, the children cowed into silence by the solemnity of the occasion. A band, paid for by the *Star*, played the 'Dead March' from *Saul* and the people of Freedman's Village took up their own version, singing the slave songs of their youth. None of them had known Tom Durham personally, but they knew he wrote for the *Star* and they knew the *Star* spoke for the Union and for black emancipation and for every cause that was worthy and good.

Among the many who had turned out to pay their last respects to Thomas Durham was a little black lady, in neat black trim and matching parasol. The townsfolk of Freedman's Village knew her well and most of the women curtseyed as she walked by them. Sojourner Truth acknowledged their recognition with her crooked smile and a gentle nod of the head, but her own attention was elsewhere, as it had been for the past two days. She was watching the lovely black girl walking ahead of her. And she knew that something was not right. Everyone dressed appropriately for a funeral, especially for a 'character' like Tom Durham. The adults were swathed in black satin and crepe. Their children wore white. And whatever the persuasion and the tendency of the mourners, this was a day when black men and white men could walk together, exactly as it had been for Lincoln.

But the lovely girl was different. Sojourner had first seen her a couple of days before. She had met that nice Englishman, Mr Batchelor, in the street, and had thanked him again for helping her on the streetcar. She had told him, with a twinkle, that she had been arrested twice since then, for the same offence that was not an offence and the judge, ever a patient man, had threatened her with some serious jail time if it happened again. Batchelor had introduced her to his associate, the Yankee captain, and the pair had gone on their way. It was then that Sojourner had noticed the girl.

She had been lurking in the shadows of an alley off L Street and, when she thought that Grand and Batchelor had got far enough away, she followed them. *Then* the girl was dressed for the night, with a cloak over her tight-fitting scarlet. She dripped with jewels and swung her hips like she used them for a living.

Today, the girl was dressed down. She still wore the cloak but under it was a respectable day dress, plain and charcoal, sweeping the ground in perfect decorum. Sojourner's old eyes weren't what they had once been, but she could see the girl's quarry well enough in the distance. The Englishman and the Yankee captain were walking up the hill under the flowered archway, past the rows of white markers, the head-bowed cherubs and the broken columns that marked the last resting place of the great and the good.

Sojourner took her place at the edge of the crowd. From here, she could see Grand and Batchelor, equally far back, watching everybody as she watched them. At one point, Batchelor tipped his hat to her. But they couldn't see the black girl from where they stood, only a blur of hats and feathers. Thomas Durham had no family, but there were a disproportionate number of weeping ladies sitting on the neat rows of chairs at the graveside. The priest began the service.

Sojourner manoeuvred herself into position. She had taken a shine to the Englishman who had got himself into a jam for her, and she didn't want to see him come to harm. She saw Major Richards of the Metropolitan Police and her own personal *bête noire*, Inspector Haynes, alongside him, but approaching them, she knew, would be a waste of time. After all, what had the black girl actually done wrong? It was, despite the evidence of the past two hundred years, a free country.

And when she judged the moment was right, Sojourner struck. 'What you at, girl?'

The black girl turned, startled, then frowned at her. 'Go to Hell, gran'ma.'

'Oh, I've been there, child.' Sojourner grabbed her arm and pulled her behind the trunk of a yew tree. 'Why you following them white boys?'

'What's it got to do with you?' the girl snarled at her, thrusting her hip out and resting a hand on it. 'And just which white boys am I supposed to be following?'

'The Englishman,' Sojourner said, 'and the Yankee captain. You ain't fixing to rob them; or, if you are, you're the worst damn pickpocket I ever did see.'

'It wouldn't be seemly,' the girl said, arching an eyebrow, 'for me to knock an old lady over, especially at a funeral and all. So, get lost.'

'Sure,' said Sojourner. 'Just as soon as I've had a little chat with my friends in the police over there.'

The girl flounced past her, panic written all over her face, and crossed to where Grand and Batchelor were preparing, along with everybody else, to leave.

'Julep,' Batchelor tipped his hat.

'Mr Batchelor,' she smiled, 'Mr Grand. Did your friend get to her mother's all right?'

Grand smiled and muttered something general, ignoring Batchelor's searching look.

'I've got a message from Luther,' she continued. 'He hasn't heard from you.'

'We've been busy,' Grand explained.

'He said to remind you, sugar-plum, who's picking up the tab. Tomorrow night. The Wolf's Den.' And she was gone. As she swept past Sojourner Truth, she half turned. 'Maybe now you'll mind your own business, you old witch.'

Sojourner watched her go, shaking her head. 'Honey,' she said to herself, 'you're putting back the cause of black girls by a hundred years.'

Neither Grand nor Batchelor had really expected to learn anything new at Thomas Durham's funeral. Even so, they had watched and waited. Anyone in that crowd could have been his killer, one of the eleven names on Durham's list that still had no faces. The police had been there, for the same reason that Grand and Batchelor were, hoping for a chance remark, an unguarded comment; *something* that would have given them a lead. Neither of them had seen Wesley Jericho there. Batchelor had not seen Caleb Tice, the name crossed out on Durham's list, the name that would not leave his head. Grand, who knew Stanton by sight, had not seen him there either. And of course, Madison Mitchells was still in Philadelphia.

The superintendent of Durham's apartment block had not been at the funeral either. He could never leave the premises, he told Grand and Batchelor later. There were few men in Washington who took their jobs as seriously as he did. He looked out for his people, mended their plumbing and watched their cats while they were away. He was shocked and appalled at what had happened to Tom Durham. Oh, and by the way, he saw everything and missed nothing. Nobody came or went without him being aware. Had he seen anybody visiting Durham in the days before his death? No. Had he seen Grand and Batchelor arrive the day they found the body? No, he'd never seen them before in his life. Had he perhaps noticed the Metropolitan Police officers tramping all over the place in their hobnailed boots? Well, er, no, not exactly. And, having been enormously helpful, the superintendent put his bottle-bottom glasses back on and closed the door.

Both the enquiry agents burned the midnight oil at the Willard that night, thumbing through the back numbers of the *Star* in case young Aloysius Cottrell had been even half right. Had Tom Durham so libelled someone in his column that they had sought revenge – not by due process, but by stoving in his head? And were any of the libelled politicians on the list that was now missing; perhaps one of the names that now neither of them could recall?

If the superintendent of Durham's building had been all three wise monkeys rolled into one, the clerks and chambermaids at the Willard were even worse. As subtly as they could, Grand and Batchelor quizzed them all, from the manager to the boot boy, and nobody could shed any light on anyone who might have visited their rooms and left no calling card. The last thing the pair wanted to do was to tip their hand and admit that their room had been trashed. That would mean the police, and sooner or later even a clod like John Haynes would have got wind of Durham's list and what it meant. Faced with brick wall upon blind alley, their only hope that next night was Luther Baker.

Marble Alley was darker than usual, the street lights spluttering as the rain started from the west. One or two of the Wolf's Den visitors were alighting from their gigs as they arrived; everybody, in the tradition of the Division, ignoring everybody else. If there was a face you recognized here, you kept quiet and swore – if it came to it – that it was a trick of the light.

Julep was draped around Luther Baker in the upstairs room and the only sound was the repetitive thud of a headboard from next door.

'How did you enjoy the funeral, boys?' Baker asked.

'Wouldn't have missed it,' Grand said.

'Mind telling me why you were there?'

Silence. Apart from the thud.

'Julep, honey,' Baker sighed. 'Would you give my compliments to the senator from Wisconsin and tell him to shut the Hell up. I'm sure his business is pressing, but it's not as pressing as mine.'

He waited until she had gone. There was the sound of a door being flung open, a scream and a curse. Raised voices. Then silence.

Baker smiled. 'Now,' he said, pouring drinks all round from a bourbon bottle on the table. 'What's the connection between Cousin Laff and Tom Durham?'

'You knew Durham?' Batchelor asked.

'Only by reputation,' Baker said.

'He'd offered to help us,' Grand told him. 'With Cousin Laff's case.'

'Using a newshound?' Baker's eyes squinted in the lamplight. 'Risky.'

'*I'm* a newshound, as you put it,' Batchelor said. 'You're using me.'

'Don't feel so put-upon, Batchelor,' Baker chuckled. 'And anyway, I sent for Grand here. You came along for the ride.'

'Was that what it was for?' Batchelor asked. 'Silly me. I'd forgotten.'

'What I don't need is a smart-mouth,' Baker hissed. 'What happened in Knoxville?'

And Grand and Batchelor told him; nearly all of it. Some things that happen in Knoxville have to stay in Knoxville.

It was altogether an older case that Grand and Batchelor investigated next. And that was the case of Caleb Tice. His name had been crossed out on Durham's list. But there was something intriguing, not to say sinister, about a man who was supposed to be dead, sitting and looking surprisingly chipper in a bordello in the Division. The problem was that neither man who had told Batchelor that Tice was dead was in the mood for talking. Luther Baker had admitted that he had killed Tice and had thrown him into the Potomac. John Haynes had fished the man's body out of the Potomac. But he still had Grand and Batchelor in the frame for Tom Durham's murder. And he wasn't likely to be exchanging confidences any time soon.

But there was another name that Batchelor remembered, a fourth man who was there when the Bakers and Tice had cornered the assassin John Wilkes Booth.

'Colonel Conger?'

The man with the hard eyes and drooping moustache didn't look up. 'You'll find the chests through there, boys. Take care now; there's many a slip between here and Ohio.'

'I'm sure that's true, Colonel, but that's not why we're here.'

Conger looked up from his ledger, eyeing his visitors carefully. One was tall and good-looking, in a duster and wideawake. The other was wearing a foreign suit. Neither of them looked like hauliers. 'I'm sorry,' he said, getting up. 'How can I help you gentlemen?'

'We are investigating the death of an old comrade of yours,' Batchelor said. 'Lafayette Baker.' He passed his enquiry agent card across the desk.

'You're a long ways from home, boy,' he said. Everton Conger was surrounded by boxes and travelling cases. The only items of furniture not yet parcelled up for the road were the chair he sat on and the desk in front of it.

'You and Baker were friends?' Batchelor asked.

Conger laughed. 'A rattler's got no friends, Mr Batchelor,' he said. 'I'm guessing you're Batchelor.'

The Englishman nodded.

'So I guess you're Grand.'

'I do my best,' Grand said.

'No, Lafayette Curry Baker died owing me several thousand dollars. The son of a bitch had some cockamamie hotel scheme in mind, and persuaded me to part with some of my reward money.'

'Reward money?' Batchelor sat down, uninvited, on a packing case.

'You know, for capturing John Wilkes Booth. I don't guess you Limeys know much about all that, huh?'

'I was a journalist, Colonel Conger,' Batchelor said, on his dignity. 'I know a great deal about it.'

'Did you kill Baker?' Grand cut to the chase.

Conger sat stunned for a moment. 'Get outta here,' he said, but a smile played around his lips. 'I didn't like Laff Baker but I was happy to ride with him. Lieutenant Colonel of the First District of Columbia Cavalry. You boys have mounted cops in England?'

'Yes, we do,' Batchelor said.

'Well, we were a peculiar mix, really. There was a war on, so we had to be mounted, just to get from A to B. The Army of course looked down its noses at us, and the Metropolitan Police didn't give us the time of day. Still, you learn to be thick-skinned when you ride with Lafayette Baker.'

'How long had you been with him?' Grand asked.

'Let's see.' Conger scratched the little hair he had left. 'Let's see.' He was dredging his memory. 'I got wounded the second time crossing the Staunton in Virginia. They mustered me out of that man's Army then, so I volunteered to join Baker's outfit. Bunch of misfits, every one, but I managed to instil *some* soldiering into them.'

'When did you see Baker last?' Batchelor asked.

'Hell, now you've asked me,' Conger conceded. 'That'd be after the Stanton business. We all got our marching orders then. First the First DC Cavalry, then the National Police Detectives closed down. End of an era,' he sighed.

'The Stanton business?' Batchelor needed clarification.

'Well, I don't guess it'll hurt any,' Conger said, 'you boys knowing. It's all a matter of public record anyhow, if you know where to look. Stanton ordered us, the National Detective Police that is, to snoop on President Johnson – those two never did see eye to eye. Johnson got wind of it and all Hell broke loose. Baker had to appear at a commission of Congress, after which they fired him. So, you see, it's all along of Stanton.'

'Yes,' Grand said, 'we've heard that before.'

'Exactly where the diary fits in all of this, I just don't know.'

'Diary?' Grand frowned. No one had mentioned a diary.

'John Wilkes Booth's diary. Somebody picked it up after the barn caught fire, just before Booth was killed. Laff handed it to Stanton. The next time he saw it, when he asked to borrow it to write his book on the Secret Service, there were eighteen pages missing.'

'There were?' Batchelor was trying to make sense of all this.

'According to Stanton, on his honour, the pages were missing before he got the diary. On *his* honour, Baker said they weren't.'

'Who do you believe?' Grand asked.

Conger chuckled. 'You're between the Devil and the deep with those two,' he said.

'And what about Caleb Tice?' Batchelor asked.

'My God.' Conger sat back on his one remaining chair. 'That's a name I haven't heard in a while. Man's dead.'

'So we believe,' Grand said, straight faced. 'What was his involvement with Baker and Wilkes Booth?'

'He was my second-in-command in the First DC Cavalry. Held the rank of major. Was he more soldier than cop? More cop than soldier? Who can say? But he was a slippery son of a bitch, that's for sure.'

'How did he die?' Batchelor asked.

'How well do you know Luther Baker?' Conger asked.

'We've come across him,' Grand said.

'Well, Tice and Luther had some bad blood between them. Don't ask me what; I don't know. But it was something to do with a woman. Oh, and nearly losing Booth of course.'

'Losing Booth?' Batchelor wished they had tracked Everton Conger down sooner. The man was a mine of information.

'Well, it wasn't his fault, exactly. Tice had something of a reputation as a tracker. Booth had broke his leg when he landed on the stage at Ford's. Blind man could have followed the trail he left. 'Cept Tice lost him. We found him again, sure enough, but if he'd gone any further into Virginia, we'd never have caught up to him. Cobb lost him in the Zekiah Swamp. He and Luther had one helluva row over it.'

'Cobb?' Grand blinked. It was a name he had heard before. From a madwoman who had once been a maid at Lafayette Baker's house.

'Caleb Tice,' Conger explained. 'Everybody called him that.'

# FIFTEEN

J ames Batchelor felt a little guilty stringing Aloysius Cottrell along but he had, after all, a murderer to catch, and if the reporter had stars in his eyes for a little while longer, that could be construed as a good thing. So, the back editions of the *Star* were made readily available and young Cottrell felt he was doing his bit in the cause of international journalism. In fact, it was he who found it.

'Here we go.' He held up the relevant edition in the dark, damp basement of the *Star* offices. All morning, Batchelor had shaken his head at the parlous state of the old newspapers. They were falling apart with moisture, where the swamps of Washington seeped ever upwards, turning the walls to a mildewed green and curling the edges of the pages. 'Eighteenth January, 1866.' He cleared his throat, about to read aloud, when Batchelor unceremoniously snatched it from him.

'"A body",' he read, '"presumed to be that of Major Caleb Tice, formerly of the First District of Columbia Cavalry, was found floating in the Potomac this morning." Presumed to be?'

'All right,' Grand said. 'So, we know when he was fished out of the river. When did he go in?'

And the search began again, all three of them flicking furiously back.

'Got it!' It was Batchelor's turn to triumph. 'Or have I? "An eyewitness spoke of her horror yesterday" – that was the fourth of December – "when she saw a gunfight at the Naval Dockyard. Two men, neither of whom could she identify, became engaged in an argument and shots were fired. One of the men fell into the Potomac. The body was not recovered."'

'Does the witness have a name?' Grand asked.

'Undoubtedly,' Batchelor said, reading on. 'But it's not written down here.'

'*Star* policy,' Cottrell explained, a little sheepishly. 'Retaliation is a deadly thing. The District Attorney would rather have eyewitnesses to murder, alive; you know, so they can appear in court.'

'Amen to that,' Grand murmured. 'James, the finding of the body; was there an autopsy?'

Batchelor dug out the later edition and his face broadened into a grin. 'No,' he said, winking at Grand, 'but there was a post mortem.'

'Man, that was two years ago,' Charles Williams muttered, wrestling with his mountains of paperwork. 'Have you *any* idea how many bodies I've handled in that time? Oh, it's not as many as New York, I'll grant you. But it's enough.'

'Can we narrow the field a little?' Batchelor asked. 'Body found in the Potomac. Gunshot wound.' He thought he ought to add one final fact, 'Male.'

Dr Williams looked aghast. 'Of course, male,' he said, outraged that this foreigner should imply that Americans shot women. 'Ah, oh no. That's the wrong month. Ah, here we are. January, you say?'

'The eighteenth,' Grand confirmed.

The doctor held the paper up to the light. It was his own handwriting and he still found it difficult to read. 'Male. Aged between thirty and . . .' He turned the paper to Grand. 'Does that say forty-five, would you say?'

Grand nodded. 'Or ninety-five. Forty-five makes more sense.'

The doctor agreed. 'Forty-five. Cause of death, single gunshot to the head. I won't bore you with occipital and temporal, gentlemen – that's the kind of thing only we medical men understand. Suffice it to say he was shot with a pistol at close range.'

'Pistol?' Grand queried.

'Says here a .44 calibre. Yes, I remember now. I dug the slug out of his cranium myself. I'm no gun expert, Mr Grand, but I'd guess Army Colt, Remington – something like that.'

'How do you know it was Caleb Tice?' Batchelor asked.

'Says so here.' Dr Williams was an inveterate believer in his own testimony.

'Yes, but how do you *know*?' Batchelor persisted. 'Our information is that Tice was probably shot on the fourth of December. The body wasn't found until the eighteenth of January.'

'That's five weeks in the water, Doctor.' Grand did the sums for him.

'Well,' Williams had the grace to concede, 'it's true the body was pretty battered about. A lot of post-mortem bruising. The river will do that. If I remember rightly, Inspector Haynes believed he had been killed on the quayside at the Naval Dockyard. His body was found, according to my notes, at James Creek. He hadn't travelled far, but far enough.'

'The current?' Grand checked.

'Sure,' the doctor said. 'Something must have held him down, though – ropes, anchor chains, something of that sort. Or he'd have floated clear to the Anacostia.'

'Do you remember, Doctor,' Batchelor asked, 'was the face recognizable?'

'Not to me,' Williams said. 'What with the bullet, the bruising and the fish-nibbling. You'd have to ask Inspector Haynes. He was pretty sure about it.'

'Oh yes,' Grand smiled. 'Thank you, Doctor. We will.'

Julep had lost them. Or rather, him. For a while, before and after the incident with Arlette McKintyre and the baby, Grand and Batchelor had gone about like Siamese twins joined at the hip. She'd trailed them to the *Star* offices, then to Dr Williams's, then back to the Willard. Now, as the sun began to set, gilding the columns of the Treasury building and the White House, she sat on a bench along Pennsylvania Avenue and waited. He hadn't told her who to follow in the event of the twins separating, so she tossed a coin. It had come down Batchelor and so she went for that. He had gone into a tobacconist's and had not come out. How long could it take to buy a cigar? Then she remembered. The tobacconist had a back entrance and he must have taken it and gone along D Street. Shit!

She hauled up her skirts and barged her way through the sidewalk throng. Then she slowed down. The last thing she wanted now was to draw attention to herself. Black girls walking alone in this upmarket part of town were not commonplace. She didn't want to stand out more than she had to. She checked behind her that goody two-shoes Sojourner Truth wasn't breathing down her neck, and when she faced forward again, she ran straight into James Batchelor.

'Julep,' he tipped his hat. 'Fancy running into you,' he said, although it had actually been the other way around. 'If I didn't know better, I'd swear you were following me.'

For the briefest of moments, Julep panicked. Had that mad old busybody Truth been shooting her mouth off? She was mighty friendly with white folks these days; but then, who wasn't? 'Why, sugar,' she smiled her best smile, 'you don't wanna be so forward. This ain't about you, you know.'

'Of course not,' Batchelor said. 'Think nothing of it. Actually, I'm glad we met. We need to see Luther again.'

'Something to report?' she asked.

'Something to ask,' Batchelor said. 'For example, why did he kill Caleb Tice?'

There was a silence. 'He ain't gonna tell you that,' she murmured.

'What about you, Julep?' Batchelor closed to her. 'Are *you* going to tell me?'

'Me?' she laughed. 'In the middle of D Street in broad daylight? Honey, I want to stay alive.'

Batchelor became serious. 'I don't want to make life difficult for you, Julep,' he said. 'More difficult than it probably already is, at any rate. But Grand and I are up to our necks in this now. And you know more about Caleb Tice, I suspect, than anyone.'

'I do?' Her eyes widened.

'You were the one who took me to meet him; remember, at Madam Wilton's?'

She looked deep into his eyes. 'It's not gonna help you,' she said. 'With your case, I mean.'

'I'll be the judge of that,' he said. 'Can we go somewhere?'

They could. And, as night drew on, Julep lit the lamps in her little apartment. This was the Island, a part of Washington Batchelor had never been before, and it was hardly salubrious. But it was not in the Division and it was not under the watchful eye of Luther Baker.

She sat him down in a comfortable horsehair chair and handed him a glass of bourbon.

'Can I ask you a question, Julep?' he said. 'A personal one, I mean?'

'You can ask, sugar,' she said, sitting opposite him and showing rather more ankle than he was comfortable with.

'Are you Luther's woman?'

Julep roared with laughter. 'I ain't nobody's woman, honey-child,' she said; then she paused. 'And everybody's. Is that as personal as your questions get?'

'Tell me about Tice,' he said.

'Tice was a soldier,' she told him. 'Just about everybody was, back then. He got himself mixed up with Lafayette Baker's National Detectives – don't ask me how. He and Luther didn't exactly get on. Hate at first sight, you might say.' She sipped her bourbon.

'Was there more to it?' Batchelor asked. 'Luther said it was a matter of honour.'

'Yeah, well, I think that's a pretty fancy name for it. Luther also said he didn't want to talk about it.'

'You're remarkably well informed,' Batchelor said.

'That's why I'm still here, baby,' she purred, 'with my own place and an account in my own name at the First National Bank. You gotta stay ahead of the field. And the way to do that is to be "remarkably well informed".'

Batchelor smiled. For a girl from the bayous of Louisiana, Julep did a passable British accent. 'How much?' he sighed, hauling out his wallet. He didn't choose to remind her that this was Luther Baker's money anyway.

She screwed up her face. 'Let's get one thing straight, sugar,' she said. 'Look about you. I can buy you twice over. I don't need your money. I can also outdrink, outsmoke, outpoke and outshoot you. So this ain't no level baseball field. You came to me, remember?'

That was a moot point, but Batchelor let it go. 'So, you're going to tell me what I want to know for free?' he asked.

'Oh, there ain't no such thing as free, honey.' She shook her head, smiling. 'I'll be sending you my check when I'm good and ready. And you might not see it coming.'

'Fair enough,' Batchelor said. 'Luther and Tice? What happened?'

'They fell for the same lady.' Julep got back to her drink. 'You'd think, with both of them closing down the war and hunting President Lincoln's killers, they'd have enough on their minds; but us women – well, we've a way of getting under men's skin, ain't we?'

Belle Boyd floated into James Batchelor's mind but he shook himself free of her.

'They got into a scrape over her one night. She was mighty free with her favours and both of them wanted more. Luther said he'd kill Tice if he ever saw him again, and he was to leave the lady alone.'

'And he did see him again?'

'Sure. You got duelling in your country, Mr Batchelor?'

'It's against the law,' the Englishman told her, 'but it used to be a problem.'

'Here too,' Julep said. 'Tice was an honourable cuss, all Southern gentility. He called Luther out.'

'Challenged him to a duel?'

'Yep. Fields not far from here, at Bladensburg.'

'And?'

'Luther turned him down.'

'He not being an honourable cuss?' Batchelor felt he had to check.

'Luther's pretty handy with a gun, but he couldn't go up against Cobb in broad daylight. No, he waited until dark.'

'So, it was murder?'

Julep's face hardened. 'I don't know nothing about the law, honey,' she said, 'except how to stay one step ahead of it. When one cuss shoots another, that's murder. When thousands of 'em put on uniforms and do it, they call it war. Go figure.'

'Julep,' Batchelor put down his drink and leaned forward, 'did you see it? The shooting, I mean?'

'Sure.' She topped up her glass and took a swig. 'Luther got wind that Cobb was going to be at the Naval Yard one night. The National Detectives had been disbanded by then and it was everybody for himself. Luther went to find him.'

'And he took you along?' Batchelor couldn't believe it.

'Wanted witnesses,' Julep said. 'Only it didn't quite turn out that way.'

Realization dawned and he clicked his fingers. 'You're the eyewitness,' he said, 'speaking of your horror.'

'What?'

'The *Star*'s account. I knew that was it. The report said that a woman saw the shooting but that she couldn't identify either man involved.'

'I may have been a little confused there, sugar,' she smiled.

'I could, of course, identify them both. The original plan was that Luther should kill Tice and I could be on hand to tell the law that it was self-defence. When Cobb fell backwards and hit the water – well, that was it. There was no body. Or, if there was, it would just be another poor victim of the Potomac.'

'So why didn't both of you just leave?' Batchelor asked. 'Go home? Forget it?' Not that he, as a true blue Englishman, could have done any such thing.

'There was a beat cop patrolling,' Julep remembered. 'We couldn't tell if he'd seen what happened, or whether he'd seen me with Luther, but he'd seen me right enough, so I had to come out with the *Star*'s version.'

'But Tice wasn't dead?'

Julep took a deep swallow. 'I damn near died of fright,' she said. 'It must've been a couple of months later, a time certainly after all the hoo-ha had died down and they'd found what we all assumed was Cobb's body. He just showed up at Madam Wilton's one night, bold as brass and asked for me.'

'You work for Madam Wilton's as well as the Wolf's Den?'

'I told you, honey,' she wagged a finger at him, 'I don't work for nobody. And I work for everybody. Cobb knew better than to come to the Den. Luther had all but moved in by then.'

'Did Tice get nasty?' Batchelor asked. 'Threaten you?'

'Uh-huh,' the girl shook her head. 'Like I said, he was a Southern gentleman. He wanted Luther, not me. Besides, he had other things on his mind.'

'Like what?'

'You'd have to ask him that, sugar,' Julep said.

'I'd like to,' Batchelor told him. 'How do I find him?'

'Leave that with me,' she said.

'All right. And thank you, Julep.' Batchelor got up. 'You won't take my money?' She stood up with him and shook her head. 'Then at least take this.' And he kissed her on the lips, a kiss more lingering than it should have been, for all sorts of reasons. She smiled when it was over and led him to the door.

With his hand on the doorknob, he turned. 'Two more questions before I go,' he said. 'What did you mean about Caleb Tice being a Southern gentleman? If he rode with Luther Baker, he fought for the North, surely?'

'Again, honey,' she said, 'you'll have to ask him. The Mason-Dixon line ain't so wide and only the Potomac separated North and South back in the day. What's your other question?'

'The lady,' Batchelor said. 'The lady that Luther and Tice argued over. Who was she?'

'Why, didn't I tell you?' Julep arched an eyebrow. 'It was Jane Curry Baker, Lafayette's wife.'


Grand stood at the door, hat in his hand, polishing his toecaps on his calves as he had so many times before, waiting to be let inside. Old habits died hard. He looked the butler up and down and the butler returned the compliment.

'Captain Grand, sir,' he said, with no inflection. 'I hope you have been keeping well, sir.'

'It's plain Mr Grand now,' he said, realizing as he did so he had no idea what this man was called. Years in London had changed his attitude to things and he didn't think it was too late to ask. 'And what should I call you? After all these years?'

The butler looked mildly affronted. He kept himself to himself, he was sure, and he had never asked for too much attention from the snooty bastards he served. 'Lulworth, sir,' he said.

'Like the Cove,' Grand said, pleased to have retained some English geography.

'Possibly, sir,' said the butler, who had no idea what he was talking about. 'Are you here to see the mistress, sir? Or Mrs Mitchells?'

'Either. Both.' Grand had had a rather difficult interview with Arlette's parents when he had turned up in a cab, with her and little Johnson. Although he was by no means responsible for their daughter's drug-addled state, or the fact that their only grandchild was close to being starved to death, as well as becoming a hopeless imbecile through the addition of laudanum to his diet, he was nevertheless at first treated like the dirt on their shoe. Then, Arlette had rallied enough to tell them how Matthew had come in like a lion and borne her and her child away from a house of horrors and he was the white-haired boy again. He heard a distant cooing, that could only be Mrs McKintyre.

'Matthew? Is that Matthew Grand I hear?'

'Yes, Mrs McKintyre,' he said, peering round the butler. 'I've come to check on the progress of Mrs Mitchells and young Master Johnson.'

'Oh, so formal!' Mrs McKintyre appeared through the dimness of the hall; all frills, furbelows and a smell of slightly old lavender. 'Come through into the parlour. Arlette and little Jack,' Grand was happy to hear that his nickname for the poor child seemed to have stuck, 'are in here. Come through.' She gestured madly. 'Come on through.'

Arlette sat in a low nursing chair, her baby in her arms. She was back in her pink and her frills and her curls bounced under a lace bonnet. The baby was swaddled in a snow-white shawl, its little face pinker now than when Grand had seen it last, and a chubby fist, escaped from the bonds, waving in the air. The sunlight touched their heads softly and the golden threads of their hair gave it back in spades. It was a very pretty picture and Grand paused in the doorway to enjoy it for a moment.

He became aware of tweeting at his elbow and looked down into the radiant face of Mrs McKintyre. He smiled at her and she grabbed his arm excitedly.

'Matthew, Matthew, look at them. Are they not the prettiest things you ever saw? Thank you, for bringing them back to us. That evil man, that Mitchells, he told us that Arlette was too busy with the house to come over. I knew it was wrong, but Mr McKintyre would listen, you know. He thought so much of that . . . that . . .' In the absence of words, she stamped her little foot. 'But don't let us fret. They're back now and Hell itself will not part me from them. My babies.' She squeezed Grand's arm in a surprisingly strong grip, and then suddenly let go, backing off. 'I'll let you youngsters get reacquainted,' she said, archly. 'Mr McKintyre is at the courthouse as we speak, seeking an annulment.'

Grand thought the baby in Arlette's lap was perhaps reason enough for that application to fail, but said nothing.

'I'll rouse Bella to get Arlette some tea. Would you like some tea, Matthew, or would you like something stronger?' She gave him a roughish tap in the ribs.

'No, Mrs McKintyre,' Grand said, unused to his new status of honoured guest. 'Tea would be just wonderful, thank you.'

She trotted across the hall and pushed on the green baize door. 'Bella!' she bawled. 'Tea for Mr Grand and Miss Arlette.'

An answering holler came up from the depths.

'No,' she answered it. 'Just for two.' Then, suddenly, she was back at Grand's side. 'You don't want an old woman like me here, when you two young things want to talk things over, do you?'

Grand, who had hardly been able to get a word in edgewise, was now truly speechless.

'Anyways,' she said, 'I'll be in my sewing room if you need me for anything.' She stroked his arm and leaned her head against it for a moment. 'It's wonderful to have you back, Matthew.' And before he could answer, she was gone.

As soon as her footsteps died away, Arlette lifted her head and looked at Grand, her eyes full of cunning. 'Matthew,' she said, in her old hectoring tone. 'Over here a minute, hmm?'

He went across the room, walking gingerly. In all the danger that he and Batchelor had been in, might still be in, he realized that this was probably far, far worse. It would take all of his skills to get away unscathed. He stopped a few paces away and leaned forward to admire the baby. 'He looks well, Arlette,' he said, diplomatically. 'And you, of course. The picture of happy motherhood.'

She curled her lip at him. 'Likely so,' she said, and her arm snaked out like a rattler and she had the edge of his coat in her hand before he could step back. 'Now, Matthew Grand, my deliverer. Have you got any consarned laudanum on you or haven't you?'

'Arlette,' he said, prising her fingers from his pocket, where they rummaged fruitlessly. 'I most certainly do not have any laudanum on me, nor do I intend to carry any. You are here to get well.'

She stood up, putting the baby all anyhow in his crib, so he gave vent to a howl that at least showed his lungs had come to no harm. 'Matthew Grand,' and her face was full of venom, 'you saved me from one Hell and brought me to another . . .'

Before she could reach him, he was across the floor of the drawing room and heading for the door. In one silent and fluid movement, the butler opened it and passed him his hat. And, not for the first time, Matthew Grand found himself outside the McKintyre house, listening to the screams from within.

\*    \*    \*

'What I want to know is, when you two monkeys are going to make a move against Stanton.'

Luther Baker was feeling less than even-tempered that night. The tab that Grand and Batchelor were running up was getting out of hand and, so far, they'd been tinkering at the edges. They had talked to the widow, Jane Baker. They had talked to a nurse and a maid. They'd stumbled – literally – over the body of Tom Durham. And they'd taken themselves off for a sightseeing tour of Tennessee, during which they'd come across some lunatics who liked to dress up and scare the black folks. All in all, Luther was throwing good money after bad and he'd had enough of it.

Grand took the plunge. 'We're not convinced,' he said, 'that Edwin Stanton is involved.'

'Not involved?' Baker snapped. 'Of course he's involved. The only reason I bought you two misfits in in the first place is that I can't reach him. The War Office, the Treasury, the Supreme Court building – if I so much as set foot in any of them, I can kiss my ass goodbye in the Old Capitol Prison.'

'On what charge?'

'On what charge?' Baker mimicked him, although not so well, it had to be said, as Julep had. The girl was nowhere in sight tonight. In his more hospitable moments, Batchelor imagined her safely wrapped up in her Island apartment, knitting or doing crewelwork. Then the conversation brought him screaming back to reality. 'This is America, mister. What do the fancy dans call it? Postbellum America? Well, it's all gone to Hell in a handcart, I can tell you. When Lincoln died, his Vice President went to pieces. Turns out Johnson was a secret Southerner anyhow, judging by the way he wants to draw a line in the sand and forget that four years of war ever happened. No, it wasn't just Washington that was under Stanton's law, believe me; it was the States as a whole. And he's still pulling the strings. Somehow. Behind the scenes.'

'He's out of office,' Grand reminded him.

'Yeah, and I'm William Tecumseh Sherman. So the next man in the White House'll be Ulysses S. Grant. And who'll be pulling his strings? That'll be Edwin Stanton.'

'All right,' Batchelor said. 'Let's get to specifics. What did

Stanton have on Lafayette? And don't give us any generalities about knowing where the bodies are buried.'

'That ain't no generality!' Baker shouted, then moderated his tone. Even here at the Wolf's Den, walls had ears. *Particularly* here at the Wolf's Den. 'Take John Wilkes Booth. There are only two men alive now who know where *he's* buried. I'm one. Stanton's the other. The third would have been Laff. And that's precisely why you boys are here. Now, when you gonna start earning your keep?'

There was a silence while everybody looked at each other.

'I suppose,' Batchelor said, 'I could approach Mr Stanton, in my usual guise as reporter? Piece on great Americans, that sort of thing, for the *Telegraph*.'

'Great Americans!' Baker growled. 'All right. Do that. It's not likely the old snake in the grass'll give much away, but when you see him, be sure and ask him why he turned down the President's invitation to Ford's Theatre that night, the night they got Lincoln. I'd like to hear the answer to that. Then I'd like to hear which cowardly son of a bitch he got to kill Cousin Laff.'

'He'll only see one of you,' Julep whispered, 'not both.' It was difficult trying to talk sotto voce above the rattle of a streetcar and the snorting of the horses. The noises from Pennsylvania Avenue didn't help and the crowds were building at the end of the Washington office day. As a black, of course, the girl who worked for nobody and for anybody could not ride inside the jolting vehicle. She was no Sojourner Truth with a crusade to win. She meekly followed the white man's laws by day and broke most of them, not to say God's commandments, by night.

'Let's let Mr Lincoln decide,' Grand said, getting ready to flip a dollar from his pocket.

'When he says one of you,' Julep kept an eye out for the guard, 'he means you, honey.' She was looking at Batchelor. 'A face he knows, you understand.'

Batchelor did. So did Grand. 'When?' the Englishman asked. 'Where?'

'Eleven sharp,' she told him. 'Madam Wilton's.'

'There's not going to be a police raid tonight, is there?' he asked.

Julep laughed. 'No fear of that,' she said.

'Well, then.' Grand put his dollar away. 'Over to you, James, my boy. And give my regards to Major Tice.'

Julep's laugh had attracted the streetcar guard, who wandered over to her. 'What you looking at, cracker?' she hissed. 'Ain't you seen a gorgeous piece of black ass before?'

# SIXTEEN

Madam Wilton's was just as Batchelor remembered; the brass shingle burning by the ornate door, the strains of a violin playing a saraband somewhere within its portals. It still had, despite the sudden arrival of the Washington Metropolitan Police not so long ago, the air of a finishing school for young ladies.

This time, Batchelor had gone alone. There was no need for Julep to be on hand, although increasingly, both Batchelor and Grand had come to believe that the woman was on hand constantly, one of the many shadows that filled the Washington night. The lights flickered in the hallway, reflecting myriad points in the sparkle of the chandeliers, and he reached the door of Room Nineteen. It opened to his knock and he was in.

This time there was no elegant gentleman sitting at a table, no pistol muzzle levelled at his head. The room was empty. Batchelor whirled this way and that. At times like these, he half wished that he was as *au fait* with guns as Grand, but this was not the time to be ruing a misspent youth. The door had closed behind him with a click that made the hairs on the back of his neck stand on end. Now there was no sound but the ticking of the clock. Four minutes past eleven. Perhaps Major Tice had a different definition of the word sharp.

There was an envelope on the mantelpiece. And it had Batchelor's name on it. He tore it open and read the letter's contents. 'Contraband shacks,' it read. 'You have fifteen minutes.'

Batchelor's brain reeled. Where the Hell were the Contraband shacks? Matthew Grand had never taken him on his promised tour of this great city and Batchelor was literally lost. He hurtled down the stairs, colliding with a couple of Congressmen on their way up, and was out into the street.

There was a cab waiting a hundred yards away, the horse dozing in the traces, and Batchelor ran for it.

'Do you know where the Contraband shacks are?' he called up to the cabbie.

'Sure thing, mister,' the cabbie said, readying his whip. 'But are you sure you want to go there?'

'Positive,' said Batchelor, and got in. He didn't take much notice of his surroundings, intent as he was on the time. Every other minute he checked his hunter. Was the cab going backwards?

They hurtled up a gentle rise and Batchelor became aware that the broad boulevards and bright lights had gone. Wooden hovels lay scattered at rakish angles and washing hung limply from rope lines strung across alleyways. He scattered a flock of chickens as he got down and felt his boots squelch in the mud.

'I guess you know your business, mister,' the cabbie was looking around him nervously, 'but if it's a black girl you're after, you'd have done better back in the Division.'

'Thank you,' said Batchelor. 'What do I owe you?'

'That's taken care of,' the cabbie said, and was only too keen to lash his horse back down the slope.

What now? Batchelor was standing in the middle of a shanty-town, the ramshackle roofs of the buildings black against the purple of the night sky. There was no moon. And the stars were far, far away. He heard them before he saw them. Two men, then three, creeping towards him out of an alley. Another crossed by a picket fence to his right and two more to his left. To a man, they were black, with hard, scrawny faces and worn clothes, patched hand-me-downs that many people had worn before. A couple of them carried sticks.

'What you doin' here, cracker?' one of them asked. 'We don't get many white callers.'

'I've come to meet someone,' Batchelor said. He was aware that they had surrounded him now and that the circle was closing in.

'Oh, yeah?' another asked. 'Who's that?'

'That's my business.' Batchelor knew as soon as he said it that he might not live to regret that remark.

'Yours and Major Tice's,' a third voice boomed. Another man, rather older than the others, with greying hair and kindly eyes, walked forward from the circle's rim. He held a note in his hand

and he passed it to Batchelor. 'The Washington Monument,' he read. 'Which way's that?' he asked aloud. 'The Washington Monument?'

'Washington Monument?' the first man stroked his chin. 'You heard o' that, Blue?'

'No, I ain't, Scip. And you know I'm Washington born and bred.'

'Me neither,' another man piped up. 'But these crackers keep on building, don't they? T'ain't safe for decent black folks to walk the streets.'

Batchelor heard the stifled sniggers, but the joke was very definitely on him and he didn't appreciate it. 'I have money,' he said, rather wishing now that he was still in that London alley with the Irish roughs.

The sniggering stopped. 'We don't want your money, white boy,' one man said, his voice thick with anger. 'You wouldn't give us the time of day if'n you didn't want something.'

'Aw, don't tease the cracker, Scip. Man's likely to shit hisself – oops, pardon my manners – soil himself.'

Batchelor stood his full height and crossed to the man, staring him down. 'I asked you gentlemen a civil question,' he said. 'You may guess from my accent that I am a stranger in your city. Now, for the last time, are you going to tell me which way the Monument is?'

The older man looked at the Englishman grimly. Then he pointed with his left hand. 'That way, mister,' he said. 'And you won't find no cabs around here. You're gonna have to run for it.'

Batchelor nodded and turned. For a moment, the circle did not break and the sticks seemed to glow white in the men's hands. Then, they fell back, first one, then two, and there was a clear run down the hill. Batchelor tipped his hat and strode off, not breaking into a run until he felt himself to be out of sight of the shacks. In the distance as he ran, he heard a harmonica open up and the mocking words of the old Civil War song rang in his ears.

'The Massa run, ha, ha, The darkie stay, ho ho. It must be now the Kingdom's coming, and the year of Jubilo!' It was followed by hoots and catcalls and gales of laughter. At least tonight, James Batchelor had momentarily lightened *somebody*'s life.

He jogged as best he could over uneven ground in the pitch dark, cursing whenever his ankle threatened to turn or brambles ripped at his trousers. He could see the city's canal lying straight and silver ahead – and he could smell it, too; the open sewer of the capital and the floating graveyard of cats without number. The park, still under construction, that he had seen in the daylight when he and Grand had talked to Luther Baker behind his tree, looked different at night. Sinister shadows extended the bushes and the night airs shifted the fallen leaves, sending them skittering across the pathways like armies of rats.

Here it was, the Monument, three times the height of a man and surrounded by scaffolding. Batchelor's lungs felt fit to burst and his legs like lead. What was this game of 'hunt the thimble' that Tice was playing? He was about to give up and plan exactly what he would say to Julep when he next met her, when he saw the paper fluttering on an arm of the scaffolding. He could barely make it out in the darkness, but a minute or two turning it this way and that revealed its secret. 'The Long Bridge'.

Batchelor threw his hat against the stonework in his frustration. This was getting ludicrous. Just then, a whistle shattered the moment and Batchelor saw a cab standing at the bottom of the hill. He ran for it.

'Long Bridge, mister?'

'You little mind-reader, you!' Batchelor still retained *something* of his sense of humour. 'Don't tell me, this ride is paid for.'

'The Hell it is,' the cabbie said. 'You want to go to the Long Bridge, mister, it's gonna cost yuh fifty cents.'

'Fifty cents?' Batchelor nearly swallowed his tongue.

'After midnight, mister,' the cabbie told him. 'City regulations. Besides, I got a wife and kids to support.'

'Hmm,' Batchelor climbed inside. 'Haven't got any relatives in London, have you? Same line of work?'

'Would that be London, Texas?' the cabbie asked.

'Probably,' Batchelor sighed, settling back and closing his eyes. 'But for now, get me to the Long Bridge, and make it snappy.'

The sentry's boots were the only sound on the planks of the Long Bridge that night. He patrolled at the regulation speed, back and forth across the entrance and one hundred paces towards Virginia. Below him, the Potomac glided silver and slick in the starlight.

Every now and then he shifted the weight of the rifle on his shoulder and toyed, in these silent hours of the watch, with lighting his pipe.

James Batchelor had not had much to do with sentries in his life. They guarded Buckingham Palace, the Tower and the Bank of England, but this one was standing like Horatius, guarding his sacred city from a determined and dangerous foe. Batchelor waited in the shadows. Stretching far away to his right, the fringes of the Island fronted the river, and beyond that the still swampy ground of the Mall and the fractured column of the Monument he had just left. To his left, the Island continued until the rook-eries gave way to open land, lying black and level in the darkness, and the grim walls of the Arsenal beyond that.

At first, he thought he'd imagined it. There was another sound mingling with the sentry's footsteps; faster, more rhythmic, and it was getting louder. Batchelor strained to look out along the bridge. A solitary figure, no more than a pair of legs with the darkness of Virginia behind them, was walking at a steady pace towards him. The figure wore a long duster coat and a muffler under a broad hat. At his approach, the sentry sprang into action.

'Who goes?' he barked, rifle at the attack and bayonet gleaming.

'Friend of the South,' the muffled reply came back.

'What colour of friend?'

'Gold, soldier,' the voice said. 'Pure gold.'

'Advance, friend.' The soldier stood to, his rifle back on his shoulder. Batchelor expected cash to change hands, some practical explanation for the mention of gold. But there was none. No gold, no silver, not even a wad of notes. The sentry stood there, as though the traveller were invisible.

'Are you there, Mr Batchelor?' he said. 'Only, I'm a little old for playing games.'

Slowly, as though the ground might give way beneath him, Batchelor stepped out of the shadows. 'You surprise me, Major Tice,' he said. 'I've been playing your games all night.'

'Yes.' Tice pulled the muffler down from his face. 'Sorry about that, but a man in my position can't be too careful. I had to be sure you were alone.'

'And what position is that, Major?' Batchelor asked. 'On top of Mrs Baker, or floating in that river down there?'

'My, my,' Tice chuckled. 'We *have* been asking questions, haven't we?'

'It goes with the job,' Batchelor said.

'I'm sure it does,' Tice smiled. 'Walk with me, Mr Batchelor.' He led the way back from where he had come, slowing to let Batchelor keep an easy pace alongside him. 'Tell me,' he said, 'how does it feel to be walking into Dixie?'

'If you mean the South,' Batchelor said, 'I've been there.'

'Knoxville, yeah, I know. Pretty place. But there's a lot more to the South than one town or one state, Mr Batchelor. I'm from the sovereign state of Alabama, myself.'

'Congratulations.'

Tice stopped walking, looking back along the bridge. 'You wouldn't think, looking at this place right now, just how busy it was back in the day.'

'Really?'

'Thousands of Contraband streaming to safety, as they thought, from the plantations. Thousands of Yankees streaming to death, going in the opposite direction. Your friend Captain Grand must have ridden over these planks many a time.'

'Fascinating,' Batchelor commented.

'I guess you're in no mood for a history lesson.' Tice shrugged and walked on.

'Did you kill Lafayette Baker?' Batchelor hadn't moved and his voice was loud in the middle of the bridge, with only the wind, the seabirds and Tice for company.

Tice walked back to him. 'Well, you cut right to the chase, don't you?' he said. 'No, I didn't kill Baker. But I know a man who might have.'

'You'll have to explain that.'

'First off,' Tice wagged a finger at the Englishman, 'I don't have to explain nothing. Not to you. Not to nobody.' He dropped the finger and the attitude. 'There again, I'm tired of running, Mr Batchelor. I'm tired of being a marked man and dodging in and out of the shadows. I've got Luther Baker on my back and half President Johnson's Federal government. I'd like there to be *somebody* I can turn my back on and not get a bullet in it.'

'I'm an Englishman, Major Tice,' Batchelor said. 'I don't carry a gun.'

'Fair enough,' Tice said. 'What do you want to know?'

'First,' Batchelor said, 'why is Luther Baker after you?'

'He's not.' Tice was walking on. 'At least, the only reason he's not is that he thinks I'm dead.'

'He killed you?'

Tice laughed. 'In a manner of speaking,' he said. 'Out there,' he pointed back to the Washington side, where the spars and stacks of the gunboats jutted like an iron forest against the pearl of the impending dawn, 'that's the scene of the crime. Murdering bastard tried to blow my head off, but I dove into the river instead.'

'He missed?'

'If I was the charitable type, I'd say it was a combination of things. It was dark and he was upset. But the truth of the matter is, he's a useless shot.'

'That's not what Julep says. She says he's – and I quote – "pretty handy with a gun".'

Tice laughed. 'Yeah, well, that's Julep for you. Loyal as a toast, that girl. All right, I'll come clean. Luther's bullet grazed my arm and I figured I wouldn't get a clear shot myself.'

'Julep also said that Luther wouldn't stand a chance against you in the daylight.'

'Good judge of ability, that girl,' Tice said. 'I've always maintained that. I just hung around, treading water under the levee until the fuss was over. I saw one of Washington's finest peering over the side and talking to Julep. I knew she'd steer the law away from us both.'

'And the body in the river?' Batchelor asked. 'The one they fished out weeks later?'

'Some bum,' Tice shrugged. 'You gotta understand, Mr Batchelor, what's happened over here. Men died in their thousands back in the day – Shiloh, Antietam, Gettysburg. Life's cheap. I didn't kill whoever that poor cuss was, but the body became available, so to speak; some shooting in Murder Bay, I understand. He looked nothing like me, but he was white and about my age and build, so I took a chance and threw him in, complete with my best frock coat, I'm chagrined to say. Well, you gotta make a few sacrifices.'

'So Luther was happy that you were really dead?'

'Seemed to be,' Tice nodded. 'Thought that left the field open for him and Jane.'

'Open, except for Lafayette.'

'Of course. Look,' Tice had stopped again. 'Contrary to the opinion you've probably got of me, I felt pretty bad about that. I'd ridden with the Baker boys and we cleaned up the cesspit that was Washington between us. Didn't seem right to be sniffing around Laff's wife. But there it is; these things happen.'

'They do.' Batchelor was thinking of Belle Boyd again.

''Course, that ain't as unnatural as Luther. Lafayette was like a brother to that man – Jane was as good as his own sister-in-law, for Christ's sake. Has to be something in the Bible about that.'

Batchelor was sure of it.

'As for the other thing – well, it's all so much water under this here bridge now.'

'What other thing?'

'Knoxville,' Tice said.

'Knoxville,' Batchelor echoed.

'You know I was there?' Tice checked.

'There's a photograph of you, in Mr Schleier's daguerreotype emporium. You and Nathan Forrest and Lafayette Baker.'

Tice chuckled grimly. 'Pretty as a picture, ain't we?' he said. 'I didn't know who Laff Baker was back then. It was the early days of the war and I was biding my time, like a lot of fellas did, seeing which way the wind blew. Baker was calling himself Munson and he was supplying guns to the South.'

'Except they were useless,' Batchelor knew the story.

'Like tits on a bull,' Tice nodded. 'No, it was Forrest I was interested in.'

'Forrest? Why?'

Tice stopped again. They were at the midpoint of the Long Bridge now, the land on both banks just hazy lines of black against the coming dawn. 'Did you happen to notice, back there, when the sentry challenged me, what I said?'

'Er . . .' Batchelor dredged his memory. It wasn't long ago, but this night had been strange and timeless; unless he really tried, he could hardly remember his own name. Then he remembered. '"Friend of the South".'

'What colour of friend?' Tice was playing the sentry's role.

'"Gold",' Batchelor answered. '"Pure gold".'

'Right. And I'm reliably informed that when you visited Tennessee, you spoke with General Forrest?'

'Not me, exactly. Grand.'

'All right. Did Forrest say anything about me?'

'Nothing that we understood,' Batchelor said. 'At least, at the time.'

'What did he say?'

'Er . . .'

'Come on, Mr Batchelor, you've impressed me so far. Don't let me down now.'

'He said . . . he said – and according to Grand, it sort of slipped out – that you were a member of the American knights. I didn't think you Americans had knights, not as in our Orders of Chivalry, anyway.'

'Hmm,' Tice nodded. 'Chance remarks get people hung over here,' he said. 'But yes, he's right. I am a knight. I am a member of the Sacred Order of the Golden Circle, Mr Batchelor. The watchword a few moments ago, to the sentry – pure gold; he's a member too. We used to have castles all over Maryland.'

'Castles?'

'Local branches, I guess you'd call them.'

'So . . .' Batchelor was trying to make sense of it all. 'You're a sort of branch of the Ku Klux Klan?'

'What?' Tice roared with laughter. 'That bunch of misfits, dressing up in their momma's nightclothes? Give me a break, Mr Batchelor.'

'But, I thought, General Forrest . . .'

'Oh, yeah, I know he's their Grand Panjandrum or whatever they call it, but I knew the man years ago, before they'd started all that nonsense. No, the Golden Circle was set up long before the war. You Limeys had abolished slavery years ago and every day there was some liberal bleeding heart bleating about the treatment of the blacks. Lloyd Garrison, Beecher Stowe – all so much hot air. At least John Brown had convictions – went to his grave to free the blacks. Lincoln, too. No, before the war, the South was under threat. Slavery wasn't a peculiar institution, Mr Batchelor, it was the natural way of life. The Golden Circle was fixing to do something about that. We wanted to set up a circle of states, all over Mexico, Central America, the Caribbean. There were to be twenty-five of them. That would be like the United States starting over. We reckoned that the Indian territories would probably join us and the North would be outnumbered, forced to rethink their position. It could have worked.'

'But it didn't,' Batchelor felt obliged to point out.

'Hell, no. That lanky son of a bitch from Illinois got himself elected President and that was it. A house divided against itself – *that's* in the Bible too, somewhere.'

'Mark. Chapter three,' Batchelor, the ex-Sunday School boy, couldn't help but add.

'Whatever. I never had much time for the Bible. After they fired on Fort Sumter, well, that was it. The Golden Circle ended up on the scrapheap. And that,' he sighed, 'is where it lies today.'

'But, if you were with the South,' Batchelor reasoned, 'if you were pro-slavery, how on earth did you end up riding with Lafayette Baker?'

Tice had stopped yet again. Now, they were within hailing distance of the southern Potomac shore, the headland of Virginia beginning to twinkle with distant lights as people stirred themselves for another day. 'Hasn't it dawned on you yet, Mr Batchelor?' the major asked. 'If I'd enlisted with the colours, thrown in my lot with Forrest or Jeb Stuart or Jim Longstreet, what could I have offered? Another rifle among thousands, another poor bastard lying on a battlefield with his guts blown out? No. I realized I could do more good in the North.'

'You were a spy.' Batchelor put it into words.

'I prefer the phrase "espionage agent",' Tice said, 'but, yes. Every step Baker took, I reported to the South. I saw to it that he was fired – the first time, I mean – by Stanton.'

'And you nearly let John Wilkes Booth go.'

'I did. I didn't know the man personally, but I applauded his actions. When Laff Baker was brought back in to head the National Detective Police after Lincoln's death, I went with him. Figured I could get Booth out of that jam if possible.'

'But it wasn't?'

Tice shook his head.

'I lost a bit of reputation there,' he said. 'Growing up in Alabama, I knew swamps like the back of my hand. Twenty miles south of here as the crow flies is Zekiah Swamp, near Bryantown. I could have navigated that in my sleep. Laff was relying on me as his chief of scouts. I pretended I'd loused up to give Booth time to get away. But that didn't come off and the rest is history.'

'Baker didn't have a problem with you before that?' Batchelor probed. 'After all, he'd come across you when he was spying in Knoxville.'

'I guess he figured he had to trust somebody sometime,' Tice said. 'And you can trust *me*, Mr Batchelor, when I tell you that you get awful tired of not having a friend in the world. And now . . .'

Suddenly, there was a pistol in his hand and it was pointing at Batchelor. For a moment, the Englishman toyed with doing exactly what Tice had done, diving into the river as the bullet went wide. But Tice was a better shot than Luther Baker, and there were no shadowy levees here where a thrashing man could hide.

'You didn't answer my question,' Batchelor blurted out, playing desperately for time.

'Question? I seem to have been answering your questions all night, Mr Batchelor.' Tice hefted the gun a little, making himself more comfortable.

'About Baker. Did you kill Lafayette?'

'I told you, I didn't do it.' Tice cocked the Remington with an accomplished thumb.

Batchelor's squawk was a little less manly than he'd hoped, but he couldn't tell how much pressure Tice was putting on the trigger. What he needed was to distract him in some way, make him forget that he had murder on his mind. 'So, you're not the Mr Cobb who paid Baker visits in Philadelphia?'

Tice's eyes narrowed. 'Which one of them told you that?' he asked. 'The Irish bitch or the maid?'

'It hardly matters now,' Batchelor said, 'but, for the record, it was the maid – Mrs Hawks.'

'Yes, although she's only mad north-northwest, that one. What did she say?'

'She said you called sometimes, after dinner. She described you, Grand told me, as "middling" in every respect.'

'That figures,' Tice murmured.

'She heard you say to Baker something like, "Our patience is running short. You haven't much time." And, as things turned out, he didn't, did he?'

'I won't deny any of that,' Tice said. 'Baker claimed he had some papers that would prove very useful to the Golden Circle. Papers that could hang some people and send others to the pen for a long, long time. But, as you said a minute ago, it hardly matters now.'

'Perhaps not, but you said a minute ago, you knew who killed Baker.'

'No, I didn't,' Tice corrected him. 'I said I knew who *might* have.'

'I don't think this is the time for splitting hairs, Major Tice.' Batchelor was rarely so blunt, but there was something about having a gun levelled right between his eyes which made him more outspoken.

'No, I guess not,' he said. 'Stanton.'

Batchelor could have screamed, except that – even now – staring death in the face, he thought that rather un-British. After all he and Grand had been through, all the people they had talked to, all the risks they had taken, he was back here again. Looking down the barrel of a .44 on the Long Bridge across the Potomac, he had come full circle.

Tice clicked back the hammer and held the gun upright before sliding it away with astonishing speed into his belt. 'No,' he said. 'Nothing would be served by killing you, Mr Batchelor. You and your Yankee friend are no threat to me. Besides, I sort of promised Julep.'

'Julep?' Batchelor blinked. He was slowly releasing his clenched fists, letting his heart crawl back down from his mouth.

'She's taken quite a shine to you. Quite a looker, huh?'

'You're fond of her too, aren't you, Major?'

'Yeah,' Tice smiled. 'Yeah, I am.'

'Even though she's black.'

'Black?' Tice frowned. 'Come on, Mr Batchelor. Julep ain't black. She's . . . well . . . Julep, I guess.'

He turned to finish his walk on the bridge. Then he stopped and half turned. 'Sure I can't interest you in joining me for a little sightseeing in Virginia? It'll be a walk on the wild side.'

'Thank you, no,' Batchelor said. 'What about you? What keeps you in Washington now the war's over? You can't hope to revive the plans of the Golden Circle.'

'No, I guess not.' Tice was walking away.

'Julep, then?' Batchelor called. 'Will you go back for Julep?'

Tice turned back. 'For Julep, no. For Jane Pollack – now, that'd be different. Except she thinks I'm dead.'

'Who?' Batchelor couldn't believe what he'd just heard.

'Jane P . . . oh, sorry, Jane Baker. Jane was a Belle of the South, Mr Batchelor, for all she married a Goddamned Yankee. When I first knew her she was Jane Pollack. Her maiden name. Mr Batchelor? Mr Batchelor?'

But James Batchelor couldn't hear him. He was running with the fleeing Contraband, the ghosts of the past, his feet hammering on the planks. He had places to be, people to see. And a killer to confront.

# SEVENTEEN

Grand had toyed with following Batchelor, but in the end decided it might endanger the Englishman. If he couldn't keep up but he was spotted, Tice wouldn't take it out on him; Batchelor would take the brunt. So he waved him off and settled down for an evening of waiting and – he didn't mind admitting it – worrying. A young, rich, handsome man loose in Washington needn't be loose for long, he knew that, but although he had a very real need for some rest and relaxation, he was no longer sure whose girls he could trust. So, he decided to go for a quiet walk in the safe, well-lit streets around the Willard. If his walk happened to take him past a saloon, so much the better. He put some money in his pocket – enough for a few drinks, but not enough to make it worth anyone's time to roll him for it – and he set off.

The mud was still coating the sidewalk, but it was drying now and crumbling away more and more with every step, making the air hazy with a low-lying, clinging dust. Grand had dressed for it, unlike Batchelor, who had stuck by and large to his London black and usually looked in need of a good brushing down. Grand's sand-coloured coat and trousers still looked smart and if he left an imprint of himself wherever he sat, well, he was certainly not alone there. But appearance is not everything and, in the end, he got tired of the constant sneezing and the feeling that even his eyeballs had collected a film of clay, and he turned into the next saloon.

It wasn't long before he had company, a sultry girl in a low-cut gown who he remembered from his other life in Washington. She remembered him too, that much was clear.

'Why, Captain Grand,' she murmured. 'Long time, no see.'

He glanced up from his drink and smiled. 'Georgia,' he hazarded.

'Good guess,' she said, not at all put out. 'I'll settle for that. What am I drinking?'

He pulled the few bills out of his pocket and spread them out ruefully. 'I suppose what these will buy and leave me a little change,' he said.

Her eyes opened wide. 'Captain Grand!' she said. 'Don't tell me you've fallen on hard times!'

'No, I won't tell you that,' he said, 'and it's just Mister these days, if that's acceptable.' He thought for a moment. 'You're not the one who only . . .' He was momentarily stuck for the word, so left it blank. 'Officers, you know.'

She laughed and slapped his forearm lightly where it lay on the bar, protecting his small stash of money. 'No, no, that's not me. But I do only . . .' and she paused for exactly the same number of beats as Grand had done, 'men with money. And that doesn't seem to be you, does it?'

Grand was as proud as the next person. But he lowered his voice; he had lost track of who knew what and did what to whom in this town, and the walls probably had more than one set of ears. 'I do *have* money,' he said. 'Just not on me.'

'We've all heard that old one, Mister Grand,' she said, getting up to leave. 'I don't do credit.'

'I don't remember asking for anything,' Grand pointed out. 'I was just having a quiet drink and you came and started talking to me.'

'And when I did that a few years ago,' the girl said, 'you didn't push me off the bar stool. Arlette McKintyre notwithstanding.'

'You remember . . .'

She smiled at him and shook her head. 'Matthew Grand, I can't believe you didn't know . . .' She looked deep into his eyes. 'You really *didn't* know, did you? Any woman in Washington would have given their right arm to have you on the other. And you chose *Arlette McKintyre*! All right, she came from the right side of the tracks, but whatever were you thinking?'

'Arlette was pretty, um . . .'

'Exactly. Pretty. Pretty dumb. Pretty vicious. Pretty much in trouble now, if what I hear is right. She's married to Madison Mitchells, at least for now. Did you know?'

Grand played it cool. 'No.'

'All the girls knew about it, *both* sides of the tracks. It's the talk of the town.'

'How long have they been married?' he said.

'Oh, it's not the *married* that's the talk of the town, more the "for now" bit. He's got through five wives, d'you know that?'

Grand shook his head.

'Five wives, dead and buried. They all had just the one child, then they turned up their pretty little toes, just like that. That's a bit strange, don't ya think?'

'Very. And Arlette – does she look after all these children? She never seemed the maternal type to me.' It had suddenly dawned on Grand that he had never wondered where the other children were.

'No, no – they all went to live with their maternal grandparents. I don't say that Madison – I mean, Mr Mitchells – didn't kick up a fuss, but in the end, that's how it was.'

'Was it? That seems a bit strange too, and I'll tell you what, Savannah,' he had suddenly remembered her name, 'it's also a bit strange that you refer to Mr Mitchells, a big man in the Treasury and outside of your usual stomping ground, if you don't mind me saying so, by his given name.'

She drew back, eyes wide and innocent. 'Indeed, I did not.'

'Yes,' he said. 'You said Madison, as sure as I sit here.' He looked at her firmly and she gave way, slumping on the stool. 'And whatever the rights and wrongs of it, Arlette's a lady. Why should you know about her comings and goings?'

'No one could ever fool you for long, Matthew Grand,' she said, 'unless perhaps they were called Arlette McKintyre. Madison is by way of being a . . . regular . . . amongst us girls. He isn't that fussed where he takes his pleasure, but he has a fancy most nights for Madam Wilton's. A good class of girl there and very discreet.'

'Most nights? At his age?' Arlette was clearly right; Madison really was vigorous for his age.

'So I understand,' Savannah said. 'Not that I keep score, you know, but he has a bit of a reputation amongst the girls. He likes . . . well, his requirements are a bit special. I expect that's why he . . .' She suddenly stopped and looked at Grand, then leaned over and pecked him on the cheek. 'I'm sorry to chat and run, Matthew, but I suddenly have to be elsewhere.' She slid from her stool and wrapped her stole around her shoulders, hugging it close. 'Getting nippy, these nights, don't you think?'

He took her wrist and held her firm. 'What's the rush?' He had felt a vital piece of information getting closer; he didn't want to lose it now.

She prised off his fingers and spoke to them as she did so. 'The rush,' she said, 'is because you know more than you should and ask more than you should, Matthew Grand, with your blue eyes, and your blond hair and your . . . well, just let's say, I don't keep a tongue far back enough in my head with you around. So, goodnight. It's been good catching up.' Then, she looked up, fear in her eyes. 'Don't follow me, please. If you want to leave here now, then do, but first count to fifty. Please?'

He waited a moment, hoping she would crack and tell him more. From what he remembered of Savannah, she always was one for talking. But she had clearly made up her mind, so he nodded and sat back, watching her go, counting to fifty slowly in his head, like a child again, before the war had turned him into a man.

Finally, he dropped a note on the bar and walked out, watching for her up and down the street, but there was no sign. As he stood irresolute in the doorway, a distant clock began to chime, followed, seconds later, by another and another and another. He smiled. Washington time; whatever you wanted it to be. Even so, it was probably a good idea to go back to the hotel and wait for Batchelor. There was no telling how long he would be with Tice and they might need to plan tonight for action in the morning. He walked off down the street and turned into an alley that would lead him to the Willard.

It had not been so muddy here, and the soft blanket of breaking clay was thinner, so he could hear his own footfalls. Then he heard something else. Another set of footsteps were behind him; slightly out of rhythm with his own, but when he stopped, so did they. He put his hand into his pocket and curled his fingers around his Colt. The cold metal always comforted him, but in these close quarters he could use it as a club as well as a gun, with his fist given extra weight. Few people got up after a pistol-whipping. He adjusted his grip and turned to face whoever was behind him.

The man was closer than he had expected, just a pace or two away. And he had a baseball bat swinging from one hand, nonchalantly, almost as if he were waiting to take his place on the plate. As Grand turned, he swung the bat up and cradled the end in his other hand, bouncing it lovingly up and down. A quick glance showed Grand that the bat was all he had to fear, though. Although the man was perhaps an inch taller, he was rangy – scrawny even – and he looked fragile; his muscles like string, his thighs spavined and thin. Grand was not an enquiry agent for nothing.

'Mr Mitchells, I presume?'

'I don't know why you should presume that,' the man said, 'but you are correct. Have I the pleasure of addressing Mr Matthew Grand?'

'You have, though the pleasure is moot. I'm afraid if you have come in search of a game of baseball, you are talking to the wrong man. I am more of a cricketer, myself, these days.'

'Mr Grand,' the man said, his voice dry and grating, 'I have no idea what a game of baseball might be. Sport is not my interest. But I understand from some of the younger men who work at the Treasury that, if you are looking to break heads with as little effort as possible, then a bat of this kind is the best tool for the purpose. This,' and he looked down at the bat, almost fondly, 'belongs to Jem, who delivers the memos in the building. If I break it, I have promised him a new one.' He smiled, thinly. 'I understand that he has already identified the one he wants, in the window of the sporting goods emporium.'

'It takes a lot to break a baseball bat,' Grand remarked.

'I don't foresee that as a problem,' Mitchells said, stepping one step nearer again. Grand stepped back, feeling carefully so he didn't lose his balance. That would be all it needed to give this stick of a man the advantage. As he spoke, Mitchells raised the bat and swung it with all his force at Grand's head, fortunately missing by a mile. Underestimating the weight of the bat, the older man allowed himself to be pulled off balance, and staggered into the roadway, turning his ankle as he did so and falling heavily. There was a loud crack and he let out a cry of pain.

Grand squatted at his side, one foot firmly on the bat, which was broken beyond repair, just above the binding for the handle. 'Hopefully for you,' Grand said, smiling, 'that crack I heard was this bat breaking. A man your age doesn't mend well when bones get broken. Also, if I can give you some advice for if ever you try something like this again, I suggest you put in a little practice. Better men than you have come after me, Mr Mitchells, though I admit I have normally had to put more effort into making them hit the deck. Was there something specific you wanted to say to me, or were you just feeling a tad murderous on your way to Madam Wilton's? Which, by the way, is in the other direction.'

Mitchells had been winded and lay awkwardly, trying to open out his chest and draw some air into his aching lungs. Finally, he managed to have enough oxygen to be able to speak. 'I came . . .' he wheezed, '. . . to tell you to stay away from my wife.'

'I have no intention of doing anything else,' Grand said.

'I know your game . . .' Mitchells was racked by coughing and Grand stood up and backed away from the paroxysms. 'I know what you want. You want Arlette for yourself.'

'God forbid,' Grand muttered, but he doubted the man heard him. Then, louder and clearer, 'I think I need to lay my cards on the table, Mr Mitchells,' he said. 'I don't want Arlette. In fact, at this remove of time, I don't think I *ever* wanted Arlette. But I won't stand by and watch you treat even my worst enemy like you treat her. There is a baby to consider as well. They are both ill; even now, one or both of them may die, and if they do, I will go to the police. But even if they recover, if I hear of anything happening to them, I will go to the police. Hell, do you know, I may go to the police anyway; I heard enough about you tonight to get you locked up for a night or two, without bringing Arlette or Jack into it at all.'

'Jack? Who in God's name is Jack?' Mitchells wheezed.

'Your son. No one in their right mind calls a little baby Johnson. The family call him Jack and that has to be a burden off his little shoulders, for a start. But since I hope you never meet him again, what everyone calls him should be immaterial to you.'

The old man lay in the drying mud, drumming his heels in fury, his finger wagging, spittle appearing at the corners of his mouth. 'Help me up, you bastard,' he said. 'Help me up and take what's coming to you.'

Grand bent down, with his hands on his knees. In his right, he held his Colt. He reached down and put the cold muzzle to the Treasury man's temple and eased back the hammer. 'You've really annoyed me now, Madison,' he said. 'I think the best thing all round is if I just put you out of your misery, don't you?'

The man closed his eyes, and muttered what may have been a prayer but what Grand suspected was a curse. He clenched his teeth then and said, through them, 'Just do it.'

Grand pressed the gun closer and squeezed the trigger. The air was split by an unearthly sound. It was the sound of Madison Mitchells screaming.

'Tsk,' Grand said. 'I forgot. My colleague Mr Batchelor always prefers it if I keep my gun unloaded when I am not actually working. Which, of course, tonight I was not. Just a drink, a little chinwag with my old friend Savannah—' he looked down at him – 'who I believe you know.' He smiled. 'Small world. Where was I? Oh, yes, so, no bullet in the gun, no dead Mr Mitchells.' He sniffed. 'You might want to do something about changing your trousers when you get home.' He stood up, brushing off his sleeve fastidiously, and tipped his hat. 'Good evening to you, Mr Mitchells. Do give my regards to your lovely servants; such pleasant people, I thought. If ever a household deserved each other, it is yours for sure.'

And, whistling 'Dixie', Matthew Grand carried on, towards the Willard.

The last of the Willard's drinkers had stumbled out of the East Thirteenth Street Corridor shortly after one. In the Division, the night was young, but Pennsylvania Avenue was virtually deserted. Grand watched a solitary cab rattle eastwards along the empty road, noting the jolt of the wheels as it left the macadamized surface and hit the rutted mud. The oppressive humidity of the swamp that was the nation's capital had gone and the Fall was bringing its chill from the north. It wouldn't be too long before the snows fell, silent and deadly, and the ice would rim the Anacostia and grip the Naval Dockyards like a vice.

He turned away from the window to where Batchelor,

shirtsleeves rolled and collar gone, was still wrestling with Lafayette Baker's code in Colburn's book.

'Can I drag you away from the fun, James?' he asked. 'We need to take stock.'

They did indeed, and Batchelor wasn't sorry to leave the printed page. His eyes felt like gooseberries still on the bush and his right leg had gone to sleep. He slid the chair back and hobbled over to the sofa.

'To be fair,' Grand poured them both a bourbon, 'she *did* tell us, in a roundabout sort of way.'

'Who told us what?' Batchelor took the glass gratefully, circled letters still reeling in the lamplight of his brain.

'Jane Baker. She told us that Lafayette was put in the frame – a phrase she had learned from her brother, a detective in the War Department.'

'Except that we didn't know then her maiden name was Pollack. And said brother is actually a detective in the Treasury Department.'

'Which seems to be a relatively new appointment,' Grand added.

'Even though I nearly ruptured myself dashing across the city last night – or was it morning? – to bring you news of the Pollack connection, I've still no real idea how all this ties up.'

'No more have I,' Grand confessed.

'When you asked Pollack about Laff Baker, what did he say again?'

'Well, that was it.' Grand reversed the upright chair and straddled it, resting his arms on the back and his chin on his arms. 'Very little. Said he heard he'd died – in Philadelphia, he thought – and that was about it. I claimed to have been an old buddy of Baker's and dropped various hints . . .'

'But nothing?'

Grand shook his head. 'At no point did he happen to mention the obvious thing – that he was Baker's brother-in-law. Now, why wouldn't he do that?'

'Because he's involved somehow,' Batchelor said. 'You met him, Matthew? Could he be our killer?'

Grand swirled the bourbon, first in his glass, then in his mouth. 'He could be,' he said. 'The man's a detective, so he's used to dealing with shady people.'

'What would be his motive?' Batchelor was asking himself, really.

'What indeed? When Baker was dismissed, by Congress and thanks to Stanton, Pollack was presumably still with the War Department.'

'Directly under Stanton.' Batchelor was crossing tees and dotting eyes.

'So,' Grand warmed to the theme. 'The motive doesn't have to be Pollack's. It merely has to be Stanton's.'

'Stanton wants Baker dead, so he sends Wally Pollack to do it.'

Grand nodded. 'I'd give my eyeteeth to know what Pollack knows about arsenious acid.' He sighed. 'And the only way we can find that out is to confront him.'

'Do you think he'll talk?' Batchelor asked.

'Only one way to find out,' Grand shrugged.

Batchelor leaned back. 'A man says to another, "Kill an enemy for me, will you? Poison him, if that's your preference." And he does. Who's guilty?'

'The poisoner,' Grand said.

'Not the man who wants the job done?'

'Him too.'

'And that him,' Batchelor said, getting up and going back over to the desk and his book, flexing his aching legs as he did so, 'the man pulling the strings, is Edwin Stanton. You're not going to like this, Matthew, but I'm more and more certain that Luther Baker was right all along. I haven't deciphered all of this, but listen. We know about New Rome – Washington. The three men who walked there, according to Baker's code, are,' he held up a finger, 'a Judas,' then a second and a third, 'a Brutus and a spy. We decided that Brutus was John Wilkes Booth; in other words, Baker is talking about Lincoln's assassination. He confirms that with his next line – "Each planned that he should be the king when Abraham should die." Now, he can't mean that literally. Booth couldn't have actually become president if Lincoln died.'

'Yes, we know all this,' Grand said.

'Ah, but I've got further now. Here, on page 185, he says, "But lest one is left to wonder what happened to the spy, I can safely tell you this; it was I."'

'He was,' Batchelor said. 'But it's the Judas we're interested in. The Brutus and the spy are dead. Listen to this – "As the fallen man lay dying, Judas came and paid respects to one he hated and when at last he saw him die, he said, 'Now the ages have him and the nation now have I'."'

'Stanton.' Grand could see it all now, exactly as Luther Baker had told them. 'Stanton became the de facto President on Lincoln's death. Stanton declared martial law in the city.'

'Yes, but it goes further, according to Lafayette. Between pages 106 and 120, it's made clear that there was a conspiracy to kill Lincoln.'

'Hell, we know that,' Grand said. 'I chased one of the bastards to England.'

'No, no,' Batchelor said. 'Wider than that. Much wider. According to Lafayette, there were eleven Congressmen involved, twelve army officers, three naval officers and twenty-four civilians, one of them a state governor.'

'Are you sure?'

'Five of these civilians were high-level bankers, three famous newspapermen – I'm beginning to look at Tom Durham in a new light now – and eleven were major industrialists.'

Grand looked at him in disbelief.

'Apparently, they raised funds of eighty-five thousand dollars to do the deed. Presumably, they'd all be rewarded when Stanton took office. Could those eleven Congressmen have swung that, do you think?'

'No,' Grand shook his head. 'Oh, this kind of coup d'état happens in the jungle all the time, I have no doubt. But this is America, James. Yes, there was a conspiracy to kill Lincoln, but Baker caught them all except one – and *we* got *him*.'

'Well, there it is, Matthew,' Batchelor said. 'That's Baker's version. He ends – if it is the end – with "I fear for my life".'

'He's raving,' Grand said. 'What did the Irish nurse say – he was daft in the head?'

'Yes,' Batchelor nodded. 'That's what they more or less said to the soothsayer who told Julius Caesar to beware the Ides of March.' He pulled a coin from his pocket and balanced it on one thumb, covering it with his other hand. 'Stanton and Pollack,' he said, 'they're both in on it. Who takes whom? Shall we let Mr Lincoln decide?'

'Put your money away, James,' Grand said. 'If you and Lafayette Baker are right, it's going to need both of us. And we may need the services of the Washington Metropolitan Police.'

# EIGHTEEN

Matthew Grand was asleep. He knew that, but was enjoying his dream too much to wake up although someone was trying his best to make that happen. He had just got to the bit where Savannah was reaching for—

'Matthew!'

Not only was there shouting now, there was bouncing, and it couldn't be part of the dream; he was nowhere *near* that part!

'Wake up!'

Cold water was dribbling into his ears; unless his dream had left its usual path by a country mile, he must be awake. His eyes flew open and met those of James Batchelor, just inches away.

'For God's sake, Matthew. It's easier to wake the dead than you. And what were you dreaming about? Your grin was a mile wide.'

Grand sat up and swung his legs out of his bed. 'I won't tell you, James. You're much too young. But if this isn't a dire emergency, I will not be pleased with you, that much is sure. So, why the bouncing, the shouting, the—' he held out his night-shirt – 'water?'

Batchelor dabbed at it ineffectually. 'Sorry about the water, but I wanted to speak to you while everything was fresh in my mind. And it *is* eight o'clock.'

Grand collapsed back on to his bed, eyes closed. 'Eight o'clock! We haven't been to bed at a God-fearing hour for nights now. I was rather hoping for a lie-in. We are not going to find Stanton or Pollack at their desks this early, and getting to see either of them at all today isn't going to be easy. Pollack will be on his guard if Mitchells shared anything about our little altercation and Stanton . . . well, Stanton is Stanton, and he isn't just going to ask us in for a chat.'

Batchelor dragged his colleague back to a sitting position. 'Yes, exactly. That's why we need to have a plan.'

'A plan, James?' Grand sighed. 'My plan is for some eggs

and bacon and getting back into this bed, not necessarily in that order.'

'My plan . . .' Batchelor said as Grand rolled his eyes, '. . . my plan is to go to the Library of Congress and look up all the people on Baker's list.'

'But there are no people on Baker's list,' Grand pointed out. 'Just numbers. So how do we look them up?'

Batchelor looked mulish. 'We make a list of our own and then . . . and then *you* tell me who is the most likely.' He stood proudly, arms folded, a man with a plan well laid.

'*Me*? Why me? I haven't been here for ages and anyway, I was just a captain in the Third Cavalry. Why should I know anyone?'

'Oh, come on, Matthew. Don't sell yourself short. You moved in the right kind of circles to know all kinds of things about people. Look . . .' Batchelor plumped himself down on Grand's bed and became conciliatory, 'why don't we just look through names . . . army lists, that kind of thing.' He looked suddenly doubtful. 'You do *have* those, do you?'

'Of course.'

'Well, we'll look through the lists and the biographies of the Congressmen, all that kind of thing,' and he waved an airy hand to indicate that nothing could be simpler. 'I was . . . no, Goddamn it, I *am* an investigative journalist. It will take us half a day, at the very most. Well, a day, perhaps. In any event, we can make appointments for tomorrow with Stanton and Pollack and be ready with some really meaningful questions for them. What do you say?'

Grand sighed and pulled the covers over his head. 'I say that you're the investigative journalist, James. Why don't *you* go to the Library of Congress and come back here and tell me all about it. You know where to find me.'

Batchelor pulled the blankets down and looked stern. 'Matthew. I know we have been working hard. I know we have been treated rather badly by rather a lot of people, but we're nearly there. I can *smell* it!'

Grand looked at his friend. The man was like a terrier when he had an idea, and actually looked not unlike one, with his bright eyes and enthusiastic expression. He gave in. 'All right, James.

Leave me alone for a minute, while I wake up properly and get dressed. Then we'll go to the library. But on one condition.'

Batchelor looked suspicious. 'What?'

'I have my bacon and eggs first.'

The newly awakened journalist smiled. 'I think that is a fair bargain,' he said. 'I'll see you downstairs in the dining room in ten minutes.' And he was gone.

The Library of Congress had seen better days but had also seen worse ones. The fires of the previous decade now a distant memory, the dust and silence reigned once more, and Grand felt, as he always did in the presence of more than one or two books, overwhelmed and under-educated. Batchelor blossomed. Grand would have sworn that the man had grown at least six inches as soon as they were in amongst the shelves, stretching on and on almost to a vanishing point.

Grand nudged Batchelor and breathed as quietly as he could in his ear. 'Where do we start?'

'Ssshhhhh!' The sound was like a scream in the paper-deadened atmosphere, and Grand jumped a mile.

A man with calf-binding coloured hair in a sharp centre parting, framing a face remarkable for a huge beak of a nose, was bearing down on them, his finger raised for silence. Batchelor was about to speak, to ask for assistance, but as he drew his breath in, the man placed a firm hand over his mouth and pointed with his other hand to a door in the corner, almost hidden in the gloom thrown by a balcony.

Having made his wishes clear, he led the way, beckoning with an upraised arm as he walked, but not looking round. He opened and then closed the door with exaggerated care, and only then turned to the enquiry agents and spoke, in a low but essentially normal voice.

'I'm so sorry for that,' he said, with a sweet smile which transformed his whole face. 'I am Ainsworth Spofford, *the* Librarian here, and although perhaps you think I exceed my remit, I walk my shelves daily, checking that all is well.' He looked at them, anxiously. 'You didn't *meet* anyone on the way in, did you? No one with . . . well, with *books* under their coats, anything of that nature?'

The two seekers after truth shook their heads solemnly. They both felt a bit shy about speaking out loud, after their initial greeting.

'I'm happy to hear that,' Spofford said. 'It's a worry. A constant worry. And when we have the new building . . .' He shook his head and looked worried, then immediately brightened. 'However, today is today; let's not worry about tomorrow. Who are you, gentlemen, and how may I help you? First of all, do you have library cards on you?'

Batchelor bit his lip. 'I'm afraid not, Mr Spofford,' he said. 'We are just visiting. But . . .' and he rummaged in an inside pocket, 'I have a British Museum reader's card here somewhere . . .'

'British Museum!' The librarian gave it a long look. 'That will be more than acceptable.' He beamed at Batchelor as at a good deed in a naughty world. Then, sternly, he turned to Grand. 'And you?' he said.

'I . . . I *don't* have any reader's tickets,' Grand said, playing for time. 'But . . . but . . . I was a captain in the Third Cavalry.'

Spofford shrugged. 'Who wasn't?' he asked, rhetorically. 'Anything else?'

Grand was stumped. And annoyed; he hadn't wanted to follow up this cockamamie lead in the first place. He held out his business card. 'All I have is this,' he said, crossly.

Spofford took it and again gave it a long look, then his face broke out into his brilliant smile. 'My Lord!' he said. 'A detective!' He looked at Batchelor too. '*Both* detectives! But, how exciting. I have just finished a re-reading of *The Rector of Veilbye*. Do you know it?'

Both men shook their heads.

'Not? It's by Steen Steensen Blicher; a little dated now, possibly, but a thoroughly engrossing mystery. I sometimes think that, had I not become a librarian, I should have liked to have become a detective. It needs the same kind of mind, you know. Attention to detail and a retentive memory.' He stood looking from one to the other as though he had just invented them. 'Well,' he said at last, 'how can I help you, gentlemen?'

Batchelor had written out the main categories of their search at the top of pieces of paper, so they could list their findings below. He explained to the librarian that they needed to find some names of various Washington worthies, for a project they were working on – sadly not crime related. The man's face fell but his inner librarian rose to the challenge.

'Come with me, gentlemen,' he said. 'I can show you the locations of the volumes you need, then I will leave you to it. Of course, as a Washingtonian myself, I may be able to shed a little light for you. Not that I'm one to gossip, you understand. Come and see me before you leave.' He looked from one to the other once more, before leading them out into the library again, with his finger once more to his lips.

Batchelor had the time of his life that day, surrounded by teetering piles of books, a pencil lodged behind his ear. Grand settled into his role of arbiter, shaking or nodding his head in response to Batchelor's pointing forefinger. By the time the shadows began to lengthen, they had a substantial list under each heading. Grand had known from the outset that there would be far more than eleven Congressmen who warranted inclusion; he had lost count at forty-seven. The army and navy lists were also long, but he needed to go through those with a fine-tooth comb and a glass of Early Times back at the hotel – sad, but true, many still in the books were dead now, or as near as made no never mind. And he wasn't the man to go and raise old ghosts for no reason. But he let Batchelor have his hour. He still had better hopes of Pollack and Stanton – as long as there was a message from either man when they got back to the Willard, he might not have to rack his brains after all.

But no such luck.


Batchelor laid out all of his pages on the desk in the suite's sitting room and looked at them, excitedly.

'Just think, Matthew,' he said. 'In these lists is the name of the man who murdered Lafayette Baker.'

Grand, sprawled out on a chair by the fire which was burning brightly in the grate, didn't turn his head. 'Uh huh.'

Batchelor walked over and stood in front of him, looming until the American opened one eye and looked up.

'What?'

'I don't think you are taking this line of enquiry very seriously, Matthew?' he said, in a tight voice.

'Well, James, do you know,' Grand said, sleepily. 'I do believe you have hit upon the one useful statement made by anyone today. No, I do not take it seriously. We have spent the whole day in a library, making lists of people who will mostly turn out to be dead or in Wisconsin or somewhere – which in many ways is the same thing, by the way – when we could have been doing something more . . . more . . .'

'What? More what?' Batchelor was tired; he was dusty. His right forefinger was stained with ink and he hadn't eaten since breakfast. Grand had gone out for a bite at around two, but by then Batchelor was too high on his dignity to go with him. Long before then he had known he was chasing a hare, but he wasn't going to admit that.

'Useful? I could also say entertaining; I have had more fun watching paint dry.'

Batchelor sat down on the second fireside chair. 'It may prove to be useful, though,' he said, a touch plaintively, 'if we get nowhere with Pollack and Stanton.'

Grand leaned forward and tapped Batchelor's knee. 'What say we go out for some supper? Not to the dining room – I'm getting fed up to the back teeth with the Willard chef's signature sauce, if I tell you the truth. Let's go find a little place where the locals go. Pick us up a steak and beans, some chilli beef.' He looked into Batchelor's face, wheedling. 'If we've got time when we get back, we'll look at the army lists. Is that a plan, now, James?'

As if in reply, Batchelor's stomach rumbled and whined.

'You know in your guts it's the right plan,' Grand said, laughing. 'Come on, now. You're a guest in my country and I've not made you welcome. Stick with me and I'll find you a meal to remember.'

Batchelor wasn't one to give in easily, but he *was* hungry and Lafayette Baker wasn't getting any deader, so where would be the harm?

'I'll get my coat,' he said.

'Good man. Bring mine too, would you, and we'll be off. Steak or fish?'

'Definitely steak.'

'Then I know just the place.' Grand shrugged into his coat and patted his pocketbook to make sure he had the wherewithal.

All present and correct, the two clattered down the back stairs of the Willard and out into the cool of the Fall night.

As they staggered along G, heading back to the Willard, full to the brim with oysters, steak, and more especially the special brew, the secret of which was only known to the cellarman at the Ebbitt Grill, Batchelor was in expansive mood. He leaned against a building on the junction with Thirteenth and waved an arm behind him.

'Wha'dda country,' he said to Grand, who nodded pleasantly. 'Wha'dda *town*.'

'City,' Grand corrected him, but was ignored.

'Back there,' Batchelor said, swinging his arm so extravagantly he nearly fell over, 'that damn big building. Looks like a castle. Wha'disit, now?'

'The Smithsonian.' Grand had drunk as much as Batchelor, if not a little more, but he had more space in his hollower, longer legs to carry it, and had also had other food that day to soak it up. Batchelor's first three pints had hit an empty stomach while they waited for the food, and they had taken their toll.

'Thassit. And that other one.'

Grand shook his head ruefully. Hard to pick one big building in Washington.

'Full of things.' This time the swing of the arm did overbalance the journalist and he fell against Grand and stayed there, leaning heavily. In a lull in the traffic, Grand piloted him across Thirteenth and down towards the Willard.

'Macey's?' Grand supposed that fitted the general bill.

'Yes!' Batchelor was impressed. 'Thassit. And now, this thing, this . . . white thing.'

Grand leaned him up against the white thing at issue. 'The Church of the Epiphany,' he said. 'Many Congressmen worship here, or so I believe. I know for a fact that Edwin Stanton has a pew, for example.'

Batchelor opened his eyes wide. 'Stanton?' he said, looking right and left. 'Stanton? Is he here?'

'No, James,' Grand said, hoisting him up under an armpit and persuading him to walk on. 'Only on a Sunday.' He adopted the voice used the world over to kittens, small babies and drunks.

'Let's keep walking, shall we? Some of these streets get a little rough after dark.'

Batchelor looked over his shoulder and then ahead, peering rather theatrically into the gloom. The piercing white frontage of the church reflected what little light there was in the sky and gave the two men a ghostly pallor. It also made the man lurking at the corner of the building more visible than he could have hoped, but he still had the element of surprise when he stepped out in front of Grand and his burden.

'Mr Grand?' The voice was familiar, but it was in the wrong place, and Grand took a moment to identify it.

'Mr Pollack? Is that you?' Grand was glad to unhitch Batchelor and he lowered him down to sit splay-legged with his back against a buttress of the Church of the Epiphany. 'We were planning to come see you tomorrow.'

'I thought I would save you the trouble,' Pollack said, stepping forward. The reflected light showed up the fact that the clerk's hair was thinning and greying at the temples. It danced off his glasses but one thing it did not do was make him look at all threatening. Grand reached down to haul Batchelor back to his feet.

'Don't do that, Mr Grand,' Pollack said. 'I don't have any argument with your friend there. Better leave him where he is.'

'Argument?' Grand was perplexed. Unless this was going to turn into a confession, he couldn't imagine why Pollack had any argument with either of them. 'Have I given you offence in some way, Mr Pollack? If so, that was surely not my intention.'

'No, indeed, Mr Grand. I enjoyed our little chat. But, it transpires, you are not friends with Mr Madison Mitchells. Not at all, in fact. I would go even further . . .' it was not hard to tell that Pollack was a public servant, '. . . you beat him savagely a few nights ago, an unprovoked and desperate attack in a dark alley.'

Grand held up a hand. 'Whoa, Mr Pollack. Let me stop you right there. Mr Mitchells attacked *me*, with a baseball bat borrowed from one of your office boys. He missed, because he is an old man who had probably never held a bat before in his life. And the only injury he sustained, if he sustained anything at all, was in falling over when he missed his mark.

And, of course, the injury to his dignity, when he pissed himself with fear.'

Pollack looked a little less sure of himself, but didn't move.

'Does that sound like the Mr Mitchells you know, Mr Pollack?'

The clerk said nothing, but put his hands in his pockets, in an attempt to look nonchalant.

'I'll take your silence for assent, Mr Pollack,' Grand said. 'A man who bullies women and babies isn't likely to do his own dirty work. Tell me, Mr Pollack, were you not available when he came looking for me the other night? Has he sent you now to finish off what he tried to begin?'

Pollack came to a decision, and pulled his left hand out of his pocket and pointed it at Grand. From knee level, Batchelor cried out, 'He's got a gun!' He struggled to his feet. If he was going to die tonight, it wasn't going to be sitting on the ground.

'Mr Pollack,' Grand said, all sweet reasonableness. 'Put the gun away and let's talk this over. If you need to prove to your boss that you hit me, I don't mind a black eye. I wouldn't agree to taking a hit in the face as a rule, but I can see you don't really mean me any harm. You are just in a difficult position.'

Pollack looked amazed and not a little chagrined. 'Mr Grand,' he said. 'That's mighty big of you, but I'm afraid Mr Mitchells will accept nothing less than your dead body. I'm sorry. I want you to know that this is nothing personal.' He levelled his Smith & Wesson and pulled back the hammer, slowly.

Grand nodded towards Pollack's left shoulder. 'You might want to look behind you first, Mr Pollack.'

Pollack sneered. 'I stopped falling for that one when I was in knickerbockers, Mr Grand. There's no one there. I checked before I hid that I was alone.' Then, his heart nearly stopped dead in his chest. A velvet voice was purring in his ear.

'You didn't check careful enough, though, did you, honey? I been alongside you or just behind ever since you left the Treasury building. That was just personal curiosity; I wasn't to know you were after my good friends here, Mr Grand and Mr Batchelor.' Julep waved a satin-gloved hand over Pollack's shoulder and Grand grinned back. He had known she was there for several minutes, but Batchelor stood there transfixed.

'Mr Pollack was just doing a little errand for our friend

Mr Mitchells,' Grand supplied any information the girl had missed.

'I gathered that much,' she said. 'Is that Mr Mitchells whose wife I met with you the other day?'

'The very same,' Grand agreed.

'Hmm.' The girl leaned nearer to the clerk, whose brow was now sheer with sweat. 'Do you feel that?' she said and he jumped. 'It's the muzzle of my Derringer and I don't intend to show it to you – nice girls don't carry guns, do they? You'll just have to take my word for it. Now, you'll hand your piece to Mr Grand there.' Pollack reached forward and Grand took the gun, unloaded it into his hand and then put it in his pocket. 'Now, you'll apologise to Mr Grand.'

Pollack was silent, now as white as a sheet but still stubbornly on Mitchells' side.

'Do. It.' Each word was accompanied by a jab from the Derringer.

'I'm sorry, Mr Grand,' Pollack said, through gritted teeth.

'That's better,' she said. 'Now, off you—'

'No!' Batchelor had suddenly rediscovered the power of speech and coherent thought. 'We were going to come to see you tomorrow, anyway. We may as well ask you our questions now. Save us a journey. Save you an embarrassing visit from two enquiry agents. I shouldn't think the Treasury takes very kindly to investigators through its portals.'

'That's a good plan, sugar,' Julep said in the man's ear. 'Why don't you do that? What is it you want to know, James?' She treated him to her sweetest smile and he basked in it for a moment, before stepping in front of Pollack.

'Why didn't you tell Mr Grand here that you were Lafayette Baker's brother-in-law?' Batchelor started as he meant to go on. Washington was still swaying in his vision, but he wasn't about to let Pollack know that.

'He didn't ask me.'

'I mentioned Lafayette, though,' Grand pointed out. 'Asked after him. What could be more natural than for you to tell me you were his wife's brother? And how sorry you were at his passing.'

Pollack shrugged. 'We don't talk family in the Treasury building. Mr Mitchells doesn't like it.'

'I didn't notice him there at the time,' Grand said. 'So, I ask again, why didn't you say anything?'

Pollack just shrugged and looked at his feet. Julep gave him another poke with her Derringer and the clerk yelped in fear.

Batchelor put his hand out to the girl. 'Step back, Julep,' he said. 'He isn't worth dying for, I know that. Putting a bullet in him won't solve anything.'

She looked at him for a long minute and then did as he said, stepping back and leaning languidly on the cool white stone of the church.

Pollack swallowed hard and looked at the three of them, one at a time, weighing up his chances. The black girl may be further away now, but that didn't make that much difference to a bullet. Her gun was still trained on him and she looked as though she knew how to use it. The men were younger than him, fitter; and the American, the one who had come to the Treasury, looked as strong as an ox. Taking everything together and weighing up his chances – he had none.

'I didn't tell you because . . . because I killed him.'

The sounds of the city seemed to recede and become muffled. The others leaned forward.

'What?' Grand could hardly believe his ears.

'I killed him. He trusted me and I gave him poisoned beer – Wenlock Oatmeal Stout; my favourite and his.' A slow tear ran down his cheek. 'I had to do it.' He actually wrung his hands and Julep's Derringer came slowly up, aimed at his head. She thumbed back the hammer almost as slow as a dream. Batchelor held out a hand to stop her going the extra fraction of an inch.

'It was for the good of the country, don't you see?' The clerk turned his head this way and that, trying to make them understand. 'Who knows what he would have done had he lived? I *had* to do it!'

Grand looked at him, dubiously. 'Was it your idea?' he asked.

Pollack laughed, a single, grating bark. 'No! I love my sister. I didn't want to put her through all that pain, but . . .' He dropped his voice. 'It was top secret. He told me I had to do it and tell no one. He gave me the crystals to put in his beer. He checked each time to see if I'd done it and then, finally, that night at

Murphy's Rooming House . . .' the words caught in his throat, 'Laff died.'

Batchelor stepped forward, excitedly. 'When did you see Stanton, to get your orders and the poison?'

Pollack looked puzzled. 'Stanton?' he said. 'I didn't—'

There was suddenly a deafening sound, reverberating from the walls of the church and making the bells shiver and ring. When it had died away, Pollack lay on the sidewalk, in a puddle of his own blood, black in the night. It ran slowly towards the gutter, yellow gleams glinting off it from the distant streetlamp as it left Pollack's body and soaked into the mud.

'Julep!' Grand spun round to the girl, but she stood there as stunned as the other two. And almost as stunned as Pollack.

'It wasn't me! Count my bullets if you want to. Look!' She turned the gun and handed it butt-first to Grand.

'It couldn't have been Julep,' Batchelor said. 'Look, he's been shot in the chest and she was slightly behind him and to his left.'

'You're right, sugar.' The girl had recovered her composure. 'I'm *good*, but I ain't *that* good!'

Grand looked around him, at what the corners and cornices might conceal, but there was no one there, no movement, no sound, no dull gleam from a barrel in the dark. He looked down at Pollack. 'He's beyond our help,' he said, 'and last time I checked, there are usually more bullets where there is one. No one run, just walk. But walk fast. Julep, can we walk you home?'

But she had already faded into the shadows.

'It's no good looking for her, Matthew,' Batchelor said. 'You couldn't find her if you tried all night. I think the best thing we can do is get back to the hotel and try to be surprised if we hear this news from someone else. Yes?'

Grand shook himself and looked at Batchelor. 'You've sobered up quickly,' he said.

'Yes. I don't recommend it as a cure, but it will do for now. Shall we?'

And with speed but as much composure as they could muster, they set off down Thirteenth, heading again for the sanctuary of the Willard.

# NINETEEN

It had been a long time since Matthew Grand had put on his uniform. To be fair, it wasn't his now, but one lent to him by his old acquaintance, Henry Rathbone. Henry wasn't the man Grand remembered. His arm had been slashed by John Wilkes Booth in the Presidential box that night in Ford's Theatre, the night Lincoln fell beside him with a Derringer slug in his brain. The experience had changed Rathbone for ever. He was nervy, distracted – and, according to Arlette Mitchells, intent on killing his wife.

Even so, he hadn't asked any awkward questions when Grand had come calling, to renew old acquaintance, chew the army fat and borrow his dress uniform. True, it was infantry blues rather than the more flamboyant option of the Third Cavalry of the Potomac, but the major's epaulettes glinting at his shoulder almost made up for that. It was also too small and Grand was forced to leave his top button undone. He hoped that Stanton's minions wouldn't notice.

Edwin Stanton was a shambles of a man, the greying hair curling in oily ringlets around his ears, and the beard, streaked grey and black, reaching halfway down his chest. His skin, Batchelor noticed, as they stood in his law office off Pennsylvania Avenue that morning, was the colour of parchment, and his clothes hung on him as though they had been tailored for someone much larger. But the mouth was hard and grim and the eyes clear and penetrating behind the gold-rimmed spectacles.

'I think there must be some mistake.' He peered at his visitors. 'I was told there was a message from General Grant.'

'Grand,' Grand corrected him. 'And that's merely Captain, I'm afraid. Well, just plain Mister to be precise.'

Stanton had not moved from his chair. 'A captain in a major's uniform who is not a captain. Do you suffer from delusions of grandeur, Mr Grand? And should I call my security?'

'I wouldn't do that,' Grand said. 'Neither would I reach for the pistol you probably have stashed in your desk drawer.' He patted the holster at his waist. 'I think you'll find mine is faster.'

'Very well.' Stanton put down his pen and leaned back in the chair. 'You're not a major, not even a captain, and I assume you were not sent by General Grant. So, what is the purpose of your visit – and is your friend here mute?'

'On the contrary, Mr Stanton,' Batchelor said. 'Most people seem to find I say too much.'

'Well, well,' a smile creased Stanton's careworn face, 'an Englishman. How very quaint.' He picked up the pen again. 'Unless there is something you wish to say, gentlemen,' he said, 'I suggest you leave. I'm a busy man.'

'Precisely,' Grand said, and sat down opposite Stanton, uninvited. 'We'd like to know how busy you've been. Especially in relation to Lafayette Baker.'

Stanton blinked at the mention of the name. He put the pen down again and took off his glasses, cleaning them furiously with a cloth. Batchelor crossed to the door and locked it. 'Congress fired Lafayette Baker,' the former War Secretary said, 'for exceeding his powers in the context of the President.'

'Yes, we know.' Batchelor took a chair alongside Grand's. 'He was spying on Johnson, on your orders.'

Stanton's mouth hardened. 'I was the greatest President this country never had,' he said. 'Andrew Johnson is a drunk and a pardon-seller. Before Congress impeached him, he was all for forgiving the South, restoring the Confederacy's old powers as if there had been no war. Well, there was one – and I fought it.'

'So did I, Mr Stanton,' Grand said quietly. 'Not from an office in Washington, but from the foxholes in the field.'

'Well, then.' Stanton was still riding his high horse. 'You'll appreciate more than most that there are times when hard things must be done. Risks must be taken. Baker was a loose cannon. All right, I appointed him chief of detectives; I gave him the power in the first place. But in the end, I confess, he got away from me. He had to go.'

'Is that why you had him killed?' Batchelor asked.

Stanton frowned. His glasses were back on his head now and his eyes were cold and cunning. 'Did you know I used to train snakes, Mr . . . er . . .'

'Batchelor.'

'Yes, when I was a boy back in Steubenville. Wormsnakes, hog-noses, earthsnakes, ribbon snakes, garter snakes – it was only the rattlers you couldn't control. They're wayward, unpredictable, treacherous. Lafayette Baker was a rattler. I knew that, of course, when I took him on, but . . . you were there, Grand. You remember how it was. When Lincoln died—'

'Yes,' Batchelor said, interrupting. 'About that. Why didn't you go to the theatre that night?'

'The fourteenth of April, 1865,' Stanton remembered, suddenly very far away. 'Easter Sunday. Contrary to what you've probably heard, gentlemen, I am a God-fearing man. I do not approve of theatres, especially on the Lord's Day. That baboon in the White House knew that. I'm astonished he had the brass neck to ask me.'

'You were saying,' Grand reminded him, '"When Lincoln died . . ."'

'When Lincoln died, there was panic. Chaos. We all sat in that damned room in the Petersen house and our chief was dying. I took one look at that long, lanky body of his and I knew there was no hope. Mrs Lincoln was hysterical, wailing in another room. The doctors were wringing their hands. I've never seen so many ashen-faced politicians in my life. Whatever the grief they felt, whatever they had done or had not done during the war, the common cry that night was "Whatever shall we do?" The house was falling that night, gentlemen. There had been eight plots against Lincoln that I know of, but no one – *no one* – had ever killed a President of the United States before. *Somebody* had to take charge. That somebody was me.'

'So you became a tyrant?' Batchelor said. 'John Wilkes Booth thought he'd killed a tyrant. And you took his place.'

'Welcome to Washington, Mr Batchelor,' Stanton said. 'Democracy's a wonderful thing, isn't it? Oh, we pride ourselves on its fairness and we make speeches about the will of the people. That's why there are still contraband shacks all over Washington and blacks can't ride inside streetcars and that damned Monument is still unfinished after three decades. There was no place for democracy after Lincoln died. It needed a firm hand. Decisions. Times. Places. People. I called in Lafayette

Baker to turn this Gomorrah into a Jerusalem. And it worked for a while. If that's tyranny, all right, I'm guilty. But the Union has held. The house isn't falling any more. As to whether it's still divided against itself – well, we'll just have to wait and see.'

'But Baker knew too much, didn't he?' Batchelor persisted. 'Knew where the bodies were buried.'

'Yes, but he was out in the cold, powerless.'

'And his book?' Grand asked.

Stanton laughed. 'Yes, I enjoyed that. One of the best works of fiction I've come across.'

'What about Booth's book?' Grand asked.

Stanton blinked. 'What book?'

'The diary,' Grand said. 'The one found on his body at the Garrett farm. The one Baker gave to you. The one with eighteen pages missing.'

'What about it?' Stanton asked. 'Am I missing a point here?'

'It's all about a third book, really,' Batchelor said. 'A trilogy, in a way, which forms a circle. Colburn's *United Service Magazine* for 1864.'

'What relevance has that?' Stanton wanted to know.

'It's not the book itself,' Batchelor explained. 'It's the code contained in Lafayette Baker's personal copy. It makes it pretty clear that you orchestrated the plot on Lincoln's life. Booth was just the gunman.'

'We spent a most useful day in the Library of Congress yesterday,' Grand said, ignoring Batchelor's startled glance. 'Mr Spofford was help itself. He told us, among other things, that you pardoned Private Corbett of the Sixteenth New York Cavalry, the man who shot John Wilkes Booth. Why was that, Mr Stanton, when Lafayette Baker had ordered that Booth be taken alive? Did you slip Corbett thirty pieces of silver to make sure that Booth never lived to testify in court?'

'Come to think of it,' Batchelor took up the tale, 'none of the conspirators testified in court, did they? You wouldn't want that to happen, in case your name came up. Isn't that what those missing eighteen pages are all about? When you read the diary, didn't you find, to your horror, that *your* name was there, Judas to Lincoln's Christ.'

Stanton pulled his glasses off again, as though he were suddenly weary of the world. 'As I told Congress at the time,' he said quietly, 'the eighteen pages were missing when I got the diary.'

'On your honour,' Batchelor remembered the words.

'On my honour,' Stanton repeated. He slid back his chair and shuffled over to the window. His walk was slow and hesitant and Grand and Batchelor hadn't realized until now how very ill he looked. But Stanton wasn't looking out of the window at Washington teeming below him. He was looking at a small, oak casket on the sill and he picked it up. 'Here,' he said softly, 'are the ashes of my daughter, Lucy. She died twenty-seven years, three months and four days ago. And there isn't a day goes by but I don't think of her.'

He put the box down and turned to face them. 'I'll be seeing her again soon, gentlemen, if there is, as I trust, a good and loving God. The doctors tell me I have just months to live. General Grant has promised me a seat on the bench of the Supreme Court, but I doubt I will live to see it.'

Grand and Batchelor looked at each other. The arrogant tyrant of a few moments ago, the man who had held the United States of America in the palm of his hand, was suddenly small and old and just a man.

'Yes,' Stanton said, 'Lafayette Baker knew where the bodies were buried, as you put it. But so did dozens of people on the Hill, in the War Office, the Army, the Navy. Have I had them all killed? I did what I had to do when Lincoln died and I make no apology for it. I would do it again.' He pulled himself to his full height and the effort cost him dearly. 'Now,' he said, 'if you think I am guilty of the murder of Lafayette Baker, you can send for the police and have me arrested. Hell, why not speed up the process, Mr Grand, and use that pistol of yours?'

Grand and Batchelor stood up and Grand unbuttoned the holster strap. For a moment, Stanton's life flashed before him – the snakes coiling in Steubenville, Lucy running and laughing in the spring meadows, the marching dead of the great and terrible war and the body of a President on a bier, under the flag they both loved. Grand flicked open the holster's flap. There was no gun. Whatever retribution Edwin Stanton had to face, for whatever crimes he may have committed, the instruments of that retribution would not be Grand and Batchelor.

Neither man had spoken on their way back from Stanton's offices. For weeks now they had been starting at shadows, trailing ghosts. One man's truth was another man's lie and yet another's cryptic code. They both remembered the puzzled look on Wally Pollack's face just before he died, the puzzled look when he heard the name Stanton. And they had both come away from the great man's offices convinced that, whatever else he had done, Edwin Stanton had not ordered the death of Lafayette Baker.

When they reached their rooms, Grand grabbed Batchelor's sleeve.

'What is it now?' Batchelor asked. He had had enough of Washington skulduggery and there seemed to be no end to it. 'The last time you behaved like this, our rooms had been—' He froze as Grand slammed back the door and held his Colt at arm's length. A beautiful black girl stood there, in their living room.

'Julep,' Batchelor said. 'Why are you here?'

'And, more importantly, how did you get in?' Grand added.

Julep half smiled. 'I've been here before, honey,' she said, waving a nail file in the air. 'And I'm sorry about turning the place over.'

'You?' they chorused.

'Nobody ever accused me of being tidy,' she smiled, 'but now you gotta get out.'

'Of the hotel?' Grand asked.

'Of Washington,' she said, looking around for the suitcases. 'Out of the States.'

'Why?' Batchelor asked.

''Cos it's over, sugar-plum,' she said, gathering up what belongings she saw strewn around. 'You got what you came for. The man who killed Lafayette Baker. He admitted it, back there by the church. Luther'll be happy with that. And I can tell him. No need for you fellas to bother.'

'What's your hurry, Julep?' A voice made the men turn. And Julep hadn't looked up. 'I'm afraid these gentlemen and I have a little business.' John Haynes was holding a Remington in his hand and it was pointed at Grand. 'Anything in the holster?'

Grand raised the flap to show that it was empty. 'The pocket piece, then, Mr Grand. On the table. Now.'

For a moment, Grand hesitated, then he slid the Colt free of his tunic and did what he was told.

'Now, the Derringer.'

Grand bent over and freed the second gun from the strap under his stocking.

'Thanks, Julep,' Haynes smiled. 'I'll take over now. Get lost. We'll settle up later.'

The girl stood there for a moment, emotions raging in her head. Then she swept past Batchelor, pausing just once. 'I told you to go,' she whispered. 'Why didn't you go?' And she was gone.

'I don't understand,' Batchelor frowned. 'Julep works for you?'

'For me, for Luther Baker, for Wesley Jericho. Even – and I didn't know this until you obligingly told me about him – Caleb Tice. I expect she gave you the "I work for nobody and anybody" speech. It's her trademark. In her own little whorehouse way, she's another Goddamned Sojourner Truth. God save us from black bitches on a crusade.'

'Why are you here, Inspector?' Grand asked.

'Murder, Captain Grand. Good to see you back in uniform, by the way, even if it is someone else's. You and the Limey here have been poking your noses into Washington affairs since you got here. I could turn a blind eye to trouble on the streetcars, visiting brothels, but Tom Durham was different. And now you go and oblige me by killing Wally Pollack. And that had to be you, Grand, because Mr Englishman here doesn't carry a gun. Isn't that right, Mr Batchelor?'

'So, what happens now?' Batchelor asked. 'The precinct house?'

'Oh, no, James,' Grand said, a strange smile playing around his lips. 'I don't think Inspector Haynes is going to bother with all that this time, are you, Inspector? At best, it'll be Room Nineteen at the Old Capitol Prison.'

'And at worst?' Batchelor wasn't following the drift of the conversation now.

'At worst, it will be two bullets – one in your head, the other in mine. And I'll lay you any odds you like that the calibre of those bullets will be the same as the one Dr Williams will dig out of Wally Pollack.'

'You?' Batchelor's mouth hung open. 'You ordered Baker's death?'

'My God,' Haynes chuckled. 'It's taken you long enough to get around to that. We all know there were no witnesses to Pollack's death, apart from you two, Julep and his killer. So how else could the dear old Metropolitan Police be involved? It would have taken you minutes to figure that out, if either of you had a brain, that is. Oh, I could probably have kept the pretence up for a while, long enough to take you into custody. After that . . . yes, you're right. Room Nineteen. Well, the safety of the country is involved, isn't it? Can't have the constitution subverted by a man who resigns his commission and leaves a girl in the lurch. Especially one who consorts with a *foreigner*. It's so . . . un-American.'

'Just tell us why,' Grand said, wondering how he could get that gun away from Haynes, 'why you wanted Lafayette Baker dead.'

'Revenge,' Haynes said. 'A dish, or so the cliché goes, best served cold. Back in the day, I went to see Laff Baker, offered my services with the National Detective Force. He turned me down. Not only that, he laughed in my face. Him! The most deviant reprobate I've ever come across. Lining his own pockets, torturing people to death. Know what he told me? He thought my morals left a little to be desired. Well, he'd picked on the wrong cuss to turn down. I bided my time. Watched while he fell foul of Johnson and Stanton, watched while he fell from grace. Then I persuaded that simple-minded idiot Pollack that he was a danger to the nation, that he had secrets which could undermine the state, fragile as it is after the war.'

'Arsenic was your idea?' Batchelor asked.

'Difficult to diagnose,' Haynes said. 'I knew Rickards could be trusted to keep his mouth shut. He, like Wally, was bought and paid for.' He chuckled and shook his head. 'And you bought Luther's drivel about Stanton. You poor, sad . . .' and he clicked back the Remington's hammer.

A single shot rang out, shattering the moment. Haynes stood bolt upright, the gun still in his fist. Smoke drifted across the room, but it had not come from the Remington. His eyes crossed and he pitched forward on to his face, blood oozing from the dark hole in the back of his head. Grand and Batchelor looked up. A beautiful black girl stood there, a Derringer in her hand.

'Sorry to interrupt,' she said. 'I forgot to say goodbye.'

Julep worked for everybody. And for nobody. And they worked for her. Nobody in the Willard came to investigate the gunshot on the second floor. And no one noticed when two very large men turned up with sacks and ropes. They took their heavy bundle down the back stairs to a waiting cart. And, after dark, they drove it to the Potomac. And threw it in. And watched it sink.

'If ever you're back this way, sugar,' Julep said to Batchelor, 'I'd be proud to let you buy me a drink.'

'If I'm ever back this way,' he said, 'I'd consider it an honour.'

She smiled and kissed him. And was, this time for ever, gone.

For a while, the two enquiry agents sat silently opposite each other, over the low embers of the fire. Occasionally one would raise his head and then, seeing the other lost in thought, would return to introspection. A report would have to be written for Luther Baker, but just what it would contain was a mystery. Batchelor thought that Grand – as the one who understood Washington and its people – should write it. Grand was equally certain that it was a job for a journalist. And so the stalemate continued as night came and settled its wings over Washington, waiting for the grey feathers of dawn.

Batchelor raised his head. 'Did you hear something?' he asked.

'James, you must calm down. It's over. Really over this time. And I really think that you are the man to write this report.'

'Yes, yes,' Batchelor flapped a hand. 'But there was something outside, I know it. Have you got your gun?'

'That's not a question I hear often from you, James,' Grand said, ferreting down the side of the chair and coming up with the Colt in his hand. 'But I feel I must tell you now that I won't be going far without it in the future.'

'Well, come with me while I check outside the door, then,' Batchelor said. 'I definitely heard something.'

The two crept across the room, which seemed suddenly to

have become very wide and very empty. The door was firmly locked still, so it couldn't be Julep – and anyway, her goodbye had seemed very final this time. Batchelor turned the knob with glacial slowness, then flung it open, Grand's Colt levelled at the space beyond. On the carpet lay two envelopes.

'Really!' Batchelor said, exasperated. 'What is wrong with people in this country? Can they not knock?' He snatched them up and slammed the door. 'It's for you,' he said, passing the bigger of the two envelopes to Grand. It was pale lilac and smelled strongly of violets. The other, smaller and plain white, also had a perfume, one that Batchelor recognized and made his heart beat faster. It was addressed to him.

Each man took their letter to their chairs and read them silently.

Grand dropped his envelope on the floor and folded the letter into six and thrust it into his inside pocket. 'I find I must go out,' he said, abruptly. 'I'll be back as soon as I can. We have an early start tomorrow, what with booking our passages and all.'

Batchelor was still engrossed in his letter, although from across the hearthrug, Grand could see it was written on just one side of the small notepaper. Then, suddenly, but with more care, Batchelor also folded his letter, but within its envelope and just one gentle fold. 'Indeed. I find I have an appointment too. I'll see you in the morning.'

They both sat there for a few more minutes and then, as one man, got up and strolled nonchalantly for the door.

Grand was gone first, bounding in his usual exuberant way down the stairs, two at a time. Batchelor's exit was, as always, more circumspect, but it could afford to be; he only had to go three doors down the hall and tap lightly for admittance. The door opened, letting out soft lamplight and a waft of lilies and vanilla, the scent of a woman.

Batchelor smiled. 'Belle,' he said.

Grand had further to go, but not much. Savannah was waiting for him outside the Willard, in a fur coat that was more for show than warmth, although the night was chilly. Grand had a sudden wave of homesickness for London, for the damp smell of the river, for the sheets of slippery plane leaves covering the pavements; for the slow advance of winter, with no threat of ice on the Thames.

'Savannah,' he said. 'This is a surprise.'

'I've been thinking a lot since we spoke,' the girl said. 'About this and that. About Madison Mitchells and Arlette. Don't get me wrong, Matthew,' she grabbed his lapel and pulled him close, 'I don't like Arlette, never did, never will. I know my position is . . . tricky . . . but if ever our paths crossed, she treated me like something on her shoe. She's a nasty piece of work and you're well shot of her. But . . . well, he can't be allowed to go on treating women this way. We don't have much in this Godforsaken place; the least we can do is look out for each other.'

'Do you know something?'

She leaned even closer and kissed him on the lips, light as a sigh. 'I know *everything*,' she said. 'Pillow talk, you know.'

Grand looked at her in amazement. 'So, you and Madison Mitchells . . .?'

'Of course.' She hitched her fur coat closer around her ears and tucked her arm through Grand's. 'Where are you taking me, Matthew? Somewhere nice, I hope. I don't come cheap.'

'I see.' Grand's voice was cold. 'So this isn't for the sake of my lovely blue eyes.'

'No,' she said. 'Everything comes at a price in this town.'

'And yours is?' he asked her.

She leaned in close and whispered in his ear, then pulled back, her head cocked, waiting for his reply. 'Why, Matthew Grand,' she laughed. 'I do believe you're blushing.'

Grand cleared his throat. 'I think I can meet your price,' he said. 'Is it payment in advance, or . . .?'

'Afterwards will do,' she said. 'But for now, let's find some-where quiet for a chat. Have you got a notebook or something? You'll need to write this down.'

It was late – very late – when Grand reached the precinct station house. He found it in a state of unusual activity for such a late hour, and reflected that he might be one of few civilians in Washington who knew why. He asked a flurried police officer if he could see Inspector Haynes. It seemed politic to go through the motions of posing as an innocent man.

The policeman looked even more flurried, and hummed and hawed before passing Grand on to a colleague. Who did the same. When Grand had been passed from pillar to post for a good half an hour, he stopped in his tracks and held up a hand.

'Whoa there,' he said, in tones as hick as he could make them. 'There seems to be a problem here, gentlemen, and it's not my place to ask just what that might be, but if you could just take me to see someone, that would be kind. Then, I'll be on my way.'

'Well,' said the latest policeman, 'there's the superintendent, Major Richards. But he's very busy.'

At last! 'I won't keep him long,' Grand promised. 'And then I'll be on my way and leave you to deal with . . . whatever you are dealing with.'

That seemed a good idea to the policeman, who had already gone past the end of his shift by a full three hours. He led Grand up two flights of stairs and then knocked on a door.

'Go away!' a voice thundered. 'I'm busy!'

'He always says that,' the policeman lied. 'In you go; can you find your own way out?'

'Surely,' Grand said, and pushed open the door.

'I said go away.' Richards didn't look up. 'So go.'

'I'll just say my piece and then leave,' said Grand, undeterred.

'Does your piece have anything to do with where Inspector Haynes has got to?' Richards said.

'No. It has to do with how a Treasury official is a partner in a string of brothels and saloons; how he takes ten per cent off the top of any contract; how he has murdered five wives and possibly one or two of his children and is planning to murder a sixth . . .' Grand paused for breath and waited for a reaction.

Richards had still not looked up, but his pen stopped moving across the papers on his desk.

'Take a seat, young man,' he said. 'You have ten minutes.'

The next morning, neither Grand nor Batchelor went into details about the night before; they were, after all, according to their various upbringings, gentlemen both. But Grand did tell

Batchelor the bare bones of his visit to the precinct as they packed for their forthcoming voyage. It seemed to put a full stop to their visit to Washington and, if they avoided a certain patch of carpet as they moved to and fro from wardrobe to trunk, it was perhaps coincidental.

# TWENTY

I t wasn't quite London smog, but it would do. James Batchelor breathed it in, standing on the dockside at Liverpool. Behind him, Matthew Grand was supervising the unloading of the luggage and looking for a cab.

'My God!' Batchelor was suddenly nudging Grand in the ribs. 'Look there. Getting into that cab. It can't be. But it is! My God, it is!'

'Whatever's the matter with you, James? You can't be *that* glad to be home. It's only Liverpool, after all.'

'That's Charles Dickens!' Batchelor mouthed the words, as though he was afraid that if he spoke loudly, the bubble would burst and it would all be revealed as a dream. 'The most brilliant novelist of the age. Of any age.'

'That's not how he sees himself,' Grand commented.

'What? How do you know how he sees himself?'

'Well, he happened to mention it one night on the deck. The American tour's taken it out of him. He's not a young man, you know.'

'American tour? What American tour? Deck? How do you mean, deck?'

'James,' Grand frowned, looking the man in the eyes. 'Are you sure you're all right? Do you seriously mean to tell me that you've spent eleven days on board the same ship as Charles Dickens and you didn't notice him?'

'Notice him? Of course I didn't notice him. Why didn't you tell me?'

Grand sighed. 'Mostly because you spent nine of those eleven days adding appreciable volume to the Atlantic Ocean. I hardly liked to intrude. What was it you said? "Leave me alone. I want to die."'

'I didn't mean it,' Batchelor shouted. 'If I'd known . . .'

'Well, if it makes you feel any better, Mr Dickens wasn't too well either. Kept to his cabin, mostly. I obviously caught him on a good day.'

'Oh, for God's . . . Mr Dickens! Mr Dickens!' and Batchelor ran the length of the quay as Dickens's cab was about to pull away. He was stopped when he ran headlong into a very large man in an Ulster. 'I'm sorry, sir,' the man said. 'Mr Dickens doesn't give autographs.'

'Autographs? No, no,' Batchelor gushed. 'You don't understand. I'm a huge, huge fan. And a novelist. Well, I'd like to be a novelist . . . I—'

'Not today, sir, if you please.'

'My card,' Batchelor fumbled for it. 'At least, give him my card, could you?'

The man in the Ulster glanced down at it before opening the cab door and getting in. 'I'll see if I can find the time,' he said, and the cab lurched away.

Grand and Batchelor were almost home and Batchelor was still not speaking, except in monosyllables when strictly necessary. He was perfectly content; he knew the mood would pass as soon as the next enthusiasm came along, and he was actually quite excited to be nearly home. He had left a lot of memories behind in America, but that was then. He had loved his time there, but he wouldn't miss the dog-eat-dog of Washington's politics. In their absence, there had been an election, and that nice Mr Gladstone was at Number Ten.

'What could be better?' Grand had asked Batchelor, 'than to have a prime minister who speaks fluent Ancient Greek, chops down trees for a hobby and picks up fallen women of an evening? Back to normality, huh?'

And as for Grand, he wasn't sorry to have left Washington either; Alsatia and his enquiry business – that was his future. He looked around him as the cab dropped them off on the corner.

'It's odd, James, isn't it,' he said, with no expectation of a reply, 'how the memory plays tricks? I hadn't remembered the old place as being so busy.'

And it *was* busy. The street was crammed with people, most of them pushing carts or carrying baskets, and the smell was appalling. It was as though Smithfield had come to Alsatia and gone rotten into the bargain.

Batchelor looked up. 'It wasn't so busy,' he said. 'And why are all these people cats'-meat men?' He looked again. 'And women? And children?'

A memory surfaced in the brain of both. They were, after all, not enquiry agents for nothing. It was a memory of Mrs Manciple, cooing over kittens. Saying, as the eighth made an appearance, how they would soon have enough . . .

Leaving the cabbie standing over their luggage, they both broke into a run. They had to employ some tried and tested tactics to get to their front door, and were rather smeared with offal and worse by the time Batchelor managed to turn his key in the lock.

The smell inside was, if anything, worse than that in the street. On every surface, there were cats. They flowed in a velvet stream up the stairs, and kittens clung with pin-sharp claws halfway up the curtains, batting invisible flies from the air with an outstretched paw, their mouths open in silent mews. A tom, big with lust, was stalking a flirty female on Grand's desk while a previous recipient of his attentions quietly gave birth in the cold hearth.

'Mrs Manciple?' Grand called. 'Mrs Manciple, we're home!'

From the kitchen came an incoherent cry of delight and the housekeeper appeared, her arms full of a huge tabby, which looked at the two men with baleful green eyes.

'Oh, sirs!' she said, dropping the cat unceremoniously to tumble angrily amongst the throng. 'You're back. And look – almost enough cats! You won't need to go out looking for them any more! You can get on with your writing, Mr Batchelor. And you can . . .' She was stuck. She had never been quite sure what nice Mr Grand did for a living, when not out looking for felines.

Grand looked at Batchelor, who nodded.

'I'll go and fetch the ambulance,' he said. 'It's not the nearest, but I think the Bethlem . . .?'

'Tell them we'll pay, James. But most of all, tell them to be *quick*. And leave the door open on your way out, hmm?' Batchelor nodded and ran. 'Now, Mrs Manciple,' Grand crooned, in the voice he reserved for kittens, small babies, drunks and, now, mad housekeepers, 'let's go and sit down, shall we, and I'll tell you all about our trip. Mr Batchelor nearly met Charles Dickens, you know . . .'